"What would you have me telling people? That less than an hour after discovering you were a widow, you were in the arms of another man?"

The heat rushed into her cheeks. "A momentary lapse of judgment, I can assure you. You may attribute my actions to the overwhelming toll of mourning."

He grinned. "Come now, Louisa. You don't have to play the grieving widow with me."

She stiffened, exclaiming, "I beg your pardon!"

He continued as if he hadn't heard her. "Both of us know that you've never even met the man."

Louisa stiffened, her spine becoming ramrod straight, her chin rising ever so slightly. "Sir, you appear to think that your position as my bodyguard allows you to take certain...personal liberties."

His brow rose, reminding her that the two of them had been about as "personal" as two people could be...!

* * *

The Other Groom
Harlequin Historical #677 — October 2003

Praise for Lisa Bingham

THE OTHER GROOM
LISA BINGHAM

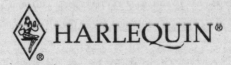

TORONTO • NEW YORK • LONDON
AMSTERDAM • PARIS • SYDNEY • HAMBURG
STOCKHOLM • ATHENS • TOKYO • MILAN • MADRID
PRAGUE • WARSAW • BUDAPEST • AUCKLAND

ISBN 0-373-29277-5

THE OTHER GROOM

Copyright © 2003 by Lisa Bingham

This edition published by arrangement with Harlequin Books S.A.

® and TM are trademarks of the publisher. Trademarks indicated with ® are registered in the United States Patent and Trademark Office, the Canadian Trade Marks Office and in other countries.

Visit us at www.eHarlequin.com

Printed in U.S.A.

To Jane, my agent and my friend.
I will always be grateful.

Chapter One

The moment was here.

So much planning and preparation had led up to this moment, Louisa realized. The real Louisa Haversham had long since donned the name Phoebe Gray and headed for the wild and wooly West, while Phoebe—or rather *Louisa,* as she would be known for the rest of her life—had waited for her husband-by-proxy to show himself.

Not for the first time, Louisa felt a burst of pique. When she had agreed to assume the life and destiny of her friend, it had all seemed so simple. The daughter of the Marquis of Dobbenshire, the real Louisa Haversham had been married by proxy to a wealthy American businessman, Mr. Charles Winslow III. That was how the two women had met. Louisa had needed a companion to accompany her on the journey from England, and since Phoebe had been on her way to America as a "mail-order bride," she'd been hired to take the position.

Her lips twitched in a quick smile. Who would have suspected that the two women had been so unhappy with the intended course of their lives that they would consider switching places? Her friend had longed for a life of adventure, while Phoebe...

She wrinkled her nose. As far as she was concerned, she'd had enough ''adventure.'' Her mother had died in a typhus epidemic when Phoebe had been but a toddler. Since then, she'd endured a series of orphanages and charity schools, where she'd been trained for service. She'd been a nanny, a governess and, most recently, a paid companion. But when the untoward advances of a wayward husband in London had resulted in her termination without references, Phoebe had been in dire straits. Weary of the life of a servant, she'd impulsively agreed to marry Neil Ballard.

Dear, sweet Neil. They'd been so young when last she'd seen him. How long had they proved to be an inseparable team at the orphanage? Two years? Three? Then, finally, his aunt had sent for him and he'd moved to America to become a farmer in Oregon. Yet even then their friendship had endured, through years of correspondence. Indeed, Louisa would hasten to wager that they had each revealed more about themselves in their letters than they ever would have in person.

Shifting uncomfortably, she pushed away the wave of guilt that threatened to be her undoing. In hindsight, she realized that she never should have agreed to marry her old chum. By the time the travel arrangements to America had been made, she'd begun to regret her hasty action. The thought of living in the untamed wilderness of the American Territories and becoming a farmer's wife had filled her with trepidation. She was tired of living hand-to-mouth. Moreover, Neil had made it clear that he was looking forward to having a woman to help ''take care of his property.''

Drat it all! By marrying him, she would have doomed herself to a lifetime of servitude.

Absently patting her bonnet and smoothing a hand down the front of her bodice, she pushed aside her misgivings about her cavalier treatment of an old friend.

She would have been a horrible homesteader, there was no doubt about that—and the real Louisa Haversham had been equally distressed about being locked into the predictable routine of a woman of privilege.

Was it any wonder the women had stumbled upon this solution? The fact that they both had similar builds, auburn hair and blue eyes had seemed foreordained. It was as if heaven above had planned their meeting.

Briefly closing her eyes, Louisa pressed a hand to her fluttering stomach and offered a quick prayer. Any moment now, her husband would arrive and her new life would truly begin. More than ever, she would have to be on her guard. She couldn't allow even the tiniest mistake to reveal her original background and identity.

You're Louisa Haversham Winslow now. You will be Louisa Haversham Winslow until the day you die.

So why was it still so hard to remember that she no longer had to struggle to survive? Even the tardy arrival of her husband had proved no hardship. A note from Charles's solicitor had informed her that accounts had been set up for her with the hotel and local businesses. At the solicitor's urging, she'd been able to spend her time augmenting her wardrobe, visiting the theater and ballet—even obtaining a lapdog and a lady's maid. In an amazingly short amount of time, she had been able to don all the trappings of a wealthy woman.

But her delight in amassing such luxuries had begun to wane. As the days of waiting had become weeks, she'd begun to despair of Charles ever making an appearance. She'd tortured herself with her own imaginings—that Charles had the temperament of an ogre or the age of Methuselah.

Finally, this morning, she'd received a telegram stating that she should meet the noon train.

With the help of her new maid, Chloe, Louisa had dressed in exquisitely embroidered undergarments, had laced her corset to a point where she could barely breathe and had donned a delicate white gown dotted with tiny pink rosebuds and adorned with yards and yards of ruffles. Her hair had been upswept in an intricate coiffure of braids and curls, and a perky straw hat bedecked with lace and ribbons tipped rakishly over one eyebrow. As a final touch, she'd indulged in a pink silk parasol and reticule, and white kid gloves and high-buttoned shoes.

She, Phoebe Gray, was a living, breathing fashion plate.

No. Not Phoebe. She was Louisa now.

Louisa Haversham Winslow.

Her pulse knocked erratically against the stricture of her stays and she took several quick, panting breaths. Dash it all, she shouldn't have laced the thing so tightly!

What would he be like, Mr. Charles Winslow? Would he be kind and gentle? Handsome and forthright?

More than a thousand times, Louisa had fantasized about Charles—so much so that she'd formed an ideal picture of the person she hoped to encounter. He would be of a certain age—not too old, but not too young. Judging by his attention to business, he would be quiet and studious, with the manners of a true gentleman. Despite the marriage by proxy, he would woo her gently, insisting on a proper church wedding before taking Louisa to his bed.

She felt a warmth flood into her cheeks at the mere thought. Although she'd resigned herself to the physicalities of marriage, she still hadn't been able to think of her wifely duties without blushing.

If only…

If only…

A disconcerting restlessness rushed through her veins. A sense of foreboding.

Seeking a diversion from her fears, she darted her gaze around the crowd of people who waited for the train from Charleston, then found it fixed on a huge giant of a man.

If only Charles could look like him.

The moment the thought slipped into her head, she pushed it away, scolding herself for being completely unhinged. How could she possibly be thinking of a stranger when her husband-to-be was destined to arrive at any moment? Had she lost all reason and decorum? Charles was bound to be a wonderful man, a handsome man, a kind and considerate…

No. She could not believe that particular flight of fancy. If the truth were told, she already knew enough about Charles to know that "consideration" was not one of his attributes. If it were, he would not have arranged to marry by proxy and she would not have been imprisoned in her hotel suite cooling her heels. And as much as she had comforted herself with the thought that he'd been occupied with important business, she couldn't help wondering what sort of business would keep a man from his own wedding.

She tapped her toe impatiently on the wooden platform even as she sneaked another peek at the giant. He really was larger than any man she'd ever seen before— though not in a bulky way. No, his body was that of a warrior, all whipcord muscle, much like the heroes that populated the penny novels she loved and hoped one day to write herself. Nevertheless, the breadth of his shoulders and the impossibly narrow span of his hips made him seem that much larger.

Her breath caught in her throat at the thought of being swept into the arms of such a man. What would she have done if *he* was Charles?

Her body was suddenly suffused with chills and then a strange, enervating heat. Feeling a blush rising to her cheeks, she gave a tiny shake of her head and quickly dislodged the disloyal thought.

She was Mrs. Charles Winslow III. She was Mrs. Charles Winslow III....

But the silent reminders merely inspired another rush of anxiety. Would she meet with his expectations?

Biting her lip, she despaired that Charles might be disappointed with her flaming red hair or the voluptuousness of her figure. Heaven only knew that she'd had more than one employer sniff in distaste about the "flamboyancy" of her God-given attributes. After years of service, during which Louisa had been eyed, judged and frowned at over and over again, she couldn't help feeling a measure of apprehension and dread.

Momentarily distracted by the blast of a whistle, she turned and caught sight of a plume of smoke darkening the sky above the jumble of buildings in the distance.

Once again, her stomach lurched.

He was here.

Her husband was finally here.

Convulsively, her gaze swung to the stranger who had caught her attention. Somehow, in the scant amount of time that she'd been preoccupied with her own thoughts, he'd stepped closer to her.

So close…

Although he was still a yard or two away, she felt his presence in a way she'd never encountered with another human being. It was as if her body was attuned to him in an elemental way. As if she knew him…

Despite the huffing of the approaching train, she studied the man more closely. Why, of all the passengers milling on the platform, was he the only one to capture her attention so completely? There was nothing about him that should have inspired such interest. He was dressed in rough buckskins, with his dark hair left long so that it tumbled across his collar. Indeed, there was something…heathenish about him.

No. That wasn't right. Not heathenish. Untamed. Elemental.

Unconsciously, she moistened her dry lips. The man looked as if he had recently arrived from the American wilderness. Undoubtedly, he lived the very life that she had shunned—one that was fraught with hardships.

So why did she find him so intriguing?

For a split instant, their eyes locked. Louisa was stunned by the flurry of sensations that tingled at her extremities and traveled inward to settle with a molten heat deep within her.

In that instant, she felt more feminine and beautiful than ever before. Beneath this man's regard, she didn't rue the less-than-fashionable curvaceousness of her body or the brilliant copper color of her hair. Instead, as she watched his eyes warm, she felt a measure of pride in her tightly tailored clothes and elegant appearance. Her only regret lay in a niggling reminder that she wasn't free to indulge in a bit of harmless flirtation.

A frown crossed her brow at her own audacity, just as a loud bang split the noontime air. Before Louisa could fathom what was happening, the giant in buckskins launched himself toward her.

In a rush, she saw the looming shape of his body, felt the impact of sheer muscle and bone. Then she was falling, falling, her body banging against the rough boards of the platform, the giant's frame protectively covering hers.

The world seemed to screech into slow motion, each sensation becoming sharp and distinct. Distantly, she heard the startled cries of the other passengers, the screams of fear. Tiny rocks bit into her back and arms.

But most of all, there was the heat, the strength, the power of the manly form stretched over hers. A whiff of something like pine. The gentleness of his breath as he whispered, "Easy, easy." Even in the terror of the moment, her mind honed in on the weight pressing into her, the scent of soap and the inexplicable wave of possessiveness emanating from this man's body.

Then time seemed to stop completely. There was only this moment, this stranger. Louisa became suddenly aware of the face looming over hers, the angular jut of his chin and cheekbones, the chocolatey darkness of his eyes.

Those eyes…

Why was there a part of her that seemed to recognize them—as if she'd known him in another life? She felt as if she were melting into their depths. Instinctively, she gripped his arms. And when he began to close the distance between them, she did not resist.…

Dear sweet heaven above, how could she resist?

The sudden shriek of a train whistle caused them both to start. In an instant, the noise shattered the intimacy that had twined around them like a spider's snare.

Horrified at her own reaction, Louisa pressed her

hands against the stranger's chest—only to encounter the hard contours hidden by his clothing.

Was this what a man felt like? So unyielding? So… arousing?

A flush seemed to spread from her fingers through her entire body. The effect was so startling that she began to fight, thrashing beneath him, knowing that if she didn't free herself immediately, she would…

She would what?

Swoon?

Or surrender?

Just when she feared that what little control she still possessed would vanish, the man rolled gracefully to his feet. In an instant, he'd lifted her and set her upright, his arm lingering about her waist in a too-familiar manner until she regained her balance.

Just as quickly as it had stopped, time rushed forward like a tidal wave. Louisa became aware of a multitude of details—the curious stares of the crowd, the horrified expression of her maid, the shriek of the oncoming train.

What had she done?

Inwardly, she berated herself for being so weak that she had let herself be affected by the first man she'd encountered on her long journey. She mustn't allow herself to forget who she was. There could be no hint of impropriety or even the smallest weakening of her resolve. She was *Mrs.* Charles Winslow III, and she mustn't forget that fact.

Louisa wrenched free of the man's grip. Yet even as she steeled herself against his regard, the warmth she saw in his gaze was so beguiling, so unexpected that she feared he had sensed a portion of her confusion.

Knowing that she must regain control of the situation immediately or wither into a mortified ball, Louisa scrambled to wrap the remnants of her pride around her. In a heartbeat, she assumed the same imperious tone she had employed to put many a recalcitrant child in line.

"How *dare* you, sir!" she exclaimed in a voice barely more than a whisper. Then, needing some outlet for the unsettling mixture of embarrassment, exhilaration and awareness that still thrummed through her veins, she lifted a hand and slapped the fellow across his cheek.

Although she'd put every ounce of strength behind the gesture, he barely moved. She was beginning to believe that he was no mere man at all, but a slab of granite.

"How could you…*why* did you—" Unable to formulate a coherent sentence, she stamped her foot in fury and slapped him again.

Rather than appearing cowed, the stranger bowed his head ever so slightly in apology. But the effect was minimized by the humor that sparkled deep in his eyes.

"My apologies, ma'am." He bent to scoop her parasol from the ground, pressing it into her numb hands before grabbing his hat. Slapping the brim against his leg, he dislodged most of the dust. Unfortunately, a betraying breeze carried the cloud of dirt in her direction, causing Louisa to cough and sputter.

"*Mon Dieu,* look what you 'ave done. Look!" Chloe, clucking and exclaiming in French, hurried forward to bat at Louisa's skirts. Small, dark and pretty, Chloe looked the epitome of a lady's maid in her dark dress and dainty black bonnet.

Louisa gaped in horror at her gown. No amount of brushing would ever repair the ruined dimity. She was covered in dirt, soot and far worse. One of the ruffles had been torn from the skirt, leaving a gaping hole, while smaller rips appeared at her hip.

Her eyes squeezed shut and her hands tightened

around the parasol with enough pressure to make the handle creak. Despite her efforts to control her infamous temper, she felt a white-hot tide of fury rise within her.

Vainly she tried to remind herself that the daughter of a marquess would hold her tongue, but the thought was no sooner formed than she blurted, "Have you escaped from Bedlam—or an American version of the same? What on earth would have possessed you to—to…" She gestured to her disarray with a wave of her hand.

The man had the audacity to grin. Insolently he settled his hat over the waves of his hair—hair sadly in need of a cut. He must be alone in the world. If he were attached to a wife or a sweetheart, she would have seen to his hair by now.

Stop it! It's no concern of yours.

"My apologies, ma'am. I thought I heard a shot."

Whatever explanation she had been expecting, this was not it. Louisa's mouth moved wordlessly as she fought to put words to the whirling of her brain.

"A *shot?*" she finally echoed.

"Yes, ma'am."

She saw a hint of a grin again.

Her speech grew clipped in disbelief. "What sort of shot?"

"A gunshot."

She stared at him, completely unable to fathom how the sound of gunfire should inspire this man to leap forward, passing a half-dozen other women, to throw *her* to the ground.

"You can't possibly think me so naive as to believe such a—such a crock of nonsense."

Briefly, she remembered the sharp retort, but a glance in the direction the noise had come from confirmed that a crate of eggs had fallen from a large pile of baggage.

A gooey mess was already beginning to soak into the weathered floorboards.

"Eggs," she said through clenched teeth. "Not a gunshot, but eggs."

"So it would seem."

The stranger's tone was so calm, so unflappable that she could have screamed again. How could he stand there, looking at her so blandly when she was...

A new wave of dismay swept through her body when the full import of her appearance sunk into her consciousness. Uttering a soft cry, she glanced over her shoulder just in time to see the noon train screeching to a halt amid a billow of steam.

"Chloe, help me!" Louisa turned to her maid in panic. But as the petite woman began fussing over the wrinkled flounces and repinning the bonnet to her tousled curls, Louisa knew that the maid's efforts were in vain. She was about to meet her husband—a very wealthy and powerful Bostonian businessman—looking like a waif who had just crawled out of the gutter.

Her anger sparked anew. Without thinking about the consequences of her actions, she rounded on the man who had caused her current disaster.

"How *dare* you? How *dare* you! Today of all days when it is imperative that I look my best!" As she advanced toward him, she poked his chest with her index finger to drive her point home. "A gunshot? Hah! I should have you arrested on the spot for lunacy if not for incompetence!"

But her anger offered no comfort for her situation. Louisa felt the prick of tears behind her eyes—as much from the debacle of her appearance as the fact that her tirade hardly seemed to dent this man's aura of confidence. Knowing that uttering another word might break the dam to her emotions, she swung her parasol at his arm, then whirled and strode away from him.

Slowly she made her way through the concerned onlookers. All the while, Chloe patted and tucked and pinned in an effort to repair some of the damage.

Louisa didn't need a mirror to tell her that the maid's efforts had done little to help the situation. She was a mess!

What if Charles took one look at her and sent her packing?

Louisa bit her lip to keep a sob from spilling free.

What if he took one look at her and knew that she was a fraud?

A chill swept through her body. Drat it all! Why hadn't she held her tongue? The daughter of a marquess wouldn't have railed at a stranger like a fishmonger. She would have withered him with a single glance before demanding that he be arrested for his actions.

Louisa groaned aloud when she remembered her parting shot. Surely she had revealed her coarse upbringing in that unguarded moment. A woman of the aristocracy would not lower herself to such an undignified display.

The train had come to a complete stop now. Steam ebbed into the humid air as the locomotive panted and heaved after its arduous journey.

Opening her parasol with a determined pop, Louisa studied the passengers beginning to step down to the platform.

Which one was Charles?

She had imagined so many versions of this first encounter that she wasn't sure what she should expect. Would he travel alone or with an entourage? Would he be tall or slight, thin or stout?

Would he be a kind man?

Would he learn to love her?

She shivered as if a goose had walked upon her grave. The tiny hairs at the back of her neck prickled, her body suddenly alert.

Looking out of the corner of her eye, she stiffened when she discovered that the horrible stranger hadn't dissolved into the crowd as she had believed.

Instead, he'd followed her.

Chapter Two

London

"Tell me everything," Horace Haversham said as he looked up from his ledgers at the man who had just entered the door.

Thomas Ritchie approached the desk, his heart knocking against his ribs in an anxious tattoo.

When Ritchie had first answered the advertisement for the job of private investigator, he'd thought little of what tasks might be required. He'd assumed that he might be asked to follow a wayward wife or find an old business acquaintance. For a man who had spent a lifetime devoted to petty crime, he'd thought that the situation accentuated his God-given talents for skulking in the shadows.

What he hadn't expected was to become embroiled in a web of intrigue and murder—a web that he was powerless to avoid without implicating himself in the worst possible light.

Was it only a month earlier that Horace Haversham had employed Ritchie? Was it only a few weeks since

Ritchie had discovered that Horace Haversham was a man who had literally risen from the dead?

Twenty years earlier, it had been reported that Horace had gone down in a ship destined for Hong Kong. He'd been on his way to set up trade agreements for the family shipping business. When the ship never arrived, it was assumed that Horace and all hands on deck had perished. The family title and fortune had immediately reverted to Oscar Haversham, Horace's twin and younger brother by a mere hour.

"Well? Out with it! What do you have to report?"

Ritchie cleared his throat. Hooking a finger beneath his cravat, he attempted to loosen the constraint.

"As I have explained before, a servant in Oscar Haversham's employ has become my informant. According to him, your brother's health continues to worsen. Although he had hoped to reach Italy—and the warmer climate—his ship is still docked in Liverpool. There are rumors that his business dealings are deteriorating with amazing speed. According to one of his servants, Oscar is toying with the idea of journeying to America in the hopes of obtaining a loan from his new son-in-law, Charles Winslow III."

There was no reaction on Horace's face.

"And the girls? Have they been eliminated yet?"

Ritchie's throat constricted and he wondered briefly if he would be shot for bringing bad news.

"No, milord." Ritchie unconsciously employed the title that Horace had forfeited long ago. "The elder twin, Louisa Haversham Winslow, has been holed up in her hotel suite waiting for her husband-by-proxy to collect her. Although she has often ventured out of the building to shop and enjoy the theater, her situation has proved… awkward."

"How so?"

Ritchie fumbled for a logical explanation. Dear sweet heaven above, they were casually conversing about murder!

After spending decades marooned on an uninhabited island, Horace Haversham had grown embittered and savage until, finally, he'd been rescued and returned to England. Determined to have his revenge on a brother who had failed to search for him, Horace intended to have his title back. But rather than claiming it as his right, he had decided to eliminate all possible heirs first, and thereby destroy his brother and exact a revenge he'd dreamed about for years.

Which meant that Oscar Haversham and his daughters would have to die.

Horace scowled impatiently. "*Why* has the task proved difficult?"

"T-too many prying eyes, I believe. The person you hired to…take care of the matter…has not had an opportunity as of yet."

Horace grunted in irritation, but did not press the point. "What of the other one? Phoebe. The one destined for Oregon."

This was the moment that Ritchie had been dreading. "In that respect, I have some bad news. Your…" Ritchie searched for the correct euphemism to employ before finally continuing. "Your…*people* failed in the attempt."

Horace's hands clenched around the arms of his chair and his whole body became rigid with fury. "What do you mean?"

"I—I mean that the plot was discovered. Your assistant—Mr. Badger, wasn't it?"

"Yes, yes, go on," Horace said with an impatient wave of his hand.

"Mr. Badger traveled to America to orchestrate matters for you and…ensure that each of the tasks was…completed to your satisfaction." Ritchie could feel the sweat gathering on his upper lip and between his shoulder blades. "This morning, he sent a telegram saying that the…the attempt against Miss Phoebe Gray was unsuccessful."

Fearing that he would be punished for bringing the disappointing tidings, Ritchie threw the telegram onto the desk, then took two steps backward.

Scowling, Horace read the slip of paper, then swore, crumpling it into a ball that he threw to the floor. Jumping to his feet, he strode to the opposite side of the room and peered from beneath the blinds to the street below.

A stark sliver of light revealed his features. Not for the first time, the similarities between this man and the Marquis of Dobbenshire struck Ritchie. If the marquis had not been afflicted with consumption, he would have looked like this—tall, rugged, fierce. And yet…there was a cruelty to Horace's features. One born from years of solitude and survival.

"The servant you spoke to…" Horace began.

"Yes?"

"Was he sure that Oscar intended to journey to America?"

"Yes, sir. Haversham's business situation is so grave that there seems to be no other choice. Unless Oscar can obtain the money he needs in short order, his business empire will crumble."

If Horace was concerned about his brother's financial ruin, he gave no sign. Instead, he said decisively, "Send a telegram to Mr. Badger. Tell him I'm on my way to

America. If Oscar is bound for Boston, then I intend to arrive there first. We'll book passage on a steam sloop to save as much time as possible. Tell Mr. Badger that I want him to delay matters with Louisa Haversham until I get there.''

"Sir?"

"Don't you see, Ritchie? I want my brother to sail for America thinking that he has a hope for redemption. I don't want the girl killed until he is in Boston. Then I can watch his reaction when he discovers his efforts were all for naught."

"Y-yes, sir."

"In the meantime, tell Badger that I insist he take care of the other girl immediately."

Ritchie's sweat turned ice cold as the harsh cast of Horace's face intensified.

"I want her dead before I set foot on American soil."

New York

Louisa quickly cast a glance around the crowd lingering on the platform. She'd already born the brunt of their curiosity and she didn't relish making a scene again. Not when passengers were beginning to disembark.

Her hands balled into tight fists. Although she'd sworn that she wouldn't speak to this stranger again, she had no alternative but to whisper tightly, "Go away."

She could have been talking to a post. He stuck to her side like a burr.

"I thought I'd better stay to help you explain things," he murmured, his voice a low rumble.

Louisa stiffened in horror at the mere idea of meeting Charles for the first time with this giant at her side. She was having a difficult time concentrating already. Her body ached from the fall and her skin still retained a portion of this man's heat. She didn't need a flesh-and-blood reminder of what had occurred. Especially not when the mere memory had the power to make her body grow warm and heavy.

"That isn't necessary," she hastened to assure him. Although it galled her, she added, "But thank you for your thoughtfulness."

When he didn't move, she glanced nervously at the train, then again at the stranger. "I really must insist that you leave," she said desperately. "If you were to stay, it would make things…"

"Awkward?"

She released a quick breath of relief. "Immensely awkward."

"Ah." The stranger looked at the crowd. "Exactly who are you meeting?"

Were all Americans so blunt, so intrusive, so…forceful?

She refused to answer, but when it became apparent that he didn't intend to leave without an explanation, she said, "My husband."

"Ahh." His eyes narrowed ever so slightly.

Louisa felt her balance momentarily desert her at his careful inspection.

"You don't look like a married woman," he stated bluntly.

She swallowed hard, wondering if the man had managed to tap into her thoughts somehow.

"You look…untouched."

Louisa gasped, scrambling to think of a scathing retort. But at that moment, she became aware of a stocky, balding gentleman who had stopped a scant yard away.

He was staring at her with such open dismay that she flushed anew.

Was this mousy-looking fellow Charles?

Disappointment made her speechless for a moment. Somehow she'd thought that such a successful businessman would have a different air about him. There was something…subservient about the man, not forceful, as she had imagined.

"Charles?" Louisa breathed, ignoring the giant at her side and trying not to compare the two men.

Taking a step forward, she extended a hand for his kiss. But when the man took it, his touch was cool and restrained. He held her hand awkwardly, then offered a little shake rather than a kiss.

"You are Louisa Haversham Winslow, I presume?"

"Yes."

The man released her and dug into a leather portfolio he carried, offering her a neatly printed card.

"My name is Grover Pritchard."

So he wasn't Charles. Louisa felt a wave of relief.

"I am Charles Winslow's lawyer."

"Lawyer?" Her lips could barely form the word. An icy fear settled in her veins. Had she been found out?

Mr. Pritchard glanced at the giant, who continued to stand behind her.

Turning pointedly, Louisa stated, "You may go now. As you can see, I've been delivered into safe hands."

The giant didn't move. Instead, he was studying Mr. Pritchard with open suspicion.

Louisa's panic increased. "I must insist that you return to your own activities. This man will deliver me safely to my husband, I can assure you."

Still the stranger offered no sign of leaving.

Huffing in impatience, Mr. Pritchard took Louisa's arm, drawing her aside.

"Who is that man?" he whispered, casting disapproving glances over her shoulder.

"I—I don't know. I…suffered a mishap a few minutes ago, and he felt it necessary to wait with me until Charles arrived."

Her explanation bordered on untruth, but she prayed the lawyer would accept the words at face value.

Mr. Pritchard gave a soft grunt, then took her elbow as if to steady her. "Mrs. Winslow, I'm afraid I have some rather…distressing news to impart."

A trembling began in her extremities and she felt the world around her lurch, but Louisa clung to her wits with every ounce of will she possessed.

Mr. Pritchard paused to glower again at the stranger behind them, before murmuring, "I really must insist that you return to your hotel room, where I can meet with you more privately."

Charles didn't want to create a public scene. He would send the police to fetch her from the suite where she'd lived for the past two weeks.

Unconsciously, Louisa clutched Mr. Pritchard's arm. "Please," she whispered through wooden lips. "Tell me now."

Mr. Pritchard looked down, clearly fearing that Louisa would react badly. "Madam, your husband…"

"Yes?"

"Your husband is dead."

Dead?

Louisa wasn't sure if she had actually uttered the word aloud. Shock shuddered through her body, robbing her of strength.

"No…" She managed to summon a faint laugh.

"There must be a mistake. I just received a…a telegram from Charles a few days ago.…"

Obviously fearing she would faint, Mr. Pritchard drew her toward a bench and sat beside her. "*I* sent those telegrams, Mrs. Winslow." He took her hand. "I hope you will forgive me, but I didn't know how to break the news in such a blunt fashion. I thought it would be best if I were here."

When Louisa continued to stare at him in bewilderment, he continued. "Charles grew ill during his last business trip, gravely ill. When I asked him whether I should send for you, he refused. He didn't want to worry you. Unfortunately, in the past week, his condition deteriorated quickly. There wouldn't have been time for you to join him even if I'd sent you a message."

"Dead?" Louisa whispered again, unable to fathom the reality of the situation. She had prepared herself for many things, but not this.

Mr. Pritchard abruptly stood, motioning to Chloe. "Please take Mrs. Winslow back to her suite. She's had a shock, and I hardly think the midday heat is good for her."

"But of course, *monsieur*," Chloe murmured, making a sad tsking sound with her tongue.

Mr. Pritchard turned back to Louisa, helping her to rise. "I'll join you directly, Mrs. Winslow. For now, I think you need a few minutes alone. I have several matters to attend to so that the bod—Mr. Winslow's remains can be brought here. Once I've finished, I'll meet with you again. At that time, we can prepare for your trip to Boston and see to funeral arrangements."

Distantly, Louisa was aware of Mr. Pritchard leading her through the station house. But even as she scrambled to make sense of the situation, a single thought stuck in her mind like a burr.

Once again, due to a bitter twist of fate, she was being forced to wait in New York until her husband—or in this case, her husband's body—arrived.

A wave of blackness swam in front of her eyes. Louisa felt herself falter, but not from grief. She did not wish to be disrespectful of Charles Winslow and his unfortunate demise. But if the truth were known, she had been given little information about him other than his name and his supposed wealth. No, what had the ability to steal the breath from her body was the precariousness of her predicament. In one simple declaration she had fallen from being Mrs. Charles Winslow III, wife of a wealthy Bostonian entrepreneur, to…

To being no better off than she'd been before leaving England.

Once again, she was alone with no means of revenue to support herself.

Somehow, through a fog of confusion, she heard Mr. Pritchard reiterate his condolences, and a bitter laugh lodged in her throat.

How can I be a widow when I have yet to be a wife?

Mistaking her choked cry for one of sorrow, Mr. Pritchard took her arm and ushered her toward a line of waiting carriages outside the station.

After giving the address to the driver, he took Louisa's hand in a manner that seemed almost fatherly. "I will join you as soon as I can. You can count on me." His voice dropped and his expression became grave. "Please, Mrs. Winslow…speak to no one until I have had an opportunity to meet with you. Promise me."

Startled by his request, she stammered, "I—I promise."

It was at that moment that she suddenly remembered the giant. Had he been listening the whole time?

She looked up and scanned the crowd, realizing that the stranger had disappeared. When he had left her, she wasn't sure.

Good riddance, she silently cried. The man was a nuisance from the moment he'd thrown her to the ground.

But as she climbed into the carriage, she couldn't help scanning the crowd for a glimpse of buckskin. And her disappointment in not finding the man was nearly as great as what she had suffered upon discovering that her marriage was over before it had ever really begun.

Neil Ballard watched from the shadows of a nearby alcove as ''Louisa Haversham'' was hustled from the railway station and bundled into a waiting carriage.

So that was the woman who was supposed to have been his bride.

Neil couldn't prevent the grin of satisfaction that spread over his lips. She was a rare beauty—even more lovely than her sister, he'd wager. With her pale skin, flaming red hair and indigo eyes, she made a powerful first impression. Who would have thought that the gawky, gangly girl from the orphanage could have grown into someone so lovely? He might have been tempted to think she was a stranger if not for her temper.

Unconsciously, his hand rubbed his upper arm. In that particular respect, Louisa hadn't changed at all. She still had a volatile nature. But he didn't mind. A woman who was quick to anger would be just as passionate in displaying other, more intimate, emotions. And that was a quality that any man could appreciate.

As the carriage melted into the chaos of the street traffic and Louisa faded from view, Neil straightened and made his way back to the station. Whistling softly to himself, he went in search of his baggage.

Only this morning, he'd feared that his cross-country journey would be for naught, and he would arrive to find his old friend already married to Charles Winslow. But the Fates had smiled upon him.

Charles Winslow was dead. Dead!

Neil nearly laughed aloud at the happy twist of events. He'd come to New York at a run the moment he'd discovered that the woman who had arrived in Oregon and claimed to be his mail-order bride was, in fact, a titled Englishwoman who had fallen in love with another man along the journey. In a dizzying series of explanations relayed to Neil by Phoebe's traveling companions, he had discovered that Phoebe Gray and Louisa Haversham were actually sisters who had been parted as babies. Each of the girls had been raised thinking that she was an only child. Moreover, they'd been completely unaware of the way their father had conspired to keep them apart....

It was only when Phoebe Gray's life had been threatened that she'd discovered the truth. And when Neil had found out that the same uncle who had tried to kill Phoebe was intent on harming his childhood friend, he'd reacted purely on instinct. Packing only essentials, he'd caught the next train for New York.

As mile after mile sped past, he'd told himself he was a fool. By the time he reached the East Coast, Louisa would be married—and what did it matter? She had rejected him for the arms of a stranger. She had married for money.

But even as he'd insisted that he was better off without her, he hadn't turned around. Instead, he'd been even more determined to bring the two of them together again

after so many years. He'd been driven by a need to see
her again, to discover if she'd changed, to tell her just
what he thought of her cavalier treatment. Yet, mere
minutes after holding Louisa in his arms, after feeling
her body soft and warm against his own, he'd learned
that there was nothing to keep him from claiming her
and taking her home.

Except her temper.

And her infinite stubbornness.

Again, his lips tipped in a wry smile. Although Louisa
had changed over the years—even going so far as to
adopt a new name and a new life for herself—some
things hadn't altered a bit. And judging by the fire in
her eyes, she wouldn't be looking too kindly upon him
at the moment.

So what should he do? Heaven only knew he couldn't
force her to return with him to Oregon....

Which left him with a second alternative, one that he
had toyed with only briefly on the journey. What if he
could insinuate himself into her life, make her care for
him, make her *want* to return with him?

Yes...yes, he liked that idea.

His whistle grew jauntier even as his brain began to
formulate a strategy. He needed to hurry. If he didn't
get to the hotel before Grover Pritchard, his plans would
be for naught.

Chapter Three

"Chloe, could you be a dear and run down to that little corner shop we discovered yesterday? I'm suddenly in need of a cup of tea, and the blend they served yesterday was so delightful. Maybe it would soothe my jangled nerves and help me think."

Chloe patted her arm. "*Mais oui,* but of course. I will return just as quickly as I can, *madame,*" Chloe said after ushering Louisa to the entrance of her suite.

"Check at the front desk for the nearest apothecary, as well. My head is throbbing. Perhaps the druggist could suggest something."

"Yes, *madame.*"

As Chloe bustled down the hallway with a rustle of skirts, Louisa wearily twisted the key in the lock. In truth, she didn't care if her maid was able to return with the items or not. She merely needed a few minutes alone.

Shutting the door behind her, Louisa leaned against the panels, wondering why it seemed as if a lifetime had passed since she'd left the room.

Had it only been an hour? When she'd last left these walls, she'd been filled with such anxiety, excitement, hope....

And now?

Tossing her parasol onto one of the velvet-tufted settees, she closed her eyes. The quiet was a balm to her spirit.

To say Louisa was shocked and dismayed by recent events would be an understatement. Even now, her stomach churned with nerves. But as the reality of her situation sank in, she soon realized that it wasn't her "widowhood" that bothered her most. No, what caused her the greatest amount of distress was the fact that she had been relegated once again to the gilded prison of her hotel room, where she would be forced to return to wearing black. And it was only a matter of time before she would be penniless and out on her ear.

Stop it! How selfish can one person be?

Biting her lip, Louisa sank onto the edge of a chair, gripping the armrests. Thoughts bubbled in her brain like a mountain spring, jumping from her predicament to the stranger at the train station to Charles's lawyer.

What would happen to her in the next few days? Mr. Pritchard had mentioned that Charles's remains would need to be shipped to Boston by train.

Louisa shivered at the mere thought. Apparently, she would be expected to accompany the body to Boston and arrange for a funeral....

Arrange for a funeral...

If she were about to be tossed onto the streets, Mr. Pritchard wouldn't be looking to her for such niceties.

Did that mean her secret was still safe?

She grew still, a glimmer of hope chasing away the chill in her bones. As much as she might want to summon genuine grief for Charles, he was a stranger to her, nothing more than a name. How could she mourn for someone she'd never known?

Louisa pressed a hand against her lips to still the trembling that racked her body. She surrendered to a gamut of emotions—regret, fear, hope and…relief.

Relief?

Yes. Relief.

Suddenly, she saw her predicament from another perspective. She was a widow. She didn't have to live with a stranger—or a husband. She was free. *Free!*

Living a life of service, Louisa had noted that widows were allowed a certain amount of latitude in society. If a widow was too flamboyant, it was attributed to her grief. If she wanted to travel alone, it was seen as a need for solace. If she immersed herself in wild escapades, it was a longing for diversion. As long as a woman followed the dictates of good taste and maintained an aura of soberness, she was left alone. If it weren't for the inky-colored wardrobe she would be expected to wear and the lack of any sort of male company, a person might long to be in Louisa's position.

A knock sounded at the door and Bitsy began barking from the side of the bedroom. Louisa quickly schooled her features, knowing that Mr. Pritchard must be on the other side. Heaven only knew she mustn't reveal her true feelings to the man. She would shock him to the tips of his puritanical toes if she were to display anything but the most mournful demeanor. For the next few weeks, she must continue her charade with utmost care. If Mr. Pritchard were ever to suspect she was an imposter…

Louisa twisted the knob and swung the door wide. ''Mr. Pritchard, how kind of you…''

The words trailed away into a choked silence as she realized it wasn't Mr. Pritchard who stood before her, but the stranger from the station.

''Oh!'' As she stared at the man on the threshold,

Louisa's exclamation was little more than a puff of air, but it was clear he'd heard her.

He touched the brim of his hat with two fingers. "Mrs. Winslow."

How did he know her name? Where to find her?

Louisa shook herself. He must have heard it at the station. How else could he have known where to find her except by eavesdropping?

At a loss as to how she should respond, Louisa couldn't move, couldn't think. She could only wonder why he would seek her out.

And why her heart suddenly beat an odd tattoo.

Realizing that she was gaping at him in a manner that might be misconstrued, she frowned. "Haven't you already done enough to ruin my day, Mister..."

"Smith. John Smith."

She cocked an eyebrow in disbelief. She never would have imagined such an unusual man to have such a common name.

"You've come at a bad time, Mr. Smith." Another spurt of shrill barking underscored her claim. "I'll have to accept your apologies another—"

"I haven't come to apologize."

Before she knew what he intended, he stepped into her sitting room and closed the door behind him.

Louisa gasped, her chin lifting a notch. "Mr. Smith, I don't know what business you think you have with me, but I really must insist that you leave." When he didn't move, she added pointedly, "Now."

To her horror, he ignored her. Moving past Louisa, he opened the door to her bedroom and peered inside, then began looking behind the larger pieces of furniture as if he expected someone to be skulking in the shadows.

Her spine stiffened in outrage. "What in heaven's name do you think you're doing?"

"My job."

Her mouth worked wordlessly before she finally managed to say, "If this hotel—"

"I don't work for the hotel. I work for your husband, Charles Winslow III."

Louisa's mouth hung open and she stared at him dumbly. Charles? "But Charles is…"

"Dead. Yes, I know. I heard Mr. Pritchard's announcement at the train station."

So this man *had* been eavesdropping on a conversation that was meant to be private.

"Mr. Smith—"

"You may call me John, if you wish."

"Mr. Smith—"

"After all, we'll be spending a great deal of time together."

Again she was at a loss for words. Then, with a helpless wave of her hand, she dismissed his outlandish statement.

"If you are aware of Charles's death, then you must also know that any business you had with him is over. You will have to make an appointment with Mr. Pritchard if you are seeking payment." Sweeping her skirts aside, she moved toward the door.

"I have already been paid. In advance." His eyes became piercing, forcing her to stop midway. "Charles hired me to be your bodyguard, Mrs. Winslow."

Louisa huffed softly in disbelief. "If this is a twisted effort to finagle money out of me—"

"I can assure you, Mrs. Winslow, that I am your bodyguard."

"I—it's preposterous."

"Not at all. As the wife of a wealthy businessman, you could be at risk. Your husband was naturally concerned about your welfare."

"But…a bodyguard? Surely he wouldn't have gone to such extremes."

"Obviously you aren't familiar with the hazards to be found in America, Mrs. Winslow. For all our outer gloss and polish, this is still a new country. A wild and somewhat untamed country. Even the civilized trappings to be found in New York and Boston haven't completely dispelled a thread of lawlessness that runs through the…baser levels of society."

Louisa unconsciously lifted a hand to her throat.

"A woman such as yourself is in danger of being kidnapped—or worse—by brigands attempting to steal part of your husband's vast fortune."

Louisa could barely breathe. "But…I don't…"

"Your husband cared enough for your safety to arrange for my services before he died. You see, Charles had received a few threats…"

"Threats?" she whispered.

"Threats against your safety."

Suddenly Louisa wasn't feeling nearly as fortunate as she had only moments earlier. "I—I can't believe—"

"You'd best believe what I'm saying, Mrs. Winslow. To ignore your husband's wishes concerning this matter could have serious repercussions. Deadly repercussions."

Louisa suddenly remembered how Mr. Pritchard had insisted that she speak to no one until he could confer with her again. Was this what he'd meant? Had he feared for her safety?

Her heart was thumping so wildly in her breast that she barely noticed John as he moved toward her. When he pulled her against him, comforting her, offering her the strength of his embrace, she didn't resist. She *couldn't* resist.

He was so warm, so broad, so protecting. It was easy to see that the man was good at his job. His mere presence inspired confidence and a sense of security.

And yet…with each moment that passed, Louisa became less aware of John as an employee and more aware of him as a man.

A tall man.

A handsome man.

A man capable of seduction.

Wrenching free, she wrapped her arms around her waist, unconsciously trying to retain the heat that had seeped into her body.

"I appreciate the fact that you feel an obligation, Mr. Smith, but—"

"I'm staying," he said bluntly.

She scowled, his intractable attitude grating against already sensitive nerves.

"Surely you can understand that, *if* I found it necessary, I would prefer to hire a person of my own choosing."

He didn't move. He merely stared hard at her with those dark eyes, as if she'd said something childish.

"I can assure you that I'll make every effort to find someone suitable."

"I'm not going away."

For the second time today, she stamped her foot in outrage. "Mr. Smith, I am a grown woman. I have seen to my own needs for some time." She bit her lip, realizing that a true daughter of a marquis would not have made such a pronouncement. Rushing on, she added, "I appreciate your situation, but surely you must understand mine. At a time of such…sadness, I would prefer to have people around me that…that I could…that would…''

She doubted he was even listening to her. Brushing past her, he opened the door and stepped into the hall. As much as she might have wished he were leaving for good, she knew she wouldn't be so lucky. He'd been gone less than a heartbeat before he returned, his arms laden with a dusty saddle, saddlebags and a rolled up blanket that she had no doubts held a firearm of some sort.

''I'm staying,'' he said again, his voice implacable.

As if to punctuate his claim, he dropped his belongings on the floor and tossed his hat on top. Then he removed his jacket, revealing a pair of pistols strapped to his hips.

Louisa was startled by the sight of the firearms, as well as the sheer strength of the man's body without the shield of the bulky leather coat.

Dear sweet heaven above. This man was supposed to protect her?

And who would protect her from him?

A potent frustration flooded her body as she was confronted with her own vulnerability. For two cents she would scream, causing a scene the likes of which he had never seen before. But even as she contemplated that extreme course of action, she knew that such behavior would hurt her reputation far more than his.

''If you will excuse me,'' she said through clenched teeth, ''I've had a very trying afternoon. I'm feeling the need to…grieve.''

Knowing that remaining in this man's presence for another moment would be more than her infamous temper would bear, she marched into her bedroom and slammed the door. Bitsy took one look at her and scampered back to her basket.

Of all the interfering, overbearing barbarians! He seemed to think that she had nothing but fluff between her ears. She had half a mind to let him know just how clever she could be. She would ask Mr. Pritchard to send the man packing—or summon a magistrate and have Mr. Smith hauled away in leg irons!

But even as she contemplated the idea, she froze. Was that what a true marquess would do? People would be expecting a woman with manners polished in finishing school. Recalling the women she had worked for in the past few years, Louisa was well aware that aristocratic ladies tended to be subservient, meek and mild. She mustn't allow her own stubbornness to give her away.

And yet…she couldn't fathom how she was going to endure more than a day or two in Mr. Smith's company. He was too…too…

Disturbing.

How in the world was she going to get rid of him?

A knock at her bedroom door caused her to jump. Too late, she realized that she hadn't twisted the key in the lock. Before she could blink, the door had opened and John Smith stood framed in the archway.

Bitsy growled from her spot on the floor.

''I arranged for the hotel staff to send up a bath. I assumed you would want to wash before Mr. Pritchard returned.''

Louisa was caught off balance at her bodyguard's thoughtfulness. She teetered on the brink of anger, exasperation and tears. A chance to clear her mind and soak her aches away was just what she needed. Only then would she be able to clear her head and think more rationally.

"Thank you," she offered in a low voice.

A fleet of liveried servants filed into her room, setting a long copper tub on the floor. With expert efficiency, they draped a linen sheet over the sides and against the bottom to protect Louisa from sharp edges. Then they proceeded to fill the tub with buckets of hot water, all the while avoiding the little dog that scampered between their legs.

Just as abruptly, the room emptied and Louisa was alone.

Not about to make the same mistake twice, she tiptoed to the door and carefully turned the key in the lock. Then and only then did she begin to feel a lessening of the tensions that had been gripping her muscles.

As her body relaxed, she became aware of the throbbing of her limbs from an assortment of bruises. Tugging the gloves from her hands, she frowned when she saw that the leather had been pierced by sharp pieces of gravel. Spots of blood dotted her palms.

Breathing deeply, she tried to quell the burst of nausea that too much excitement and nervousness invariably inspired. Since birth, she'd been cursed with a weak stomach whenever her emotions ran high.

Railing against her traitorous emotions, she unpinned her bonnet and tossed it onto the bed. Then, with fingers that trembled, she unbuttoned her bodice and wriggled free.

Normally, Louisa was tidy to a fault, but today she didn't have the energy to move any more than necessary. As she wrestled with the fasteners of her skirt, petticoats and corset, she suddenly wished she hadn't sent Chloe on an errand.

At long last she emerged from her man-made cocoon.

Taking her first real breath in hours, she drew her chemise over her head and stepped out of her pantalets.

Ruined. All ruined. Even the delicate lace of her corset and chemise had succumbed to the pressures of the day.

Again, tears gathered and a sob lodged in her throat. She never would have imagined that an afternoon could go so horribly awry.

Tearing the pins from her hair, she shook out the tresses so that they tumbled in waves to a point well below her hips. As she padded to the tub, her fingers massaged her scalp, willing away the headache that was already beginning to form.

"It's been a beastly day, Bitsy," she whispered to the dog who watched her avidly.

Two dark eyes blinked at her from a mop of silky white hair, but she stood clear of any possible splashes of water.

Draping a bath sheet over a nearby chair, Louisa reached into a jar on the bedside table, gathering a handful of scented salts and tossing them into the water.

She had just turned to step into the tub when a pain shot through her thigh, raced up her back and down to her toes. Crying out, she glanced down and saw a ghastly purple-black bruise darkening her skin from hip to knee.

Louisa collapsed onto a nearby chair just as the door came crashing open and John Smith stood poised in the opening, a pair of pistols aimed in her direction. Squealing in outrage, she felt his gaze rake the length of her body as she grabbed for the bath sheet. Jumping to her feet, she sought the first weapon she could find, a long-handled scrub brush. Whirling on the man who claimed to be her bodyguard, she rained blows on his arms and shoulders. At the same moment, Bitsy jumped from the basket. Yapping and snarling, she came to her mistress's defense, nipping at John's heels.

"You beast! You haven't got the manners of a goat…or a…" Unable to summon words caustic enough, Louisa growled in disgust instead.

Her attack had very little effect. After replacing his revolvers in his holster, he disarmed her with a deft flick of his wrist. Tossing the brush onto the bed, he scooped the dog from the floor and set it outside the bedroom, pulling the damaged door shut.

Separated from her mistress, Bitsy barked even more frantically, and the thump of paws and the scrabbling of claws made it clear that she would try her best to remove the barrier.

Ignoring the din caused by the dog, John wrapped his arms around Louisa's waist and bodily replaced her on the chair. He held her tightly until her outburst wound down like a child's toy. Then, despite her protests, he pushed the hem of the towel to one side, exposing the length of her thigh and the horrible bruise.

A long silence followed. Then he said, "I'm sorry."

Whatever she had expected him to say, his low apology wasn't it. The sincerity of his tone dissipated her anger like so much smoke, leaving her weary and trembling. His eyes drew her into their dark pools. Again, she felt a sense of familiarity she couldn't explain.

Gently, fleetingly, John examined the battered flesh. Retrieving one of the linen squares from the pile on the dry sink, he dipped the cloth into the cool water of the pitcher and returned.

Without a word, he pressed the cloth to her skin, softly, fleetingly, with only enough pressure to transfer the coolness, yet not enough to cause her pain.

"Do you have any other injuries?"

"No." The word barely escaped her tight throat. Nevertheless, he met her gaze directly, obviously searching for the slightest sign of deceit. "No! I've got a few scrapes on my hands, but nothing serious."

One by one, he lifted her palms and dabbed at them with the cloth. With the blood wiped away, it was easy to see that the wounds were superficial.

"I'm truly sorry that I caused you harm."

His voice was low and seemed to brush against her nerve ends like soft velvet. A molten fire settled deep in her body, radiating to her extremities.

This was madness. Sheer and utter madness. Louisa had been informed of her husband's death less than an hour before. Yet, here she sat in a state of total deshabille with a man who was a stranger to her. Yes, she had prepared herself to marry a man she'd never met, but this...

This encounter was more intimate, more alluring, more dangerous than anything she could have imagined occurring between a man and a woman.

Vaguely, she supposed that the emotions that swirled within her were the first whisperings of passion—an emotion that she had begun to believe she was incapable of feeling.

One of Louisa's secret desires was to write a book filled with romantic tales. She wanted to invent stories equal to the depth of emotion found in the works of Charlotte Bronte or Jane Austen. And yet, despite her romantic inclinations, Louisa had never experienced pleasure in a man's arms.

In her years of service, she had not completely escaped the attention of male visitors. Her red hair and voluptuous build had caused many a man to attempt to

woo her into submission. Indeed, it had been the untoward advances she'd encountered in one of her last positions that had caused her to journey to America. Yet
in all that time, she had never experienced the quick-
ening of her heart or this telltale shortness of breath. She
had begun to believe that she was incapable of such
riotous emotions…

Until now.

John glanced up from his ministrations, causing her
to look quickly away.

Dear sweet heaven above. She couldn't let him know
what he was doing to her. Her humiliation would be
complete if he were to sense the way he'd managed to
plow through her defenses in such a short time.

As he bent over his task again, tending to her opposite
hand, she gazed down into the tumbling waves of his
hair. Her fingers twitched with her sudden need to touch
those curls.

What would he say if she were to give in to her in-
sanity? Would he look upon her as a wanton? He
wouldn't be the first. During the attempted seduction by
her former employer, he had claimed that no woman
with such flaming hair could be anything but a siren and
a seductress.

How would John Smith react to being seduced?

The thought raced through her mind with the searing
heat of a brand, and she jerked free of John's hands, her
fingers curling into fists until the scrapes burned.

John cast a questioning look in her direction, then
resolutely tugged the sheet into place, hiding the length
of her thigh and allowing her some modicum of privacy.

"Are you all right?"

She nodded, unable to speak.

"You're sure?"

"Yes, I'm sure." Her voice was far too husky and telling to her ears. She could only pray it wasn't so revealing to his.

His eyes narrowed consideringly. "I've got some liniment in my saddlebags that will help to ease the pain. It smells like the very devil, but it will do the trick." Without another word, he stood and walked to doorway. "After your bath, we'll see to it."

We'll see to it?

The mere thought was enough to make her tremble anew. Her breathing became strident, her body flushed as she realized that this man had taken more liberties with her than any other human being she had ever encountered. And now he calmly informed her that he wished to touch her again? To tend to her injuries himself?

No. No, she couldn't bear it. Not after all she had endured today. To have him touch her again would be her undoing.

Knowing that she must not allow him to sense even a hint of weakness in her manner, she jumped to her feet, tightly clutching the towel.

"No, Mr. Smith, we will not tend to anything." She tried to make her tone frosty and her posture imperious. "As far as I'm concerned, you have overstepped your boundaries."

"I heard you scream, Mrs. Winslow."

How was it possible for her formal title to ring like a caress?

"I barely cried out!" she insisted.

He shrugged. "I thought you were in trouble."

"The sound was nothing more than a reaction to discovering the bruise. And in any event, even if my life had been in peril, you should have knocked!"

"And will you have me announcing my arrival to unknown brigands and making proper introductions before attempting to rescue you?"

She hugged her arms under her breasts, then released them again when his gaze dropped to the tautly pulled bath sheet.

"Mr. Smith." She tried again, attempting to sound as self-righteous as a dowager queen. "If you are to remain in my employ—"

"I am in your husband's employ."

"But my husband is dead!"

"Then I will wait until that time when I feel a responsible party has been brought in for your care before making any changes to the agreement I had with your husband."

"I am more than able to take care of myself."

"Not from what I've been able to see."

She gaped at him openmouthed. "I—I hardly see how you could have come to such a conclusion. I've been on my own for—"

She barely managed to stop herself in time. She'd been about to reveal that she'd been alone for years. But by admitting such a thing, she would betray her charade.

"I've been on my own for weeks."

His expression was rueful. "That hardly makes you an expert."

Her bare foot stamped on the ground in irritation before she could stop herself. "Mr. Smith, if you would examine today's debacles—"

"Today's what?"

"Debacles! Calamities, fiascoes... If you considered them, you would be forced to admit that all of my misadventures have resulted from your own overhastiness to act."

"Overhastiness?" he repeated as he turned away in apparent unconcern. "Is that truly a word?"

The moment he opened the door, Bitsy raced in, her toenails scrabbling on the wooden floor as she fought to stop her forward charge. Instead, she tumbled head over heels under the bed.

Without a second glance, John continued into the sitting room. At the man's apparent disregard for her feelings, frustration roiled within Louisa, causing the last wisps of sensuality to evaporate. Stomping after the man, she tried to hammer her argument home.

"You are missing the point. If you hadn't interfered in business that was not your own, I wouldn't have been hurt today and that door wouldn't be broken!"

John turned, his eyes dark and filled with determination. "I can assure you, Mrs. Winslow, that you are very much my business."

Before she could absorb the change in direction, he turned and prowled toward her with the stealth and determination of a cat. "I plan to see to your safety."

"But it is *you* who has made me *unsafe!*"

Before she knew what he meant to do, he whipped an arm around her waist, hauling her tightly toward him.

"Unsafe?" he growled. "You have no idea how vulnerable you are at this moment. There are those who have already declared their intentions to destroy you."

His words chilled her to her very bones. Looking up at the sharp cast of his features and the tight line of his mouth, she was forced to believe him.

"B-but why?" she whispered.

"Because of who you are…and who you are destined to be."

Then, before she could absorb his cryptic statement, his head dipped and his lips closed over her own.

Louisa felt as if she had been struck by lightning. A streak of sensations shot through her body, even as her limbs seemed to lose all strength. Unconsciously, she gripped his jacket with both hands in an effort to remain standing, while his lips moved over hers in such effortless mastery that she couldn't help but respond.

John's arms wrapped tighter around her waist, drawing her against him, pressing her to his length. Without the protection of her clothes, each muscle and ridge was imprinted in her body and seared into her memories.

Unable to stop herself, she released her grip of his clothes and plunged her fingers into his hair, delighting in the silky texture, the thick weight of the sable curls. Her mouth opened to the pressure of his tongue, and she shuddered as one of his hands spread wide to explore the swell of her hips.

And then, distantly, just when Louisa was ready to abandon all reason, she heard a scrape, a scratch…

The twist of a key in the lock!

Chapter Four

Both of them moved at once, Louisa to step away and grip the bath sheet, John to pull her protectively behind his body even as he used his free hand to whip a revolver from his holster.

Horrified, Louisa watched as the door slowly opened, revealing not only the dainty form of her maid, but the mousy figure of Mr. Pritchard, as well.

"Get out," John growled, fixing his revolver on a spot between Pritchard's eyes.

The little man gasped and backed up against the door-jamb, holding his satchel in front of him as if it were a shield.

"No!" Louisa stepped around John's body, grabbing his arm, even as her bodyguard pulled back the hammer of his revolver.

Mr. Pritchard offered a high squeak of distress.

Chloe began muttering prayers beneath her breath.

Bitsy bolted into the room, saw a new target of frustration in Mr. Pritchard and began snarling at him, trying to bite the man's trousers.

"Bitsy, please stop!" Louisa cried.

Mercifully, the dog obeyed, sitting on her haunches,

her gaze bouncing over the players in the room. It was clear that the tension in the hotel suite continued to distress her, but she'd been trained well before being sold to Louisa, and she didn't dare disobey.

Louisa turned to John. "Stop," she said again, tugging at his arm. Slowly, gradually, he released the hammer and lowered his arm.

"Get out," he said again.

Mr. Pritchard's mouth worked, but no sound came forth.

"No, I'm supposed to meet with Mr. Pritchard about personal business concerning my husband," Louisa announced.

John looked at her, then at the cowering lawyer. His body relaxed infinitesimally. "As you can see, she isn't ready to entertain your company at present."

Mr. Pritchard cleared his throat, squeaked, then cleared it again before managing to ask, "A-and who are you?"

"I'm Mrs. Winslow's bodyguard."

Pritchard blinked as if John had proclaimed he was the king of England. Then the lawyer looked at Louisa. "You hired a bodyguard?"

"No, Charles hired a bodyguard."

Pritchard stiffened. "I don't believe it. I would have known if Mr. Winslow had taken such measures."

John's pistol whipped up again, the distinct rasp of the hammer being locked in place echoing through the room.

"Are you calling me a liar?"

"N-no, no! Of course not. I just…you must understand that…" He cleared his throat and began again. "If you could provide me with some documentation, I could…"

In three strides, John closed the distance between them. Yanking the man by the lapel of his suit, John held him fast while he pressed the snout of his revolver into the lawyer's forehead.

"Is that proof enough for you? I've been hired to protect Mrs. Winslow. My services have been bought and paid for by Mr. Winslow himself."

"B-but Charles has been in South Carolina for the past three months. How could he have—"

The revolver dug into the man's skin and he hurriedly added, "O-of course, I haven't been privy to all of Mr. Winslow's business arrangements."

Bit by bit, John released his hold of the man. Clearly shaking, Mr. Pritchard ineffectually brushed his lapels, hoping to erase the creases.

"Surely Mrs. Winslow has explained to you that her husband has…passed away."

"I thought I was clear in stating that my services have already been paid for," John said harshly.

Mr. Pritchard held up a placating hand. "Y-yes, of course, but I don't see how…why…Mrs. Winslow would even need the services of…someone like yourself."

Again, John snagged the man's collar. "Then obviously, you don't know everything about Mr. Winslow's business."

Louisa rushed toward the two men as they grappled near the door. "Stop it. Stop! I won't have the two of you squabbling when anyone in the world could walk by that door and peer in!"

Finally, something that Louisa said seemed to have an effect on John Smith. Waving the tip of his pistol at Mr. Pritchard, he ordered, "Out."

"But—"

"As you can see, Mrs. Winslow still needs time to finish her bath and toilette. If she hadn't been so grief stricken that she'd fainted and I was forced to rouse her, she would have been done by now."

Louisa opened her mouth to refute the statement, but catching John's eye, she realized that he had provided her with a logical explanation for being found unclad in the presence of her bodyguard.

Playing along, she stumbled, lifting her hand to her brow. "Yes, I'm still feeling a bit dizzy."

Immediately, Chloe rushed to her side, murmuring soothing words to her in French. Even Mr. Pritchard seemed to pale when he realized he was trespassing upon the privacy of a grieving widow.

"Oh. Oh, I see!" He blushed, beads of sweat beginning to form on his upper lip. "Then I'll leave you for…until…"

"An hour will be more than enough time, Mr. Pritchard," Louisa offered, daring John to contradict her.

To his credit, her bodyguard remained silent.

"Y-yes, yes," Pritchard gasped. "An hour."

The man scurried from the room as if his coattails were on fire, securely fastening the door behind him.

Suddenly exhausted, Louisa turned away from John and gently disengaged herself from Chloe's protective embrace.

"If you don't mind, I believe I'd like to spend some time alone." She gazed pointedly at John, then patted her maid's hand. "I'll call for you when I'm ready to dress."

"Shall I bring in your tea?" Chloe asked. "I've asked the hotel staff to bring up a pot of hot water."

Louisa shook her head. "I really am longing for a bath. See if you can delay them a bit. You may return to your own room. I'll call out when I need you."

Before anyone could offer an argument, she closed the door and propped a chair beneath the doorknob to keep it in place. Only then did she allow herself to sink weakly upon the bed, close her eyes and tip back her head as if in silent supplication.

As soon as Louisa was safely ensconced in her room, Neil escorted Pritchard downstairs. He didn't really care how Pritchard intended to spend his time. Neil had his own concerns to address.

Crossing to the front desk, he asked, "Is there a way for me to send a telegram?"

"Yes, sir. If you'll fill out this form, I'll have one of the staff deliver it to the telegraph office."

Taking the sheet of paper and a stubby pencil, he thought for a moment. This was Neil's first opportunity to apprise Phoebe of what had been happening to her sister since Neil had abruptly left in search of his true bride and not the look-alike who had very nearly married him. He was sure Phoebe would be frantic for news, especially since her own life had been threatened on her journey West. He had to allay her fears and reassure her enough, so she wouldn't rush to Louisa's side. After thinking for several minutes, he finally wrote.

Louisa in my care <stop>
Posing as bodyguard John Smith <stop>
Two men to help after we leave New York <stop>
Do not contact her yet <stop>
Neil Ballard <stop>

Handing the sheet of paper back to the clerk, he took two more forms, writing brief notes to a pair of ex-army buddies.

By the time Louisa left New York, she would be watched around the clock.

Louisa's bath was far from restful. She was too aware of the man waiting on the other side of the door and the insistent ticking of the clock.

An hour. She had only an hour to gather her emotional resources.

The water grew cool around her as she stewed and worried. Finally, after little more than a half hour, she gave up all hope of coaxing her muscles to unwind. Instead, she donned a delicately embroidered wrapper and padded to the window, looking down upon the bustling street below.

Quite honestly, she had no claims on Charles or the promises he had offered his new bride. If Mr. Pritchard were completely unaware of her deceit, and if Charles had provided for her in some way as his "widow," would it be honest to accept such help?

A raw laugh bubbled in her throat, but she squelched it, lest Mr. Smith came storming into her room again under the pretext of saving her.

Honesty. Why was she worrying about honesty at this late date? She had set out to deceive everyone—Charles, his business acquaintances and his friends.

But that was different.

Wasn't it?

In exchanging identities with her friend, she had fully intended to assume all of the responsibilities and duties inherent to the situation. She had vowed to make her marriage one that would endure the test of time. She would honor her husband and make his life a happy one.

But wasn't that the crux of her angst? Maybe, after

years of serving that role, she wouldn't have felt so…deceitful in taking any help Charles might have offered. She would have considered it right and proper.

But to accept money when she hadn't even met the man…

Sighing, she wondered if she should be frank with Mr. Pritchard from the beginning, explain the situation, then hope that he wouldn't have her hauled before the nearest constable.

Her stomach flip-flopped at the idea and she pressed a hand to it, willing the sensation to go away. Damn this childish reaction from her own body. She didn't have time to baby a nervous stomach!

Groaning at the mere thought of being sick at this moment in time, Louisa called for Chloe. Although her hour of respite was only half gone, she would rather get this confrontation over with, once and for all.

When Louisa emerged again, she was dressed in sober black. Sober, depressing, smothering black. Her hair had been drawn back in a strict knot at her nape, the tresses parted in a razor sharp line.

As she caught her reflection in a mirror, she grimaced. If not for the rich fabric of her gown, she would have believed she was Phoebe Gray, governess or paid companion. Most of her former employers had believed that the "help" should dress and act with the severe piety of a nun. Two of the ladies she'd accompanied had even insisted that her hair be covered at all times.

As she entered the room, Mr. Pritchard stood. John, on the other hand, remained seated in a chair near the doorway. He tipped back his head with a lazy insolence, but there was nothing idle about the leashed energy of his pose, the intentness of his stare or the finger resting a hairsbreadth away from the trigger of his pistol.

"How are you, Mrs. Winslow?" Mr. Pritchard asked as he ushered her toward a settee.

As much as she hated to be treated like a vapid woman with nerves of glass, she allowed the man to hover over her, then sit on the edge of a chair to her left.

As Bitsy jumped onto the cushion and snuggled against her, Louisa was grateful for that small token of affection. The next few minutes could very well signal her doom.

Without thinking, she looked up. Immediately, her eyes tangled with those of John Smith. Unbidden came the memory of his arms lifting her against him and his mouth pressed to her own.

A rush of nervousness hit her stomach, and she quickly closed her eyes. Pressing a handkerchief to her mouth, she bowed her head for a moment, willing herself to relax.

"My dear Mrs. Winslow," said Pritchard as he awkwardly patted her arm. "Perhaps we should do this another time. This whole day has been such a shock to you."

Louisa shook her head, opening her eyes. Carefully averting her gaze from the man positioned by the door, she reached for a napkin and smoothed it over her lap. "I'm just...weary."

Thankfully, Pritchard seemed at ease with her cryptic explanation.

Reaching for one of the delicate cups and saucers, she inquired, "Tea, Mr. Pritchard?"

"Please."

She filled the cup with the fragrant brew. "How do you like it?"

"A bit of milk is all."

The ritual of pouring tea calmed her stomach and pushed the thought of her nerves to the background again. Handing Mr. Pritchard his tea, she paused over the second cup and saucer. Without thinking, she opened her mouth to offer a portion to Mr. Smith, then stopped herself in time. A future marquess would not take refreshments with a hired man. It simply wouldn't be done.

After preparing a cup for herself, Louisa took a sip of the brew, silently offering a prayer of thanks when the warm, familiar liquid stilled the last remnants of her nausea.

"Now, Mr. Pritchard," she began, knowing that she couldn't bear the uncertainty another minute. "What matters do you feel we must discuss so quickly?"

Mr. Pritchard set his cup and saucer on the table and reached for his satchel. With much pomp and self-importance, he used a tiny key to unlock the latch, then extracted a sheaf of papers.

"Before we begin, let me express my great sorrow at the passing of your husband."

Louisa felt a pang of pity for the man she had never met. Although Louisa and Phoebe had been indignant at the callousness of the wealthy entrepreneur who had married his bride by proxy rather than journeying to England, Louisa would not have wished him dead for the slight.

Nevertheless, her pity for the man was soon swamped by other more pressing emotions—fear, anxiety, nervousness. Louisa bowed her head in a manner that she hoped conveyed sorrow. Inwardly, however, she still vacillated between blurting the truth to this man and continuing her masquerade—a masquerade that she would live for the rest of her life.

Unsure how to respond, she waved her hand in a vague manner. Luckily, Mr. Pritchard seemed to accept such a response, because he continued.

"Normally, I would allow a grieving widow a chance to come to terms with the news of a passing." Mr. Pritchard stumbled along, obviously searching for suitable euphemisms. "But when you've heard what I have to say, I think that you will agree that time, in this case, is of the essence and the circumstances are extraordinary."

He cleared his throat and peered down at the sheaf of papers. "I have here a copy of your husband's will."

Pritchard paused, glancing up at Louisa, obviously debating whether or not she felt strong enough to take the news.

Louisa's heart pounded in her chest. If she planned to confess, now was the time—before the will was read.

But even as she opened her mouth to respond, she hesitated. If she refused the role she had promised to live to the grave, there would be unavoidable repercussions. Up to this point, she had spent Charles's money freely. Would she be accused of stealing, as well as of deceit? Even if Pritchard were generous and allowed her to leave with the clothes on her back, what would she do? She had no money, no prospects and no employment. Louisa didn't know where she could go for help. Worse yet, to reveal her identity could cause problems for the very friend that she had promised to help, the real Louisa Haversham.

Mr. Pritchard obviously took her silence as acquiescence because he removed a pair of pince-nez from his jacket pocket. Looking over the rims, he glared pointedly at Smith, obviously hoping the man would offer them a moment of privacy. When it became apparent that Louisa's bodyguard had no intention of leaving, he returned his attention to the papers.

"Mrs. Winslow, you will forgive me if I'm not completely well-versed in the situation surrounding your past association with Mr. Winslow, your courtship, or the circumstances of your…unusual marriage."

What Mr. Pritchard left unsaid was the fact that Louisa and Charles had never met. But even as she opened her mouth to offer some excuse, Louisa stopped. She had no idea what Charles had told his solicitor about her or the marriage. For all she knew, he had spun a tale of a long and involved courtship or correspondence. Moreover, a true marquess would never explain any matter so personal. Instead, she asked softly, "Can you tell me what happened to…Charles?"

The name seemed unfamiliar on her tongue, despite the many times she had practiced it.

Mr. Pritchard's expression grew grave. "I'm afraid I have little explanation for what happened. He had been suffering from a nervous weakness for nearly a year, but the doctors insisted that the condition was inconvenient more than hazardous. This spring, Mr. Winslow began a tour of his larger factories. While in North Carolina, he suddenly became ill."

Pritchard's eyes grew dark and pleading as if he feared Louisa blamed him for her husband's malady. "Naturally, he was looking forward to your arrival. But even that happy event could not offer him the strength he needed to battle the mysterious sickness. I can assure you that he was under the care of the finest physicians that money could retain, but all too soon, his body was ravaged by the sudden illness and he passed on."

Louisa pressed her napkin to her lips as if she were

fighting her emotions. In reality, she hoped to shield her features from John. Although she avoided looking in his direction, she felt him watching her intently. And there was something about the man that had the ability to completely undo her. Somehow, she sensed he wasn't completely fooled by her attempt to play the marquess, a woman worldly and sophisticated.

Mr. Pritchard tapped the papers on his satchel. "It is your husband's unfortunate demise that brings me to the point of meeting with you this afternoon."

He fiddled with his pince-nez, then offered, "With your permission, I would like to explain the contents of the will to you, Mrs. Winslow."

"I don't understand. Charles and I had yet to solemnly exchange vows in a church."

"True, true. In light of your delicate upbringing, I was well aware of the arrangements made on your behalf. I know that you had insisted on a church wedding so that you would feel more comfortable in the eyes of your faith. However, the day he learned the proxy marriage had taken place, Charles immediately arranged for a change in his personal documents."

"So quickly?"

"Yes. You see, Charles was a stickler for details. Everything was seen to as expeditiously as possible."

Which could partially explain the man's haste in insisting on a proxy marriage.

"Would you like me to read the testament verbatim, Mrs. Winslow?"

She shook her head. Her mind was already swimming with everything that had occurred throughout the day. At that moment, she feared the intricacies of legal language would be incomprehensible to her.

"If you could merely paraphrase, I would be grateful."

It was obvious from the approval in Mr. Pritchard's eyes that, in his opinion, a proper woman would rely upon the expertise of a man to interpret such a document rather than attempt the riddle on her own.

"Your husband was very conscientious about providing for your welfare, Mrs. Winslow. But due to the unusual nature of your union, he left you only a small portion of his estate, I'm afraid."

Louisa's heart had been pounding in her chest, but now it clenched in a knot. Would there be enough to see her through the next few weeks? At least until she could find a place to live, a means of employment?

"Please, Mrs. Winslow, don't regard his actions as a slight."

"No, of course not." But even to her own ears, her voice sounded weak and a little lost.

Mr. Pritchard rifled through the papers. Then he set the pince-nez higher on the bridge of his nose and squinted at the page. "If you will allow me to read…"

"Yes, of course."

"To my new wife, Louisa Marie Haversham Winslow, I bequeath the summer cottage and the five acres on which it stands…"

A house. She had been given a house.

Louisa's body trembled in relief. At least she wouldn't be thrown into the street.

"…including all of the furnishings and trappings that currently constitute the dwelling, as well as the lump sum of one million dollars."

One million dollars?

One *million* dollars?

Sure that she had misunderstood, Louisa said the

words aloud. "One million dollars?" Again, her voice sounded weak.

Mr. Pritchard shifted uncomfortably. "I'm sorry, Mrs. Winslow. I know that the amount is only a small portion of the Winslow estate."

Small portion? She couldn't conceive how anyone could have amassed even half of that amount. If Mr. Pritchard considered the bequest a pittance, what was the full estate of Charles Winslow worth?

"The bulk of Mr. Winslow's estate," Mr. Pritchard continued, "has been left to his daughter."

Daughter?

Charles Winslow had a daughter?

"For several years, Evie Winslow has been a student at the Rochester School of Learning in Boston. Charles was often away on business, so he felt it best for Evie to attend a boarding school rather than live at home."

Silently floundering, Louisa wondered how much she was supposed to know about the girl. She was certain that the real Louisa Haversham hadn't known about Evie.

But what kind of man would marry without telling his wife about the presence of a child?

The same sort of man who would marry a woman sight unseen.

"Evie is also to receive the houses in Boston and Sarasota and the apartment in Paris."

Paris?

"However, all of her holdings are to be kept in trust until Evie marries or reaches the age of twenty. Until that time, *you,* Mrs. Winslow, are appointed the girl's guardian. You have been asked to raise Evie to be a God-fearing and respectable woman of society. You will oversee all of her properties with the understanding that

Evie's inheritance is to be enhanced by any investments and improvements you choose to make.''

Mr. Pritchard paused, glancing at her over the rims of his spectacles. "In this matter, I would be happy to serve as your advisor, Mrs. Winslow, since I performed many of the same duties for your husband while he was alive."

"Yes, of course," she murmured absently.

Charles had a child—and she had just been appointed the girl's guardian. Moreover, Louisa had been charged with the task of building Evie's fortune over the next few years.

Years.

In the space of a few hours, Louisa had gone from being a nervous bride to a widow to an instant mother and financier.

Chapter Five

Mr. Pritchard must have sensed a portion of her shock because he removed his spectacles and laid the sheaf of papers next to the tea tray.

"The rest of the document contains a few small bequests of personal items to friends and employees who have served him well, but I will allow you to review such things at your leisure. I think that you've had more than enough to absorb for one afternoon."

"Yes, I..."

"I have already taken it upon myself to notify his remaining relatives and arrange for Mr. Winslow's private car to meet us here. That way you will be able to ride in comfort once we have...collected Mr. Winslow's remains. When I have received word of an anticipated arrival, I will meet with you to go over plans for the memorial services."

His expression gentled into that of a kindly grandfather. "In the meantime, I suggest that you rest. This day has been a terrible shock to you, I'm sure."

Her hand unconsciously touched her throat. "Yes, I..."

Again he patted her arm. "Please don't trouble yourself to see me to the door.'' He stood, taking a card from his pocket. ''Should you need anything, anything at all, send one of the hotel runners to get me. I have a small townhouse I use while I'm in New York. I've noted the address on the back of my calling card.''

''Thank you, Mr. Pritchard,'' she murmured, taking the embossed square, ignoring the way Bitsy stretched out to sniff it suspiciously.

''Good day to you, then, Madam.''

''And to you, Mr. Pritchard.''

Mr. Pritchard had scarcely taken three steps before John was there to hand the man his hat. With a narrowed glance of disapproval, Mr. Pritchard snatched the bowler as if he feared John meant to crush it. His scowl deepened when John opened the door wide.

As soon as John had twisted the key in the lock, Louisa offered him what she hoped was an imperious stare.

''You should have been more polite to Mr. Pritchard.''

''Politeness has never been one of my strong points.''

''Of that I have no doubt.''

Scooping Bitsy into her arms, Louisa moved toward the window, staring sightlessly through the panes, her fingers unconsciously stroking the dog's silky fur. Try as she might, she couldn't seem to grasp what had just happened. She had been told that she would be wealthy beyond her wildest imaginings. Never again would she need to fear being left destitute. Never again would she be forced to go into service. She was a free woman.

No. Not free.

The money would not come without strings. If she decided to accept it, she must also accept the responsibilities that came with it. She would become the mother of a child she hadn't even known existed. She would need to learn quickly how best to safeguard the Winslow estate and add to it. And these obligations would not end when Evie turned twenty. If there was anything that Louisa had learned in her own experience as an orphan, it was that parenthood was meant to last a lifetime. A child should never be abandoned.

"Are you thinking of the many ways you can spend your money?"

She stiffened, casting a dark look over her shoulder. "Is that what you think of me?"

He shrugged, leaning against the doorjamb. "I don't know what to think of you. Your husband was very vague in his description of his bride."

Little did John know that Charles had been vague due to simple ignorance.

"Our courtship was a very private one."

"It must have been if you weren't even aware that he had a child."

Louisa froze. How had she given herself away?

John straightened. "You needn't worry. I doubt that Pritchard noticed the way your skin lost its color. And even if he did, he's of the impression that you're a helpless soul prone to bouts of fainting."

"If he has that impression, it's because you intimated as much."

"What would you have me telling your lawyer? That less than an hour after discovering you were a widow, you were in the arms of another man?"

The heat rushed into her cheeks. "A momentary lapse of judgment, I can assure you. You may attribute my actions to the overwhelming toll of mourning."

John grinned. "Come now, Louisa. You don't have to play the grieving widow with me."

She stiffened, exclaiming, "I beg your pardon!"

He continued as if he hadn't heard her. "Both of us know that you've never even met the man."

Had Charles been this forthright with a hired man? Or was John merely guessing?

Louisa stiffened even more, her spine becoming ramrod straight, her chin lifting ever so slightly. "Mr. Smith, you appear to think that your position as my bodyguard allows you to take certain personal liberties."

His brows rose, reminding her that the two of them had been about as "personal" as two people could be. Nevertheless, she plunged on, ignoring his reaction, knowing that if she didn't speak now, she would rue the day.

As she moved toward him, Louisa realized there was nothing more liberating than money. She felt suddenly confident and in charge of her own destiny. And she knew instinctively that the time had come to dismiss Mr. John Smith.

"Mr. Smith, I realize that you and my husband had an agreement of service. However, I'm sure that you can also appreciate the fact that any contracts made between you are null and void. Since you have become privy to my financial information, I'm sure that you will appreciate the fact that I am more than able to make my own decisions concerning my safety and that of my stepdaughter."

She held up a hand when he would have spoken. "Please, there's no reason to argue the point or to insist that you must see your term of employment to its planned termination. Take whatever monies you have received with my gratitude and consider it your due in having the arrangements abruptly canceled. I am more than happy to forfeit your wages."

•

Clutching Bitsy to her chest, she regarded him regally, finally feeling as if she really were a marquess. "As for me, I've had a long day. I'm sure you'll understand if I don't see you out. I plan to retire to my room for the rest of the day, so you may collect your things—" she stared pointedly at the dusty saddle "—and be on your way." Unable to resist, she added with utmost dignity, "God bless, and Godspeed."

With that parting shot, she escaped into her bedroom and closed the door. Unfortunately, the sight of the damaged panels brought back far too many memories—the caress of John's fingers as he'd soothed her bruised hip, the infinite gentleness as he'd bathed her hands.

His touch.

His kiss.

His taste.

Stop it!

But even as she inwardly castigated herself for being a fool, she couldn't help but feel a pang of regret.

As well as a stronger wave of longing.

Dear sweet heaven above, had she totally lost all reason? This man was nothing to her, nothing. She'd known him for less than a day.

And yet...

From that first glance, the man had pulled her instinctively to him, as if she were a fly being lured into a spider's web.

Setting Bitsy on the floor, Louisa pulled the pins from her hair. She shook the tresses free, needing to free herself from the tight restraints, hoping it would ease the pounding of her head and the absurd aching of her heart.

Wishing to be alone, she didn't bother to summon Chloe from the neighboring room. Instead, she wriggled from her jacket and skirt and eased her shoes from her feet. Then, after dipping a cloth into the cool water in her washbasin, she stretched out on the bed, laying the damp square over her forehead.

Almost as soon as her head touched the pillow, she heard Bitsy's nails scrabbling against the polished floorboards, then felt a jarring sensation as the dog jumped onto the bed. Within seconds, the dog's wet nose pressed against her cheek, the tiny, furry body wriggling against her with open adoration.

Louisa felt a lightening of her mood. She'd never had a pet before, let alone something that was bred for little else than feminine appeal. The dog was small, scarcely the size of a glove box, and covered with long, fine fur the consistency of silk sewing floss. With huge dark eyes and a stubby tail, she resembled a winter muff.

Despite her small size, there was nothing lacking in the animal's devotion. For the past week, she had been Louisa's constant companion—and as such, she had been privy to many of Louisa's secrets. Today she had discovered the dog had a loyal streak, as well.

"So, Bitsy," she whispered. "You won't have a daddy, after all. Are you disappointed?"

Seeming to understand the question, Bitsy tilted her head to the side as if she were considering the idea. Then her whole body shook as she wagged her tail.

Louisa grinned. "I must admit, I'm not too disappointed myself. Especially since he's made me rich." Her voice lowered even more as if she were afraid to admit the fact out loud. "Is it wrong of me to accept the inheritance, Bitsy?"

The dog offered a short yap and pawed at the bedcovers in something akin to delight.

"I suppose that someone else might have told Mr.

Pritchard the truth.'' Louisa sighed. ''But what else could I do?''

Closing her eyes, she cuddled Bitsy close, drawing strength from the dog's warmth.

''I've done the right thing,'' she said. But her tone sounded unconvinced even to herself. ''Evie will be needing a mother, and I will not leave her alone in the world.''

As soon as the words were spoken, Louisa felt better about the course she was about to embark on. A yawn caught her unawares. Her body thrummed with weariness although it was only midafternoon. She'd fairly worn herself out with worrying.

''At least I think I've done the right thing....'' she murmured, the words little more than a sigh. Then she surrendered herself to sleep.

From his position on the other side of the door, Neil settled into a chair.

If there was one thing for which he'd been known during his time as a Union scout, it was the fact that he had the ears of a fox. He could hear a whisper half again as far as the average man. He'd had very little difficulty discerning Louisa's murmurings from the other side of the door.

No, not Louisa. Phoebe Gray. The woman who had promised to marry him.

When Neil had decided that he would assume the role of her bodyguard, he'd had two overpowering reasons. First, it would allow him to ensure her safety so that her uncle's henchmen wouldn't have a chance to harm her. Second, and even more important, he would provide a way for Phoebe to begin to care for him as a man, not merely as a name at the bottom of a letter or a skinny, frightened school chum.

Unfortunately, Neil was beginning to see that he had sorely misjudged things. He would have been better off abducting the woman and hauling her back to Oregon. Sure, she would have been angry. But now…

Now she could live a life of luxury without putting a dent in her inheritance. More troubling still, she'd been given the charge of a child. And in Neil's experience a woman's dedication to duty was never so strong as when a youngster was involved.

Damn.

Damn, damn, damn.

What should he do?

Slouching in the chair, he rested his head against the back, even as his finger curled loosely over the revolver in his lap.

Right now he wasn't sure what course to take. To reveal his identity might force his hand too soon. To point out the foolhardiness of adopting another woman's identity could cause her to dig in her heels and become even more stubborn and intractable.

He would simply have to play things by ear.

Which meant that under no circumstances did he intend to abandon his own masquerade as Louisa's bodyguard—no matter how she might protest.

Late evening shadows were pooling around her bed when Louisa woke. Beside her on the pillow, Bitsy lay on her back, her pink stomach exposed, her mouth open and her tongue lolling out as she slept in utter abandonment.

Louisa pressed the heels of her hands to her closed eyes. She had hoped that her nap would help her feel more refreshed. Instead, she was groggy and lethargic, her head pounding as she remembered the day's events.

Had she really been offered a million dollars? One *million?*

Louisa had once served as a companion to an old woman who received fifty thousand pounds a year from a trust left by her husband. She'd been the wealthiest woman Louisa had ever known, with servants and carriages, a manor in the country and a town house in the city....

One million dollars.

Louisa couldn't even comprehend the amount—and to think that she'd been made guardian of a child who had inherited even more was astonishing.

Keeping her eyes closed, Louisa rolled onto her back, resting her forearm on her brow to block out the light.

She still felt twinges of conscience in taking the inheritance that Charles had left to his wife-by-proxy. But when Evie was added into the equation, Louisa knew that there was no way she would walk away from the situation. In her mind, she couldn't think of anything more horrible than to be sent to a boarding school simply because Charles had felt his life was too busy to entertain the company of a child.

What did that action say about the man she would have married? With Charles's vast fortune, it would have been simple to hire a governess and a fleet of servants to look after the girl. At least then Evie would have been offered the comfort of living in her own home. Instead, she'd been forced to endure a life with strangers.

Hopefully, the school that Charles had chosen was a step above the charity academy Louisa herself had attended as a child. When she'd reached ten years of age, she'd been sent away from the orphanage to Milton's

School of Service. It had been a cold, drafty building run by pious educators and an even more dour headmaster. No laughter or frivolity was tolerated. Even Louisa's beloved romance novels had been forbidden. In order to read her fill of *Pride and Prejudice* and *Wuthering Heights,* she had often volunteered to walk miles each afternoon to gather supplies from the greengrocer, just so that she could read along the way and hide the books in the rickety cart used for the journey.

Now you can afford any book your heart desires.

Grinning, she wrapped her arms around her body and hugged herself in delight.

The first thing she intended to see to was a proper library of—

"Would you like to dine in the restaurant below or have your supper sent up?"

A squeak of surprise burst from her throat. Louisa's eyes flew open and she focused on the man standing on the threshold, grabbing a blanket to cover herself.

"Mr. Smith!"

"Yes, Mrs. Winslow?"

"I thought I made myself perfectly clear. You were to leave my employ at once and not come back."

John leaned nonchalantly against the jamb, his arms crossed. She saw a glint of humor in his eyes, which she was sure came at her own expense.

"You were incredibly succinct."

"Then what are you doing here?"

"This is my job."

"But—"

He pushed away from the door.

Louisa abruptly closed her mouth and shrank beneath the covers.

"You've made your wishes more than clear, Mrs.

Winslow. But as I stated before, I was employed by your husband to do a job and I intend to do it. You can argue and bully and bluster and cry all you want, but it won't change my mind."

Louisa opened her mouth, then realized that any efforts on her part would be ignored. For the time being, she was stuck with John Smith as her bodyguard.

But that didn't mean she had to like the arrangement.

Nor did it place her under any real obligation to be nice.

"Would you care to dine in or out?" John asked.

As much as Louisa would like to leave her hotel suite, she truly didn't have enough energy to cinch her body in a corset and don the many layers required by society. Moreover, she realized with a rush that she was hungry—embarrassingly so. Women of quality were supposed to have the appetite of birds. But Louisa had been so concerned about the arrival of her husband, her upset stomach had forced her to limit her meals to tea and an occasional sandwich.

Now she was famished.

"I'll dine in."

"Good. I've already got your dinner set up for you in the sitting room."

She glared at him when she realized that it hadn't mattered a jot what she had wanted. One way or another, John would have seen to it that she'd eaten in her own hotel room.

Nevertheless, when he appeared poised for argument, she merely smiled sweetly and murmured, "How kind of you to anticipate my wishes."

Just don't do it again, she wanted to add, but she didn't. The time would come for her to rebel against this man's high-handedness, but she refused to jump into the argument precipitously. After she'd had something to eat and a decent night's sleep, she would have her wits about her. *Then* she would see to dismissing Mr. Smith.

When John didn't move, she lifted her brows and tipped her chin. "If you would be so kind as to withdraw, Mr. Smith."

He didn't move for a very long time. The room grew quiet enough to echo the ticking noise of Bitsy's nails as she hurried across the room to yap at the imposing stranger.

"Five minutes," John said tightly, then stepped from the room.

As soon as he'd gone, Bitsy scrambled toward the bed and jumped into Louisa's lap. Wriggling in search of comfort, she whined disconsolately until Louisa scratched her behind the ears.

"So, Bitsy…what do you think of our Mr. Smith?"

The dog seemed to understand, because she offered a short growl, then a pair of high-pitched yips.

"I quite agree. He thinks he's a step short of the Almighty." Louisa's lips pursed together. "I suppose it's up to us to convince him he's mistaken in that opinion."

The dog barked again, her tail wagging in feverish delight.

Some of the dog's enthusiasm was contagious, because Louisa grinned—a naughty grin that would have made the matrons at the orphanage scowl in disgust and Neil Ballard smile in delight.

"Mmm. Finally, it seems that we have something constructive to do to pass the time."

Chapter Six

The moment Louisa joined Neil in the sitting room, he realized that he might have made a tactical error in insisting they dine together.

He had expected her to dress to the hilt, encasing herself in the feminine armor provided by petticoats, corsetry and layer upon layer of clothing.

Instead, she emerged wearing a concoction of lawn—a soft ruffled skirt that had more the appearance of underwear than a proper garment, with a loosely fitted jacket made of white cotton, ribbons and lace. Her hair was unfettered and fell around her shoulders in waves of fire that reached far down her back.

Louisa paused, acknowledging his gaze. Even though he knew he'd been caught staring, he couldn't bring himself to look away.

"I can send for Chloe if you want help to dress," he finally muttered, his voice emerging gruff and a bit harsh.

She raised one of her eyebrows. "I *am* dressed, Mr. Smith."

He folded his arms across his chest. "Don't you think

you should entertain a gentleman in your hotel suite in something more than your shimmies?''

He thought he caught a hint of pink touching her cheeks, but she brushed past him with the imperious hauteur of a queen.

"First of all, I am not 'entertaining' anyone. I have been forced to endure your company for a short while." She sat on one of the delicate chairs that had been pulled close to the table by the window. "Second," she continued as she shook out her napkin and spread it over her lap, "I hardly think that you can lay claim to the term 'gentleman.'" She surveyed the array of dishes set out on the table. "And lastly, I cannot be accused of wearing little more than my…shimmies?…since I happen to be adorned in the latest fashion in tea wrappers."

With that, she patently ignored him for the next hour.

Knowing that a cautious amount of distance would not be out of order, Neil took a seat on the chair he had pulled in front of the door. Yet even with the extra breathing room, he was not able to remain as detached as he would have liked. As he watched Louisa spoon small portions of food onto her plate, he was struck by the elegance of her profile and by the voluptuousness of her form. To her credit, the tea wrapper covered her from neck to toe. But the delicacy of the cotton and the intricacy of the full lace cuffs and beribboned placket still reminded him far too much of underwear. Fine ladies' underwear, like that worn by women who made a profession of arousing a man's interest.

This should have been his. *She* should have been his. Damn it, this woman had agreed to marry him—he'd all but *begged* to marry him. Then, at the first provocation, she'd decided she would rather ally herself with a stranger.

His lips pressed into a narrow line as Neil fanned his anger.

How could he have been so wrong about this woman's character? The two of them had been corresponding for years. In all that time, he had pictured her so differently. When he'd thought of his old schoolmate, he'd envisioned her to be a woman of the highest integrity. Proper. Giving. Sincere.

And yet he'd been with her less than a day before discovering that she had a very real taste for fine food and clothing. At the first hint of money, she'd abandoned an old friend in favor of...

Of what?

A dead man.

Neil's lips twitched at the irony.

"Is something funny, Mr. Smith?"

"Yes, ma'am," he drawled.

"Would you care to share your amusement with me?"

"No, ma'am."

It was clear that she thought he was mocking her, but he wasn't about to confess his thoughts or anything else about his incursion into her life. Not just yet. He would give things a few more days. Then he would either claim her as his bride and demand she live up to her promises....

Or he would leave and consider himself lucky for having avoided her none-too-subtle marriage trap.

Dear Diary,
It has been days since I've been able to write down my thoughts, and so much has happened. Just as I have since childhood, I need the art of putting pencil to paper to make sense of it all.

Dawn has finally come, and I am a nervous wreck!

Since Mr. Smith had proved so smug during my evening meal, I finished eating as quickly as I could and then pleaded a headache and returned to my room. But when I tried to barricade the door against him, John effortlessly pushed it open and took his position in a corner chair, insisting that it wouldn't be wise to let me out of his sight.

I didn't bother to argue with him. What good would it have done me? After everything I'd already endured that day, I was strung to a breaking point and knew that to open my mouth would result in a bout of tears.

Nevertheless, I was at a loss as to the best way to handle the situation. Remaining fully clothed, I stretched out on the bed, feigning sleep, resenting the man all the more because he'd prevented me from reading one of my beloved melodramas, as I'd originally planned. (I was quite sure that a marquess would not read melodramas, so I wasn't about to do so in front of Mr. Smith.)

Unfortunately, the quiet of the room and the faint sound of the man's breathing offered me no relief. Even Bitsy slept restlessly, her tiny moans not helping the tension. As the night progressed, John's presence seemed to suck the air from my lungs, leaving me breathless and anxious. I doubt I slept more than a few minutes at a time the whole night through. Worse yet, the man made me so overwrought that I was forced to rush for the chamber pot several times. On one such occasion, John even offered to summon a doctor—a fact that confirmed my theory that he might remain quiet and still, but he was not asleep.

By morning, I was so rattled that I accidentally pushed Bitsy to the floor. Poor thing!

Once again, I tried to convince Mr. Smith that I have no need of a bodyguard, and again my efforts have been for naught. Frankly, Mr. Smith is becoming much like a troublesome burr that I cannot dislodge. Indeed, he has given my objections so little attention that I would have had more success arguing with a stump!

"Did you wish to see me, *madame?*"

Louisa jumped when Chloe appeared in the doorway, and quickly slipped her diary into a drawer. She hadn't yet sent for the maid. Since John had stepped into the outer room for a moment, she'd been filling her starving lungs with air and staring absently out the window.

"I—I didn't send for you, no."

Louisa stifled her impatience. It shouldn't come as a surprise that Chloe had come to her room before being called. Within hours after she'd hired the girl, it had become obvious to Louisa that the young lady was terribly inexperienced. Although Chloe had claimed during her interview to have had experience with two other positions, Louisa now doubted the claim. Chloe's manners were rough, her tone too familiar at times. She pulled Louisa's hair when she dressed it and failed to pull Louisa's corset strings tight enough. Added to that were the times when Louisa was sure that her items had been moved—as if someone else had been trying them on. Worse yet, Chloe seemed to hover over Louisa. She smothered Louisa in her effort to please—so much so that Louisa often felt exhausted by her maid's attentions by the end of the day.

In any other circumstances Louisa would have given the girl notice and tended to her own personal needs. But she'd known that the daughter of a marquis would never travel without a lady's maid. She'd feared that the lack of a servant would call attention to her in all the wrong ways.

In the end, Louisa had put off any thought of firing the girl just yet. She'd told herself that Chloe was merely young and eager to do her best. With some training, the French girl could be an asset—and who else would bother to train Chloe if Louisa dismissed her without references? Moreover, having a servant that was so green could prove an asset. Veteran lady's maids could often be as snobbish as their mistresses. If Louisa hired a woman who was fully trained, that woman would probably determine in a heartbeat that Louisa's social graces weren't as polished as they should be.

Yet even as she told herself that she would give Chloe more time, Louisa fought a rising tide of irritation. Chloe's earnest expression was far too much like a mother hen guarding her baby chick.

And heaven only knew, Louisa didn't need someone else guarding her person.

"Are you ready to dress?"

"No, I don't..."

Chloe's face fell, assuming an expression of near panic, so Louisa gestured for her to come in. "Yes, you're right. I may as well begin my regimen. Will you help me?"

It took more than an hour for Louisa to finish her toilette. She was forced to endure the painful pulling of her hair when Chloe proved overly eager at the task.

Then, after a search of her wardrobe, she found only one appropriate costume for mourning—black shoes, hose, skirt and basque.

Grimacing at her reflection, Louisa rued the loss of her beautiful new clothes. She would have to keep to the hotel for a few days in order to display an appropriate amount of grief, but sometime soon she would need to augment her wardrobe again. She would require black, unadorned petticoats, an assortment of shoes, hosiery and accessories, as well as a traveling costume, daywear and eveningwear.

Her head spun at the mere thought of acquiring everything she would need before her trip to Boston. Once there, beneath the prying eyes of neighbors and friends, she would want to remain at home as much as possible.

"What will you do with the other things, *madame?*" Chloe's eyes darted to the pretty clothes that had been set aside as inappropriate as they'd packed her things.

Louisa felt a pang of very real pain. If she were to obey the true conventions of mourning, she would not be allowed to dress in such things for years. Years and years.

Her sigh was laden with regret—a sigh that she hoped Chloe would attribute to the passing of Louisa's husband and not to the loss of her wardrobe. She was flooded with the memory of her mother's death and the neighbor women who had huddled over pots of black dye so that they could properly adjust the few pieces of clothing Louisa had to her name.

"They can be dyed, I suppose."

Chloe uttered a soft cry. "What a shame!" She immediately covered her lips with her hand to stifle her outburst. "I am sorry, *madame,*" she whispered contritely.

Louisa offered a small smile and patted the maid's hand. "Perhaps we could…" About to suggest that they could begin the dyeing process here at the hotel, Louisa stopped.

She was a wealthy woman. A *very* wealthy woman. Why should she ruin these beautiful things when she had money enough to burn?

"We'll sort through everything later today, Chloe." She eyed her maid assessingly. "With a few alterations, several of my things should fit you well enough."

Chloe's eyes widened, her mouth moving soundlessly. Unconsciously, Louisa fingered the delicate silk of a gown that had been thrown over the end of the bed. Taking it and another, she handed them to Chloe.

"You cannot possibly mean to give them to me, *madame*," the maid breathed.

"Yes. I do," Louisa said decisively. "There are a few things I'll keep out of sentimentality—" such as the delicate undergarments, her first silk suit, the gown she'd worn to her first opera "—but it would pain me to see them dyed black. We'll simply have to make another trip to the shops."

"No."

The women whirled at the dark, masculine voice.

Seeing that John had been eavesdropping again, Louisa tipped her chin and stared haughtily at her bodyguard.

"You won't be going into town, and you won't be doing any shopping," he said, folding his arms over his chest.

She stiffened. "And who are you to say what I will or will not do?"

"I'm the man who intends to keep you safe."

"Safe from what?"

Her challenge was clear. She wanted John Smith to prove that such measures were necessary. But if she'd hoped he would rise to the bait, she was sadly disappointed. He merely responded, "From yourself, it would seem. It isn't wise for you to be traipsing about town—especially so soon after the news of your husband's death."

She was about to argue with him, but quickly reconsidered. As much as she hated to agree with him, she had already decided for herself that it would be in poor taste to be caught shopping the day after she'd been informed of her husband's demise. Nevertheless, she was determined to have the last word on the matter.

"In time, I fear that even you will not be able to prevent me from joining polite society, Mr. Smith. Although I wouldn't dream of dishonoring the memory of my beloved husband…" she paused to squeeze her eyes shut and press a handkerchief against her lips as if grieved "…eventually, there are purchases I shall need to make so that I can be ready for the trip to Boston."

"Tell me what you need, and I'll arrange for it to be brought to you."

"You will not!" Her cheeks grew hot at the very thought of this man knowing her measurements, let alone ordering pantalets and hose and petticoats.

"That's my only offer."

She huffed in indignation. "You seem to forget who is the employer and who is the employee, Mr. Smith."

He straightened from his negligent pose against the door frame and took a step toward her. His eyes grew dark, piercing. "And you seem to forget that I have been hired to keep you safe."

"From what?" She gestured at the room around them.

"So far, you haven't proved that my husband even hired you, let alone that there is a need for your services."

Without looking away, John said, "Chloe, will you leave us please?"

Chloe's gaze bounced from Louisa to John, then back to Louisa before she whispered, *"Oui, monsieur,"* and darted from the room as if being chased.

"There's no need to frighten her," Louisa said, planting her hands on her hips.

"At least she has the good sense to feel a measure of fear. You would do well to follow her example."

"Why? What should I fear?"

"Me, if nothing else." The words were low and dark, shivering with sensual overtones rather than menace.

At that moment, she did fear him. Not for his size or his strength, but for the way he could melt her inhibitions with a single glance.

"You presume far too much. Have you forgotten that I am newly widowed?"

"No." His eyes narrowed. "Although at times you seem to forget the fact yourself."

Again she felt a betraying flush seep into her cheeks.

He took a step closer. "Did you love him, Louisa?"

She knew she should reprimand John Smith for using her given name, but she feared that any sound she made would emerge as a croak, so she merely glared at him.

"You don't have the air of a grieving widow. Indeed, you seem almost...relieved."

Dear heaven, how had she given so much away? If this man had been able to guess a portion of the truth, how many others would soon realize her perfidy?

"I wish to be alone," she whispered.

"Have I touched a nerve?"

Her stomach flip-flopped with a new bout of anxiety,

and she prayed she wouldn't embarrass herself. Not here. Not now.

"I wish...to be left...alone," she said, more emphatically, measuring her words with great care as if John didn't have all of his wits about him.

Moisture pricked at the backs of her eyes and a thick lump welled in her throat. She had been so sure she could carry off her charade, and now this man threatened to ruin everything.

Tears gathered and a wave of despair washed over her. She really would be thrown into the streets if her bodyguard had anything to do with it. And why? Why did he feel that he needed to bait and torment her? What had she ever done to him?

John paused, clearly taken aback by her weeping. His eyes narrowed as if he feared they were little more than crocodile tears summoned for his benefit. But when she fought to control the shaking of her chin and the jagged breaths she took into her lungs, he finally murmured, "I'm sorry. I was out of line."

"Please," she sobbed, her anguish becoming more overwhelming, the tension of the past few weeks taking its toll. "Leave me. Just leave."

Whirling, she threw herself on the bed, burying her face in the pillow and crying as if her heart had been crushed. Long bitter moments of weeping followed until the linen beneath her cheeks grew wet. When she finally dared to look up, she realized that for the first time, John had obeyed one of her commands. The room was vacant, the door carefully closed.

A new burst of sobs racked her body.

But this time, she didn't know why she cried. She knew only that a nameless sense of loss hovered over her like a dark cloud.

Dear Diary,
There is still no word from Phoebe and I find myself racked with curiosity and guilt.

What has happened to my dear friend and Neil? Are they married? Are they happy? Has Phoebe been able to maintain her ruse?

I often worry what would happen if Neil were to discover what we've done to him. I still remember the first time I met him, when he came to Bentwood's Orphanage. His parents had recently died in a cholera epidemic and he appeared so lost and frightened. Naturally, he became the target of bullies, forcing me to take him under my wing, since I'd earned my reputation for having a fierce temper and fighting back. We became inseparable during that year—until relatives from America came to claim him. Although we continued to write to one another, and I read how he'd grown into a man, I still picture him as a boy with enormous, haunted eyes.

What does he look like now? Is he small and slight? Or has America toughened him?

And why, after everything that's happened, do I feel a faint twinge of jealousy at the thought of my two friends living as man and wife?

In the next few days Neil grew amused by Louisa's attempts to get rid of him. After that morning when she'd cried, she'd seemed to make it her personal mission to convince him to quit. She'd argued, been perverse and difficult and ordered him about as if he was the lowliest servant.

Through it all, he'd steadfastly resisted the urge to

respond in any way other than with utter calm. Indeed, he was beginning to enjoy those times when he was able to provoke her. But what surprised him most of all was his own reaction to her.

He hadn't anticipated the purely physical response he'd experienced upon their first encounter. Louisa was slightly shorter than her sister, but more curvaceous. In the past few days, she'd proved to have a feisty temper, but with a hint of mischief to her nature as well—just as he'd remembered from their days at the orphanage.

Midway through his journey east, Neil had nearly convinced himself that he was a fool to chase after his old chum. But his pride had demanded it. Didn't she realize that he'd made plans since agreeing to marry her? He had a home that needed a woman's touch. And the time had come for him to begin raising some sons to carry on the legacy he'd carved out of the wilderness.

That idea had taken root in his brain and blossomed to the point where he had a half-dozen names ready and a cradle started. Then there was the money he'd doled out for the woman's journey, and the improvements he'd made to the master bedroom on her behalf.

Once again his impatience at the entire situation resurfaced. Soon he would need to move the cattle to summer pastures. He didn't have time to invest in finding and courting another wife—nor did he care to do such a thing. He knew from the letters he and Louisa had exchanged that their relationship would be agreeable enough. Damn it, they already had a long history together, and he didn't intend to go home empty-handed!

Especially after he'd discovered that she was a passionate creature.

''Mr. Smith.''

He turned to find the object of his thoughts glaring at

him from the bedroom doorway. At her side stood that tiny dog—if it could be called a dog. In Neil's opinion the animal was little more than a fluffy rat.

"Mr. Smith, I *must* begin looking for more appropriate mourning attire and I cannot do that successfully from inside this suite!"

"All right."

His agreement took her by surprise. She had lifted a hand to shake her finger at him and now it hung in mid-air.

Her mouth opened, closed, then opened again. "Then you'll allow us to go to town?"

It was clear she detested having to ask his permission.

"If you feel the trip is necessary."

For a moment, her eyes sparkled with unguarded glee. Then, whirling, she called, "Chloe! I need your help! Quickly!"

Neil couldn't account for the way that her simple pleasure warmed him. Glancing down, he found Bitsy regarding him with dark, suspicious eyes.

"What are you looking at, dog?"

After offering a sharp, disapproving yip—one that seemed to convey that Bitsy sensed Neil's ulterior motives—the dog turned and scampered back into the bedroom.

Leaving Neil to his own thoughts.

His own desires.

As soon as the door closed behind her, Louisa grinned and hurried to gather her gloves, parasol and reticule.

Just because she'd been forced to humble herself enough to ask Mr. Smith's permission to go shopping did not mean that she had conceded the war. She still didn't understand why she needed a bodyguard. No threats had been made against her—indeed, as far as she could tell, no one had paid her any attention at all. Other than brief visits by Mr. Pritchard—who had patiently explained the details regarding her inheritance and Evie's trust—Louisa had been exiled to her suite with no company but Bitsy, Chloe, and…

And Mr. Smith.

A man who had only to enter the room to steal the breath from her body.

In the past few days, she had tried in every way she could to convince the man to leave her. She'd been perverse, sickly sweet, stubborn, unreasonable, condescending and rude, all to no avail. If anything, the fellow seemed amused rather than discouraged.

Eventually, she'd been forced to admit that her bodyguard would not change his mind due to a display of female histrionics. In truth, he seemed to expect her dramatics. Therefore, Louisa had decided to make one last attempt to show John that she had no need of his services.

She would take her bodyguard shopping.

In her experience there wasn't a man on the face of the earth who could endure a woman bent on a day of shopping. Louisa intended to bore him with "feminine preciousness."

She could only hope that her efforts wouldn't be wasted. The sooner Mr. Smith realized he had no place in her life, the better.

Chapter Seven

When Neil had agreed to Louisa's shopping expedition, he'd had no idea what an ordeal it would become. By lunch, he'd been to three dressmakers, two milliners and a shoemaker. Through it all, he'd been privy to Louisa and Chloe's heartfelt discussions about the merits of this shirtwaist and that skirt, a parasol opposed to a bonnet and veil, kid gloves or silk, slippers or boots. Holy damnation! The women had even minutely evaluated the different shades of black they'd encountered!

To add insult to injury, Neil soon discovered that he was going to be forced to join the process. Rather than being allowed to distance himself and watch the door for suspicious characters, Louisa dragged him along like a pull toy, insisting that he hold her dog, bags, wrap and reticule.

And what had they managed to buy so far?

Nothing.

Absolutely nothing.

Scowling at the pair of females who huddled over a table filled with scraps of fabric, ribbons and lace in yet another millinery shop, Neil clenched his jaw.

If the women weren't so heartfelt in their deliberations, he would have thought that Louisa was purposely trying to annoy him.

She wanted him gone, but even with the torture this day had become, he didn't intend to go anywhere. Not just yet.

As if sensing his thoughts, Louisa suddenly turned to regard him with indigo eyes. The shopkeeper excused herself to check on something in her storeroom.

"I think you're holding Bitsy a trifle too tightly, Mr. Smith."

Neil had forgotten about the dog.

He hated dogs. No, that wasn't quite true. He liked dogs. *Real* dogs. Those that were large enough to be seen and smart enough to keep out of the way.

Bitsy was neither. She was too small, too furry, too anxious and too obnoxious to be considered anything but a nuisance.

Neil instantly loosened his grip enough to cease the animal's growling, but not enough to encourage it to jump free. He'd already had the pleasure of chasing the pet through several shops.

Bitsy glared at Neil and offered a sharp growl of reprimand.

"I don't think Bitsy likes you very much, Mr. Smith."

"The feeling is mutual, I can assure you."

He wasn't sure, but he thought her eyes twinkled for a moment in rich humor, adding to his suspicions that she was purposely baiting him.

Standing, she made a soft tsking sound with her tongue. "For shame, Mr. Smith. Don't you know that a man of true heroic character adores children and small animals?"

He raised his eyebrows. "Heroic character? That sounds like something from a penny novel. Surely a woman of your social rank wouldn't be caught reading such questionable literature. With your background, one would assume that you would stick to the classics.''

A spot of pink touched each of her cheeks, but other than that, she didn't react.

"I *was* speaking of the classics, Mr. Smith—Chaucer, Plato, Shakespeare."

"None of whom ever mentioned enduring the company of a nasty-tempered mop."

She closed the distance between them, the silk of her skirts rustling like paper money, her perfume enfolding him, as rich as the scents of a garden. If he hadn't known the truth about her, Neil would have assumed that she'd been born into wealth, instead of inheriting it in a sudden windfall.

"And if I recall *my* reading correctly," he stated, "Chaucer had more than one nonheroic character, Plato was a philosopher and Shakespeare rarely had animals in any of his plays."

"Then you obviously didn't read carefully enough," she murmured vaguely, but the pink in her cheeks deepened.

She took a bonnet from a nearby hook and placed it on her head. "What do you think, Mr. Smith?"

"What do I think about what?"

"The bonnet."

"It's fine. They're all fine." But he wasn't looking at the bonnet, he was looking at the delicate sweep of her brow, her deep blue eyes, the soft curve of her cheek.

She shook her head in disappointment. "You don't seem to be grasping the severity of my situation, Mr. Smith."

He felt the warmth of her body seeping into his skin

and attempted to ignore it. "Which situation is that, Mrs. Winslow?"

"As a widow, my wardrobe must reflect my grief—"

He raised an eyebrow, but she continued on, ignoring his reaction.

"—but I must pay homage to my husband's success as well."

"Do you really think it's necessary to waste so much…energy on such decisions?"

"Absolutely."

He couldn't prevent a snort of disbelief.

Her shoulders stiffened in injured pride, and when she spoke, her words held a ring of sincerity.

"You would be surprised, Mr. Smith. Maybe in your world people aren't judged, but in mine, life is a constant trial of merit. One is rated and deemed worthy or unworthy by adhering to a rigid set of standards. Hems, cuffs, colors, fasteners—each has its proper place and time of day. A slight deviation can mean ostracism."

"Aren't you being a little dramatic?"

"No, Mr. Smith. I have seen women cut off from polite society for the slightest infraction of these unspoken rules. It isn't enough merely to be of a good family, one must also display an innate understanding of such matters. Appearance is everything."

He searched her features, realizing that it was "the marquess" who spoke, not Phoebe Gray, a woman who had been fired from her position as a companion because she had been attractive enough to capture the attention of her employer's husband.

"I should think that if your world of privilege is so narrow-minded, you would consider one with far more freedom."

"And where would I find such a place?"

He pretended to think, then said, "The American West, perhaps? Somewhere like…Oregon."

Although he thought she flinched slightly, he couldn't be sure.

"Are you so certain that…Oregon is such a paradise?"

"I can guarantee that in a place where women are still outnumbered two to one, the fabric of a woman's bonnet strings hardly matters."

"I'm sure that even the American Territories have their own brand of prejudices. If a woman's décolletage was too low, her clothes too new, her shoes too dainty…I'm sure any of those elements could cause talk, even in the wilderness."

Sadly, Neil had to concede that she was right.

"So what do you think, Mr. Smith?" She held up the bonnet again. "This one?" She pointed to a bonnet Chloe held. "That one?" The shopkeeper, an elderly rotund woman with pink cheeks, entered, and Louisa motioned her closer. "Or this one?"

Neil glanced at each of the hats. They were small and black, and he could see little difference between them.

"That one." He pointed to the hat that Louisa held, caring little which one she bought as long as she completed the task as soon as possible.

"Do you really think so?" She frowned, her gaze bouncing from one bonnet to the other. "Perhaps I would have an easier decision if I could see them modeled." She turned to the shopkeeper. "Would you mind, Mrs. Eddleton?"

The shopkeeper offered a girlish giggle. "Not at all, my dear."

She set the bonnet on her silvered curls, anchored it

in place with a long hatpin, then tied the ribbon beneath her ear.

"Very lovely," Louisa murmured as Mrs. Eddleton turned in a circle.

"Chloe?"

The maid eagerly pinned the second hat to her own golden curls.

"Mmm. I like that one, too."

Louisa stared at the bonnet in her hand, then at the two being displayed. "I really can't decide. Unless..."

Neil knew what she meant to do the moment she stepped toward him.

"No."

She gazed at him with utmost innocence. "Really, Mr. Smith, there's no cause for worry. I simply need your assistance."

She reached up.

"No."

Her frown was coy. "Are you afraid that helping me will prove a threat to your masculinity?" She turned to the other women. "We won't tell, will we?"

The shopkeeper giggled again. "I never whisper a word of what happens in my shop."

Louisa moved toward him again and Neil opened his mouth to speak, then stopped.

Louisa wanted him to argue. She was so certain that by pinning that blasted hat on his head she would cause a row, and that row would lead to a confrontation. Then she would have an excuse to demand his resignation.

Why should he give her such satisfaction? Especially since she would be forced to lift herself up on her tiptoes and place a hand against his chest to steady herself.

"By all means," he said quietly. "Use me as you will."

Clearly, she'd expected anything except his acquiescence. Momentarily flustered, she paused in midmotion, her hand warm against his sternum.

Dropping his voice so that only she could hear, he said, "Far be it for me to refuse the entreaties of a desperate woman."

At the word *desperate,* her eyes suddenly flashed and her body stiffened. Bit by bit, she lowered herself to the floor and backed away.

"No, now that I've thought about it again, I don't think I'm interested in this one. I prefer the braid to the feathers." Without another glance in Neil's direction, she turned her back to him and added, "I'll take the larger bonnet and veil, Mrs. Eddleton, as well as the supplies to make three more bonnets like those we chose in the catalog. I will enjoy a millinery project to keep my mind off…things."

Mrs. Eddleton clucked in sympathy even as she unpinned the bonnet and motioned to Chloe. "If you'll allow me to take your maid into the back room, Mrs. Winslow, I'll assemble the materials right now."

"Thank you."

The two women stepped through the curtain, leaving the room in a tension-filled silence.

Neil knew the exact moment when Louisa realized she'd made a mistake. By sending both women into the other room, she had left herself without a chaperon. He could see the muscles of her spine tighten infinitesimally, her shoulders draw back. He felt the awareness fill her body as if it were a current that stretched between them.

"You shouldn't have done that, you know," he murmured.

She glanced at him over her shoulder. "Come now, I

haven't bruised your male spirit by attempting to place a bonnet upon your head.''

"I'm not talking about the hat."

He bent to set the dog on the floor, instinctively knowing that Bitsy would run into the other room to investigate. As the dog's ecstatic yips and scrabbling toenails grew faint, the intimacy of the showroom grew more pronounced.

"You shouldn't tempt me, Mrs. Winslow."

"Tempt you?" The words were breathless.

"Mmm." He walked up behind her, coming close enough to press against her bustle and cause it to collapse.

Louisa started, her lungs filling with a quick gasp, but since she was pinned in place by his thighs on one side and the glass display counter on the other, she was unable to escape.

"Yes. You've been tempting me all afternoon."

"I honestly don't know what you mean."

He touched her shoulder with his index finger, tracing the line of the braid at her neck.

"I think you do. You've done little all day except sashay in front of me, trying on jackets and gloves and shoes—"

"Necessary actions if one is to buy clothing."

"Ahh, but I think you've enjoyed it. I'm fully aware of your tactics."

"Tactics?"

"You think that by overwhelming me with the minutiae of your errands you will bore me into leaving my post."

Her silence was answer enough.

"Little did you know that your plans would backfire." His finger dipped, following the back seam of her jacket down between her shoulder blades, then lower and lower still.

"I find it hard to believe that a married woman—a widowed lady—could be so unaware of her innate attractions."

She was breathing hard now. From his vantage point behind her, he could see over her shoulder. The sweet curves of her breasts pushed tightly against the ridge of her corset as she fought the awareness that pooled between them.

"You are a beautiful woman."

"Hardly," she said with a grimace. "I've always been told I was plain."

"No. You're beautiful—and anyone who told you differently was a fool."

The tips of his fingers slid along the delicate column of her throat to the hollow behind her ear. "You have a classic beauty, an exotic beauty." He felt her trembling against his caress. "Very tempting."

His hand slipped to her shoulder again, then down her arm to slide around her waist and draw her against him.

"Which is why I will not leave you. Not today, not tomorrow. Not until I've finished with the job that I've come here to do."

Although he'd told himself that he would not kiss her again, he could not prevent himself from turning her in his arms.

"You don't deserve to be a widow," he whispered, even as his heart silently added, *You should be my bride.*

Her fingers curled around his arms, the warmth seeping through the fabric of his shirt.

"Please, Mr. Smith." Her voice was rife with desperation. "I don't need a bodyguard. Please go away."

If she'd used that same tone to ask him anything else,

he wouldn't have been able to resist. As it was, he could not find the strength to go. This woman had woven a spell around him from the first moment he'd laid eyes on her, and he wasn't ready to abandon his original intent.

Especially not when she looked up at him with dark, rich eyes. Eyes that reflected a portion of his own wants and desires.

Crooking a finger under her chin, he tipped her face up. Slowly, lingeringly, he bent toward her, noting each nuance of expression that crossed her features. When finally his lips touched hers, she shuddered against him, her fingers digging into the muscles of his arms.

A heat grew within him, steadily, insistently, bidding him to forget where they were or how easily they could be discovered. Nevertheless, he could not release her until he'd deepened the kiss, parting her lips and tasting the sweetness to be found there.

It was Bitsy's return that caused them to part, and none too soon. Within seconds, Mrs. Eddleton and Chloe appeared, carrying several brightly colored hatboxes.

As Louisa rushed to meet them, John scooped the dog from the floor and purposely hung back.

Louisa displayed such a complex mix of emotions—being passionate but reserved, impulsive but wary. And yet... He knew she was determined to ensure that no one ever discovered her masquerade.

Somehow, he would have to find a way to change her mind.

Chapter Eight

Dearest Diary,

After the stolen embrace I shared with John Smith in the milliner's shop, I have grown increasingly desperate. John Smith needs to go. Now! If he doesn't leave, I am sure he will be my undoing. Whenever my bodyguard is near, I forget everything but the awareness that he inspires in me and the irresistible pull of my desire.

I cannot believe that I allowed myself to lose control—and in a public establishment, no less! If anyone had seen us…

I am desperate to have the man quit. I am even more unwilling to spend hours and hours sequestered with him in my hotel room. To that end, I have insisted on discreet appearances at the ballet, the opera and countless museums, all without effect. I even renewed my efforts to find a suitable paid companion, forcing John to sit with me as I interviewed a dozen prim and proper women who vied for the position.

Unfortunately, it was I who grew weary of the

task first. And rather than chasing John away, I fear that I have merely given him more reason to think that I need a keeper. As it is, I am weary. Weary of living in a hotel suite, weary of holding myself in check, fearing that I am being judged and observed. I want to read my books and devote myself to my writing.

But most of all, I long to be ''home.'' I want a place where I can ''nest'' and feel completely at ease.

In truth, I've never really felt that I could indulge in such pursuits. And now…

With the inheritance that I've been given, I have the opportunity to do whatever I want. Although Mr. Pritchard has explained that the main house is part of Evie's trust, there is a small structure known as the garden house on the same estate that has been willed to Louisa.

I have a house. A house and a fortune.

How could I have been so blessed? In the past, my fondest positions have involved households with children. I can't see how such a task—caring for little ones—could ever prove a hardship. In fact, I can't wait until I can introduce myself to Evie and bring the little girl home.

Louisa stretched, smiling softly as her thoughts chased away the last of her dreams.

She would focus on the happiness waiting on her horizon rather than on the difficulties of her current situation. In a week, perhaps two, she would have surmounted the last of the obstacles before her. Charles's body would be here any day. Once the coffin had arrived, she would journey to Boston, retrieve her stepdaughter and then organize a funeral—which would surely be a quiet, family-oriented affair.

Then her life would be her own.

Blinking against the light, Louisa took a moment to focus, then cautiously checked her room, knowing that John would be somewhere close by. When she didn't find him, she realized that he was blissfully absent from her bedchamber.

For the first time in days, she heaved a sigh of relief. With all the time they'd spent together, she would have expected to grow accustomed to the man. Unfortunately, she was discovering that "familiarity" had not begun to breed contempt. Quite the opposite. Her stomach was so tight with nerves when he was near that she continued to suffer from bouts of sickness. Worse yet, she was growing attuned to his presence, to the booming timbre of his voice. She had even begun to rely on him to feel…safer when he was near.

Safer?

Why would he inspire such a feeling when she was in no danger? Mr. Smith was constantly looking for a threat that had yet to materialize, and rather than relying on the proof of her own eyes, she was beginning to allow his views to upset her.

Which was why she couldn't relax enough to settle the nervous flip-flopping of her stomach whenever he was near. It had nothing to do with the man himself or the way he made her feel. It was merely a product of his gloomy suspicions.

Why should she be in any danger at all? It didn't make sense. No one even knew her.

So why was John Smith so adamant about keeping his job?

Pressing the heels of her hands against her eyes, she

surmised that he must need the money and was too proud to take it without performing "a job well done."

Louisa shook her head as if to clear it. Why should she allow thoughts of the man to spoil her morning?

"Chloe?" she called, sweeping the covers aside.

She wasn't so naive as to think that Mr. Smith was gone for good. But hopefully, he would be gone long enough for her to take a relaxing bath.

Within an hour, Louisa had managed to bathe and begin her toilette. For one brief moment, as she was being cinched into a corset that was kept tighter than she was accustomed to enduring, Louisa briefly wondered what would happen if she were to suddenly abandon her charade. But the moment the idea formed, she pushed it aside, remembering that she must consider more than herself. The money was payment for the duties she would perform for her stepdaughter from now on. Having been orphaned herself, Louisa refused to leave another child feeling alone and uncertain about her future.

"Good morning, Mrs. Winslow."

Louisa gasped, reaching for a shawl and wrapping it around her shoulders. Casting a disapproving glance over her shoulder, she ignored the wave of awareness that rushed through her body, making her knees weak.

"Mr. Smith, have you never been taught to knock?"

He shrugged, infuriating her even more.

Clutching the shawl even closer, she ignored the gooseflesh that pebbled her skin. Suddenly self-conscious and aware of him as a man, she found she couldn't meet John's eyes. The mere sight of him was enough to make her heart pound.

"You've received a message from your solicitor."

He tapped an envelope against his palm, and to her

horror, she discovered that although it was addressed to her it had already been opened.

"You read a letter addressed to me?" she asked incredulously.

"Of course."

She bristled in indignation. "Mr. Smith, I fail to see how continually trampling over my privacy falls into the realms of your job. How dare you take it upon yourself to read my mail and interfere in my personal business?"

John didn't respond, but he had the all-out gall to look amused rather than cowed.

"Give me the note, please," she demanded.

"Yes, ma'am."

She glared at him when his tone continued to be far from humble.

Snatching the note out of his hands, she struggled to open it with fingers that trembled.

"Your lawyer is informing you that Charles's coffin has arrived and the private Winslow railway car has been hooked onto the afternoon train to Boston in preparation for your journey home."

Louisa pressed her lips together to keep from snapping at him like a fishwife. As soon as she'd gathered her control, she turned to Chloe and said, "Would you excuse us for a moment, please?"

If she was going to lose her temper, she didn't intend to have her maid be witness to the fact.

The door closed behind Chloe, but before Louisa could say a word, John said, "I'll wait while you write an answer telling him that you won't be going."

Louisa glared at him. "I beg your pardon?"

"You'll need to tell him that you won't be leaving just yet."

"Why on earth would I do that?"

"Because it isn't safe. You shouldn't go anywhere until I can take measures to ensure your security."

She groaned, rubbing at the ache that was beginning to throb at her temples.

"Mr. Smith, we have been through all of this time and time again. You have yet to convince me that I need a bodyguard at all. Since that is the case, I refuse to stay here any longer while you dither and delay."

"Since I'm the professional—"

"No, Mr. Smith. I'm not going to listen to any more of your nonsense." With her fury building, she advanced, poking him in the chest with her finger. "You continually forget that *you* are the employee in this situation."

"Your husband—"

"My husband is dead. He is unable to give you orders."

"I think that he—"

"Mr. Smith, my husband's body is waiting at the railway station. The time has passed for his remains to be put to rest. As much as you might think that you have my best interests at heart, in this matter I will not relent." Her breath caught in an unconscious sob. "I want to go home. I have waited long enough and my husband has waited long enough, and in this I will not be denied!"

"Home? How can Charles Winslow's estate be home to you when you have never been there?"

Louisa's eyes filled with tears. Why was this man being so hateful to her? What could she have possibly done to deserve such treatment?

"Stay for a few days," he said, taking her hands.

"No."

He tugged her closer. "A day, then."

"No."

He framed her face with his hands. "Why can't you trust me in this matter? Why can't you understand that I have your best interests at heart?"

"Because I have absolutely no reason to trust you."

For the first time, something she said seemed to give him pause.

"I would never hurt you," he murmured.

She should have been reassured, but when his touch began to arouse an unsettling mixture of desire and awareness, she trembled.

"Trust me," he whispered. Then, bending toward her, he touched her lips with his, softly at first, then again and again.

In an instant she was flooded with a yearning that could not be satisfied with a quick embrace. Even as she damned herself for being a fool, she lifted herself on tiptoe, allowing him to take her weight as her arms slipped around his neck.

"Please don't do this to me," she whispered when he abandoned her lips to trace the line of her jaw, then dip down to the sensitive skin of her neck.

"Don't do what?"

She couldn't gather her wits enough to answer. Did she want to plead with him to stop ordering her about? To stop interfering in her private affairs?

Or did she want him to stop caressing her, kissing her, so that she could gather her wits again?

You're a widow. You're a widow....

But even as she inwardly repeated the words to herself, she couldn't bring herself to push him away. He was becoming an obsession, an addiction.

When he lifted his head, she clutched at him, attempting to pull him back.

"We can't do this," John whispered.

She offered a sound that was half moan, half sob of regret.

For long moments, he stared down at her, his eyes growing incredibly dark with the intensity of his need. She shuddered beneath the depth of his hunger, alarmed and exhilarated by what she saw.

He wanted her.

As much as she needed him.

Her heart beat in an odd tattoo. Her breathing became labored. She waited for the moment when his control would snap and he would make the decision for both of them.

But just when her body clamored for the unknown, he stepped away, gently removing her arms from around his neck.

"We'll go to Boston," he said gruffly.

The shock of his rejection kept her rooted to the floor. She gazed up at him, feeling both relieved and abandoned. Instinctively, she knew that a single word would be enough to bring him back. But just as certainly, she knew that to speak it would destroy the new life that she had begun to build for herself.

Bit by bit, the hunger within her waned to bitter ashes. Suddenly chilled, she wrapped the shawl around her body and huddled in its slight warmth.

Sensing her withdrawal, John dipped his head. Then, without another word, he turned and left her alone in the room.

John didn't stop until he reached the hall and shut the door behind him. Then he leaned a hand against the wall and took a deep, calming breath.

Damn it, with each encounter, he was forced to reevaluate his commitment to this enterprise. After spending only a short time with "Louisa," he was compelled to acknowledge that it would be impossible to walk away. She was a study in contradictions—beautiful yet modest, reserved yet sensual. She had the face of an angel, but the passion of a sinner.

And Neil was drawn to her in a very elemental way.

Sighing, he admitted that his attraction hadn't made his task any easier. On the contrary. The longer Louisa remained locked in her role as Charles's widow, the more complicated the situation became.

He supposed that he could tell her the truth, but he knew instinctively that it would be unwise at this point. He needed to remember that she truly was in danger. If she decided his lies were reason enough to send him away, there would be no one to watch out for her welfare.

Taking a deep breath, he tried to banish the image of her from his mind's eye. But the memory of the way she'd stood trembling in his embrace, her eyes dark, her lips parted and moist from his kiss, would not be so easily dismissed. Even now, Neil wanted nothing more than to carry her away, forcing her to return to the life she had originally agreed to adopt, but he quickly reined in his own impulsiveness.

Despite everything that kept them apart, there was one factor that weighed most heavily on his mind. He wouldn't force her to do anything. He wanted her to marry him and come to Oregon willingly.

Until then...

Until then, they would go to Boston, he thought, straightening. If nothing else, the journey would allow him to keep a close eye on her. He was growing more and more concerned by the way Louisa seemed healthy one minute, then was hunched over a chamber pot, sick, the next. She had continually reassured him, insisting she was perfectly fit, but he wasn't so sure....

If he hadn't known it was impossible, he might have thought that Louisa was suffering from morning sickness.

The moment the idea formed, he brushed it aside.

Preposterous. Louisa and Charles had been married by proxy. If she'd had an intimate relationship with anyone before that time, Neil would have found hints of it in her letters.

She couldn't be pregnant.

A knock at the door brought his thoughts to an abrupt halt. Pushing his misgivings aside, Neil drew back the hammer of his pistol and eased open the door.

A young boy dressed in hotel livery held up an envelope. "Telegram."

Neil slid his revolver into his holster, gave the youth a tip, then took the slip. As he closed and locked the door, a glance at the name "John Smith" on the front brought a chill. Only two other people knew his alias. The woman who called herself Phoebe Gray and her new husband, Gabriel Cutter.

His stomach clenched as he slit open the note and read the cryptic note.

Attempt on wife's life <stop>
Leaving Oregon on long honeymoon <stop>
Will join you after <stop>
Take caution <stop>
Gabe Cutter <stop>

Neil crumpled the paper and shoved the slip into the pocket of his waistcoat.

Stay on your guard, old boy, he told himself as he double-checked the chambers of his rifle. If someone had tried to kill Phoebe, it was only a matter of time before Louisa was in grave danger, as well.

Chapter Nine

As he bundled them into the closed carriage that he'd hired, and saw to the last of the trunks, Neil chafed at the delays that the women had already caused. He kept glancing at the teeming traffic, searching for the slightest hint of danger or a suspicious interest in the proceedings. The minutes multiplied until he felt they had made themselves so conspicuous they could have painted a bull's-eye on the carriage.

For the life of him, he didn't understand how anyone could amass so many possessions. He'd lost count of how many steamer trunks had been loaded so far. He'd already been forced to hire a wagon, since they could not fit in the carriage's small boot. Thank heavens one of his army buddies, a wizened, wiry fellow named Francis Tucker, had arrived to help keep an eye on things.

"There's altogether too many gosh dern things," Tucker grumbled in a raspy voice, taking his spot near Neil's elbow.

Neil had to agree. It was difficult enough keeping one eye on Louisa and the other on the surrounding crowd. Add to that a wagonful of luggage, a lady's maid and a rambunctious dog, and he was wishing that he'd hired a full contingency of men rather than arranging for two old army buddies to help him out.

"What about Parker?" Neil asked, referring to a tall dour man who had received the second telegram.

"He'll meet us in Boston day after tomorrow."

"Good." Neil nodded to the trunks. "As for those, get them loaded as quickly as you can. I want to be out of here before we become even more of a spectacle," he muttered, as Louisa blithely handed him the dog and moved to climb into the carriage.

Growling in self-disgust, Neil wondered again if he'd lost his mind. No woman was worth this humiliation. He should leave for Oregon and concentrate on his cattle. But even as he thought of abandoning Louisa, the possibility that she could be hurt stopped him in his tracks.

For now, he had no choice but to stay a little longer. At least until Boston. Then he would decide once and for all if this enterprise was the best way to bring home his bride.

The ride to the station was made with a flotilla of wagons, but just as he'd feared, Neil found his ability to watch for unseen dangers hampered by the presence of the dog. At any other time he would probably have tossed the animal onto the seat and been done with it, but judging by the way Louisa watched him so intently, he was sure she expected him to do so.

"She's beginning to like you," she said, gesturing to the dog.

Neil clenched his teeth in irritation. Louisa's comment was a bald-faced lie, and they both knew it. Bitsy was beside herself in her efforts to get free, wriggling and burrowing into his jacket, chewing at his gloves and losing no opportunity to nip a little deeper.

"Whatever possessed you to adopt such an animal?"

"Oh, I didn't 'adopt her,' as you so delicately put it. I bought her from a pedigreed breeder."

In Neil's opinion, that made matters worse. Only a fool would pay money for such a nuisance.

"Why did you buy this particular dog?"

She shrugged. "For the company."

Neil gestured behind them to the woman perched on the wagon seat, guarding Louisa's belongings. "You have a maid for that."

Louisa shook her head, making a tsking sound. "Even you must know that there are limits to the association that polite society will let me have with my maid. If I were to travel or visit another person's home, Chloe would be relegated to the servants' quarters." Louisa smiled indulgently at the dog. "Bitsy, on the other hand, can accompany me anywhere. Besides, I've always wanted a pet."

"Your father didn't buy you one?"

She blinked at him uncomprehendingly. "My father?"

"The marquis."

He saw a careful blankness shutter her eyes, and she glanced out the window. "No. My father was not prone to buying me pets."

"What was your father prone to doing?"

She did not answer for some time, but finally said softly, "Leaving me."

For a moment, the carriage was filled with an aching silence, one that made Neil remember the letters he'd received from this woman when she'd still laid claim to her real name.

She'd talked often enough of her loneliness and of being banished to the same servants' quarters she'd mentioned, but why hadn't he known she'd always wanted a pet?

Moreover, why had she never told him what she knew about her father? Neil was as familiar with Louisa's early years and her faint memories of her mother as he was with his own. But never once had she spoken or written about her father.

Did she know anything about the man? Did she have an inkling that her father had come from the aristocracy? If so, had the information merely deepened her sense of abandonment and isolation?

"Do you miss your father?" Neil asked, wondering if she would flinch.

But again, she studied him with a face devoid of emotion. "No."

Neil raised his brow. "That isn't the answer I would have expected from such a dutiful daughter."

She tipped her head to one side, then said, "My father had a talent for inspiring a sense of responsibility, but never affection."

Bitsy continued to worry Neil's thumb with her teeth, but he hardly noticed. Instead, he found himself gazing deep into Louisa's eyes.

"Is that why you feel you must carry out the wishes of a husband you've never met?"

If she was surprised at the fact that he was privy to such knowledge, she didn't let on.

"What would you have me do? Abandon all that I've chosen to be? Leave a defenseless girl without a guardian? Even you couldn't be that heartless, Mr. Smith."

Oh, but he could…and he would.

One day—one day soon—Neil would ask her to do just that. If Louisa was to be a slave to duty, then she'd best remember who had received her promises first.

Not a dead man.

But me.

Suddenly, he was glad they were going to Boston. The time had come for Louisa to see the life that she had doomed herself to live—one of rigid rules and social mores. Once there, Neil would be able to keep her sequestered and safely out of sight—a situation that would be demanded in any event, since Louisa was newly widowed. Once she discovered that she'd tied herself not only to the staid strictures of society but also to the obligatory prison of mourning, she would gladly turn to Neil for comfort.

And once she had begun to seek him out, it would be an easy enough matter to steal her away.

Louisa had a single goal in her mind as they arrived at the station.

She needed to get to the telegram office and check for messages. She had managed to send several notes to Phoebe while she'd waited for Charles to meet her in New York. Louisa had explained about the delay she'd encountered in waiting for her husband to arrive, and had begged Phoebe for news. But there had been no response.

Surely by now she would find a stack of telegrams waiting for her. Louisa reckoned her friend should be married and well into her new life at this point. It was imperative that she be given the news of Charles's death and Louisa's current situation.

But from the moment John helped her to alight from the carriage and handed Bitsy's basket to Chloe, it was obvious that he was not going to let her out of his sight.

"I've sent the driver to check on the status of your

personal railway car. Until then, you'll need to wait in the station house, out of the heat.''

Away from the rest of mankind, he meant, Louisa thought to herself as she was hurried out of the warmth of the afternoon and into the ladies' waiting room. However, to her delight, Louisa realized that he'd unwittingly taken her to the one place where he would not be allowed to follow.

''Mr. Smith,'' she said in a low voice when several women gasped and one elderly lady began reaching for her smelling salts. ''I'm afraid you'll have to wait in the corridor.''

''Why?''

''Because it isn't proper for you to be here.''

He scowled. ''Why not?''

''Because this is a *ladies'* waiting room.'' When he didn't respond, she hastened to explain, ''Many of these women are in the midst of lengthy journeys and they take the opportunity to…relax their strictures a bit.''

When he continued to stare at her blankly, Louisa quickly cut her eyes to a woman in the corner who had draped a blanket over her chest. A pair of tiny feet peeked out from the colorful quilt, making it clear that she was nursing an infant.

A stain of color began to seep up John's neck, and Louisa nearly laughed aloud in delight. Finally she'd found a way to unsettle the man.

''I'll be just outside the door,'' he said sternly. Turning on his heel, he marched through, slamming it behind him.

Chloe giggled, setting Bitsy's basket on the floor. ''I don't think I've seen a man leave so quickly in some time, *madame.*''

''Nor have I.''

Since she'd just left the hotel, Louisa had no real need of the facilities to be found in the women's parlor, but she began searching the lounge nevertheless. There had to be another way out. There just had to be!

To her delight, in the back room, where an area had been set aside to allow travelers to wash, Louisa found a narrow door. Turning the knob, she peered outside, seeing that she had unearthed a service entrance. A dim corridor led to several doors labeled Station Staff Only.

"Madame Winslow?"

Chloe stepped into the room just as Louisa was closing the door again.

"Is there something wrong, *madame?*"

Louisa tugged her gloves more securely onto her fingers. "No, not at all." She took a deep breath, then said, "Chloe, I won't be needing you until we board the train. Will you see to it that all of the trunks are safely stowed? I have a short errand to run."

Chloe's eyes widened. "But…I am sure Mr. Smith wants me to stay with you and…"

Louisa squeezed her hand. "Please. I have a private errand that I need to perform, and Mr. Smith won't give me leave to breathe. I swear, I'm in no more danger of being hurt or kidnapped than Bitsy, but that man won't see reason." She smoothed her skirts and checked the angle of her hat in the mirror. "Remain in the ladies' lounge for at least ten minutes. If Mr. Smith tries to retrieve me during that time, tell him I'm…indisposed and he should wait."

"B-but—"

Ignoring her maid's obvious distress, Louisa opened the maintenance door a crack and peered into the dim hallway beyond. Except for an elderly man mopping the floor at the far end, the area was empty.

Failing to alleviate the man's obvious curiosity, Louisa slipped into the hall. With her head high, she traversed the length of the dusty floorboards to another door marked Exit.

Her heart was pounding as she stepped into the afternoon warmth.

Stiffening her resolve and her spine, she damned John Smith for doing this to her. She should be enjoying her newly found freedom. Instead, she was laden with anxiety and guilt.

Guilt?

No. She wasn't guilty. She couldn't be guilty. She hadn't done anything wrong.

Other than steal another person's identity.

Ahh. But that wasn't stealing. She had the real Louisa Haversham's blessing—which was exactly why she needed to get to the telegraph office. Phoebe had probably responded by now with news of her own life. Louisa needed to instruct her friend to send her messages to Boston from now on.

"What are you doing?"

Louisa jumped, squelching the instinctive gasp that escaped from her throat.

Damn the man. Damn him! Why couldn't he leave her alone?

"M-Mr. Smith." She inwardly cringed at the defensiveness that entered her tone.

"Yes, Mrs. Winslow?"

"I merely…"

"Yes?"

The man was so smug, so all-knowing. But what angered her most was that he'd been able to read her intentions so easily. Somehow, despite her careful planning, he'd known that she intended to escape his vigilance. She could only hope that he didn't know why she had been so intent on finding a few minutes alone.

"I needed a breath of fresh air."

"Wouldn't it have been simpler to find it by returning to the ladies' waiting room and leaving via the main door?"

"I felt faint, so I thought this route would be quicker."

"Mmm-hmm."

Darn it, why was the man looking at her as if she were a recalcitrant child? She was a grown woman, not a toddler to be reprimanded when she strayed too far.

"Mr. Smith, perhaps I should be honest with you."

"That would make a refreshing change."

She glared at him, but refused to respond to the comment. "I am a woman who needs solitude on occasion."

"Then lock yourself in the ladies' washroom and stay there a bit."

Her hands curled into fists and she fought to control the urge to shout in irritation.

"I am not an animal to be penned up." She huffed in frustration. "You have yet to prove to me that your efforts are even necessary. There have been no threats against me, no suspicious characters lurking in the shadows, no letters, no notes, nothing. Personally, I don't know why you stay, unless you delight in tormenting me. You've been glued to my side for days and I've grown weary of you, Mr. Smith, completely and utterly weary. Indeed, I am beginning to wonder if you aren't a danger yourself. You have yet to prove that Charles hired you, yet you have taken unprecedented liberties with me and my staff! Frankly, Mr. Smith, I am hesitant to allow you to accompany me from this point on!"

A throng of passengers from an arriving train

streamed over the platform suddenly, so Louisa quickly dodged into their midst. As she did so, a sudden sound pierced the din of the crowd, and she screamed when a burning sensation stung her upper arm.

Dear sweet heaven, she'd been shot!

Within seconds, she felt a pair of strong arms whip around her waist and pull her to one side. Instinctively, she opened her mouth to scream again, but a hand clapped over her mouth. Then, before she could comprehend what was happening, she was pulled into a baggage storeroom and the door slammed shut.

Louisa struggled against her captor, wondering how one moment of defiance could erupt into such a disaster. She wriggled and kicked, all the while reaching for the hatpin that held her bonnet in place. She had just managed to pluck it free when an all-too-familiar voice whispered in her ear. "Quiet! *Quiet!* It's me, Louisa!"

The moment those familiar deep tones reached her consciousness, she grew limp, wondering why she hadn't recognized his body pressed to her own. As his grip loosened, she turned to throw her own arms around his neck.

"Someone shot at me!"

He smoothed his hand over her hair and then her back. "I know. I know."

Sobbing, she clung to him even harder.

"But why? How can anyone possibly want to hurt me? I don't know anyone in this…this b-blasted country except you, Chloe and a few odd shopkeepers."

John's hands were strong and broad, pulling her tightly against him, so the warmth of his body could seep into her own and chase away the sudden chill.

Her knees trembled so badly that she could no longer stand. As if he understood, John swept her up and carried her to a crate in the corner. There, he set her down and immediately turned his attention to her arm.

"It's just a scratch," he stated, sounding relieved.

Louisa made the mistake of looking down. Just as John had said, the wound was barely worth mentioning. Although her sleeve had been torn—yet another damaged garment to her credit—her arm had suffered little more than a graze. Nevertheless, the sight of the blood smearing her flesh was enough to make her stomach lurch anew.

Slapping her hand to her mouth, she vaulted off the crate and rushed across the room to a spot where several cleaning buckets had been left. But even as she propped her hand against the wall, she willed the sickness to pass. She would not disgrace herself in front of this man. Not again.

Chapter Ten

Louisa took deep, gulping breaths, pushing her queasiness aside through sheer effort of will. Her concentration was so absolute that she jumped when John pressed a cool, wet cloth into her hand.

"Go ahead. It's clean."

Nodding, she noted that he'd given her a snowy white handkerchief. Eagerly, she pressed it against her lips, then dabbed it to her brows.

"Thank you."

A moment of silence was punctuated by the continued shouts and squeals of surprise that came to them from beyond the door.

"You need to see a doctor."

She closed her eyes, growing tired of the man's repeated suggestion.

"There's no need. I am merely exhausted by the journey I've undertaken so far. I'm unsettled and anxious and… Home. I need to be home."

She looked up to find him watching her intently. "Is that what Winslow Manor is to you? Home?"

"Yes. It's where I plan to live from now on."

"Ahh, but isn't the term 'home' to be used for a place where someone has already lived for some time?"

She shook her head. "Not at all. Home is the place where one feels as if she belongs." Louisa closed her eyes, to relish the coolness of the cloth again. "I have had many homes, but none of them permanent."

The moment the words were uttered, she realized her mistake. The real Louisa Haversham would never admit to such a thing. The real Louisa Haversham had spent most of her years in a boarding school, not moving from one position to another.

Lifting her head, she pushed back the vestiges of sickness. "I want to go to my railway car now."

She had expected an argument, but received none. Instead, she watched as John drew his pistol from his holster and surveyed the room. "We'll go out this door," he said, motioning to a cargo door on the far side. "Rather than walking along the boardwalk, we'll circle around and come to the car from behind."

Not well enough to argue, she nodded her assent. When his hand closed around hers, she drew upon the strength it provided.

Someone had shot at her!

The words repeated in her head over and over as she followed John in a circuitous route through the station house and then the maze of trains. He moved quickly, searching the crowd furtively as he went. Finally, he stopped.

"This is it."

Louisa blinked. She'd been so immersed in the throbbing of her arm and the rush to keep up that she'd given little attention to the route they'd taken.

Looking up, she saw a railway car that was painted as drably as any of the others, and her heart sank. When she'd been told that she would be riding in a private conveyance, she'd imagined something more elegant.

John's hands spanned her waist and he lifted her up to the first step. Stumbling slightly, she climbed onto the landing, then opened the door.

"Dear sweet heaven above," she whispered, transfixed by what she saw.

She could have been dropped into a fairyland without being more surprised. Once she'd stepped over the threshold, she was surrounded in luxury. Crystal chandeliers twinkled in the late afternoon sunshine. Heavy brocade draperies framed the windows and a velvety Aubusson carpet covered the floor.

"As you can see, Charles spared no expense when he was traveling."

After shutting the door behind her, John moved from window to window, drawing thick shades.

Louisa mourned the loss of light, but she understood the precaution. Still feeling shaky, she crossed to a richly tufted settee and sank down upon it. As she fought to catch her breath, she rued the tightness of her corset and the black clothing she'd been forced to wear. She felt as if she were being smothered in the garments, and not just by their weight. Their somber cast seemed entirely out of place with the adventure of this rolling palace.

John squatted in front of her so that he could meet her eyes directly. "Are you all right?"

She nodded. "Yes, I'm fine."

"You're sure?"

She managed a weak smile. "Yes. I feel safer here."

He studied her features for several long seconds, then finally gave a curt nod. "I've got to arrange a few last-minute details. I'll send Chloe to you right away. Don't open the door to anyone but her or me and do not, under any circumstances, lift the shades. Do you understand?''

She nodded, feeling inexplicably close to tears. She couldn't remember the last time anyone had ever been so concerned about her well-being.

Shifting his weight to one knee, John reached beneath his pant leg and withdrew a tiny pistol.

''Can you shoot one of these?''

She blinked, hardly able to believe that he was about to give her a weapon. ''Yes.''

''You're sure?''

She nodded, even though she'd never held a gun in her life.

John cracked the derringer open to show her that two bullets were already loaded in the chambers.

''Use it only if necessary and only if someone is close enough that you can do some damage.''

He placed the gun in her hand and then stood. He was halfway to the door when he paused, then returned. Before she knew what he meant to do, he'd bent and placed a soft kiss against her lips.

''Take care of yourself, Mrs. Winslow.''

Then he strode from the train, locking the door behind him.

It wasn't until the silence settled around her that Louisa realized she hadn't been able to complete her original errand. If there were telegrams awaiting her, she had no way to retrieve them. Nor did she have the means to get word to Phoebe that she would soon be leaving for Boston.

She closed her eyes and felt her body suddenly flooded with weariness. This whole situation was supposed to be so simple. She would become Louisa Haversham and her life would be easy from that point on.

So how had the plan grown so complicated so quickly?

Groaning, she rested her cheek on her hand. She could only pray that once she was in Boston, her life would resume a more peaceful routine.

Neil had taken less than a half-dozen steps before Tucker fell into step behind him.

"I came t'see if'n yer ready t'unload the trunks."

Neil offered him a curt nod, then asked, "Did you see who fired the shot?" His fingers curled around the butt of his revolver, his eyes carefully scanning the crowd.

Tucker gave a hoot of laughter. "Tweren't aimed at the little missy, I can tell you that."

Neil paused and glared down at the man. "What do you mean?"

"The shooting didn't have anythin' t'do with the girl." He waved in the direction of the train. "It was nothin' more than a jealous husband."

Neil scowled.

The wizened man chortled. "When Mrs. Winslow dodged into the crowd, she got in the middle of a lovers' tiff. It seems that a woman from these parts ran off with her husband's hired man. He tracked 'em down and when he tried t'retrieve his bride, the hired man let off a shot. The bullet lodged into a pole not more'n an inch away from where Mrs. Winslow was situated. She must have been hit by a sliver of wood."

Neil studied the evident glee in Tucker's face, then peered down the length of the platform, taking in the sight of a pair of uniformed policemen and a knot of people.

"You're sure about that?"

"Hell, yes. They just retrieved the pair of 'em and

loaded them up in the paddy wagon. The woman followed it at least a couple of blocks, blubbering and wailing the entire time."

"So no one made an attempt on Mrs. Winslow's life?"

"Not this time."

As Tucker hurried off to unload the trunks, Neil squinted into the sunshine, his eyes again searching the crowded platforms.

He'd been watching Louisa for more than a week, and today had been the first hint of danger. Unaccountably, when Neil had heard the shot, he'd felt a pang of relief. Finally Louisa's uncle had played his hand and given Neil a target to follow.

But if Tucker's account was correct, that meant that Louisa's uncle still hadn't made his move. Until he did, Neil was in the dark about who or what to protect Louisa from.

Lifting his hat, he swiped at the sweat gathering on his brow, then turned in the direction of the telegraph office. It was time to wire Oregon and get more information from the real Louisa Haversham.

The figure lingering in the shadows near the station turned away from John Smith as the man strode into the station.

The weight of the pistol pressed into the assassin's leg. The scuffle on the platform had kept any shots from being fired at Louisa Haversham Winslow.

"It won't be that easy or that quick. Not anymore."

The assassin whirled, then relaxed.

"Mr. Badger. What are you doing here?"

"We've received new instructions."

"I haven't been able to get her in a position where I could—"

He held up a hand. "No matter. Our employer has decided we need to delay things."

"Delay things?" The assassin wiped at moist palms, not willing to be caught with evidence of a weak will.

"Horace has made plans to come to America. We're to wait until he arrives before killing her."

The assassin scowled. "Why?"

Badger shrugged. "Don't ask questions. You've been paid generously for your time." His eyes narrowed. "Just make sure you're ready to make your move the moment your services are required."

"She has a bodyguard with her."

Badger's eyes rose. "So? Let the man stay. There are ways to ensure a person's death that are subtler than a bullet. If he were to suddenly disappear, it would cause more questions than we can afford right now."

Once the train had left the station and the journey to Boston had begun, Louisa started to relax. Slowly the icy fear that had gripped her since being shot at the station melted away.

She was safe now. She'd left New York behind her.

Rising from the settee where she'd collapsed, she explored her surroundings, discovering to her delight that the car actually contained three small rooms.

The first was the elegant sitting room. Here it was easy to imagine that Charles had entertained his business clients. The space was complete with a small bar, an array of liquors, teas and coffees, plus several boxes of assorted chocolates. Beyond that room was a small bedroom complete with an overstuffed chair and a narrow bed, and to the rear of that, a cramped closet and dressing area.

Standing in the curtained archway that led into the closet, Louisa felt gooseflesh rise at the base of her neck. Staring at the dark suits hung on the rod, she eerily studied the staid garments, feeling like an interloper.

He would have been your husband, a tiny voice whispered in her head.

Closing her eyes, she absorbed the scent of tobacco. Pipe tobacco.

Grimacing, Louisa realized that she'd never been fond of that smell. It reminded her too much of her first position as a paid companion, to a woman whose husband had been a drunken brute. The man had terrorized his wife and frightened Louisa to death.

Shaking off the memory, she turned her back to the clothes and moved to the edge of the bed, where she stripped off her dress and petticoats.

A cistern was mounted on the wall and she dampened a cloth from a nearby stack, gently pressing it to her wound. Immediately a sharp pain shot down her arm into her fingers, but she gritted her teeth, refusing to let so much as a hiss leave her lips. If she did, she had no doubts that John would come bursting through the door—with Mr. Pritchard right behind him, no doubt.

Again she grimaced. If she'd known that the lawyer intended to accompany them, she would have…

Well, she didn't know what she would have done. Since John and Mr. Pritchard ignored her complaints, she doubted she would have been able to prevent the arrangement, but at least she could have tried. As it was, she'd left the men glaring at each other from opposite sides of the railway car.

Which was all the more reason why she should take advantage of her excuse to rest.

Unfastening the top hook of her basque, she took a gulp of air, then sank onto the chair.

Why had someone shot her? Why?

"You won't get much sleep in that chair."

Louisa didn't even bother to open her eyes. Although she'd hoped that John would respect her need for privacy, she hadn't really expected him to do so. "I don't think I can sleep. I'm still…rattled."

He didn't reply to that. He merely knelt beside her, taking her arm and examining the long, narrow wound that had already begun to scab over.

"It's shallow enough that it won't leave a scar."

He held up a coil of bandages.

Louisa eyed them ruefully. "Don't tell me that Chloe sacrificed one of her petticoat flounces for a dressing."

"Not at all. We found some medical supplies in the galley."

"You've been prying into the cupboards?"

"Not necessary. Mr. Pritchard has ridden in this car on several occasions and he seems quite familiar with all it has to offer." John's lips curved wryly. "He's already lit the stove and begun a pot of tea, if you'd care for some."

It was the first pleasant idea she'd heard all day. "I would love a cup."

He pointed to her arm. "I want to see to this first."

She stared down at the angry scratch, wondering how something so shallow could cause her arm to throb so mightily. "Very well."

She bit her lip as he took her arm and gently bandaged her injuries. Through it all, she forced herself to ignore his touch…the heat that spread through her veins…the way her body grew heavy and languorous.

When he'd finished, she reluctantly opened her eyes and stared up at John through her lashes. His gaze was no less intent than hers.

"Don't," she whispered.

"Don't what?"

He knew what he was doing. There was no need for her to clarify.

"I think it would be best if you left me alone now." When he didn't move, she said, "Please. After all I've been through today, I simply can't endure anything more."

The tiny room seemed to pulse with the intensity of their awareness. Louisa found herself praying that John would walk away, yet wishing with nearly the same intensity that he would draw her into his arms and make her forget her aches and worries.

Was he able to read her mind? Just when she felt she couldn't endure another moment, he reached out to stroke her cheek, wiping at a lone tear that she hadn't even known was sliding down her cheek. His touch was infinitely gentle, filled with the same rife awareness that tumbled through her body.

Then, taking a deep breath, he stood. "I'll send Chloe in with your tea."

The moment he slid the pocket door closed behind him, Louisa wrapped her arms around her waist, the tears coming in earnest.

What was she doing? Playing with fire? She should have railed at the man for taking such liberties. Instead she had,…

Melted at his touch.

Sobbing, she squeezed her eyes shut.

Once she reached Boston, things would be different, she promised herself.

They had to be different, or she would be lost.

Dearest Diary,

Although I have the privilege of riding in my own personal railway car, I have already discovered that such luxuries do not hasten an end to my journey in any way.

When the locomotive pulled out of New York, I had supposed that the trip would be made in a minimal amount of time, barring one or two stops for passengers. Within an hour, I realized my assumptions were naive. Passengers at every town and whistle-stop from here to Boston use this particular line. I doubt that we have traveled uninterrupted for more than thirty minutes at a time. In addition to passengers, we have also had to take on coal, water, mails and make repairs. Add to that animals on the tracks, rock slides and maintenance—as well as the need to pull onto a siding to allow other trains to pass—and we've made very slow progress indeed.

As one day slipped into two, I've grown more accustomed to the opulence of my surroundings. Unfortunately, the elegance of the train has fueled my fantasies about what I will find once I arrive at the Winslow estate. If the train is this grand, what will Winslow Manor look like? A palace?

With each hour, my curiosity has grown—and strangely, with that curiosity comes a surge of confidence.

I am Mrs. Charles Winslow III. And judging by

the elegance of the private car, I am the wife of a very important man....

The pocket door slid open and Chloe stepped inside, carrying a fresh bucket of water to fill the cistern so that Louisa could wash.

"Any news of our progress?" Louisa asked as she slid her diary beneath her pillow and pushed the covers off her legs.

From her spot on the pillow next to her, Bitsy yawned and turned her face to the wall, unwilling to end her nap as long as the train was underway.

"According to Mr. Smith, we should arrive in Boston by lunchtime."

Louisa's heart skipped excitedly. "Really?"

Chloe's smile was wide. "Yes, *madame.*"

"Wonderful!"

Chloe brought her a stack of fresh towels, then, in deference to the swaying of the boxcar, filled a basin only halfway.

Louisa quickly washed, then sat on the edge of the bed so that Chloe could brush her hair.

"Would you like me to change the bandage first?" Chloe asked, gesturing to the strips of cotton wound around Louisa's arm.

Actually, that was the last thing she wished. The throbbing ache of her wound had kept her up most of the night. Louisa did not want to see that it had torn open again or that it was red with the beginnings of infection. Nevertheless, she couldn't show such fears in front of her own maid.

"Yes, thank you, Chloe."

Gently, Chloe untied the knot and unwound the bandages. Except for a slight stinging sensation when the cloth was pulled free, Louisa was relieved that the scratch offered her no more trouble. Glancing down, she discovered that despite her worries, the gash had not bled, nor had it grown puffy with infection.

"You were lucky to have escaped with little more than a scratch," Chloe offered softly as she dabbed at the wound with a damp cloth. "The other gentleman was not so lucky, I fear."

Louisa straightened. "Other gentleman?"

"*Oui, madame.* I ran out as soon as I heard the noise, so I was able to clearly hear the policemen when they arrived."

Police? Had John notified the police of the attempt on her life?

Chloe giggled. "It is quite funny, don't you think?"

"What is?"

"The way the two men were fighting over that woman as if they were dogs after a bone."

Louisa stared at the girl, confused. "Chloe, what are you talking about?"

"Didn't Mr. Smith tell you? No one tried to harm *you.*" She bent close as she wrapped a fresh bandage around Louisa's arm. "There was this woman, you see, a Mrs. Alexander. According to the snippets I overheard, she was…unfaithful…with the stable master who worked on her husband's estate. The two of them vowed to run off together as soon as her husband was away on business. But the man returned much quicker than expected—mere hours after his wife had left him—and he hurried to the train station to intercept them."

At Louisa's open astonishment, Chloe laughed openly. "No one was trying to hurt you, Mrs. Winslow. It was all a mistake. Apparently, you dodged into the crowd at the same moment that the husband took aim at his rival. His first shot went wild, causing a beam to shatter mere inches from your arm. The other shot hit the stable master in the…nether regions.''

A slow anger began to brew in Louisa's stomach. ''And Mr. Smith knew of all this?''

''*Mais oui!* After he took you into the baggage room, the police questioned him to be sure that he had not been involved in the ruckus.''

Louisa pressed her lips together to keep from shouting in indignation.

John Smith had lied to her! It may have been a lie of omission, but it was a lie nonetheless. He'd allowed her to continue to believe that her life was in imminent danger and she was doomed to an early demise if she didn't follow the man's instructions to the letter.

Which was exactly what he wanted, no doubt.

Louisa jumped to her feet, ready to storm into the sitting room and demand an explanation, but she froze without taking a step.

No.

No.

If she railed at the man now, she would lessen her own power over the situation. But if she kept her silence, she would have the upper hand. He would think that she was frightened and willing to become his timid puppet. If she played her cards right…

She might even be able to lead the man in a merry dance.

Chapter Eleven

As the train pulled into the Boston station, Neil checked the chambers of his revolver and slid the loaded weapons back into their holster.

Grover Pritchard regarded him with wide eyes. "You're not really going to wear those into town, are you?" the man squeaked

"Yes," Neil replied shortly.

"B-but it will look as if…"

Neil speared the man with a steely glance. "As if what?"

"As if you're expecting trouble."

"I am."

Pritchard's face lost some of its color. "Do you honestly think that Mrs. Winslow is in danger?"

"I know it for a fact."

Refusing to explain anything more, Neil turned his back. Unfortunately, his new position gave him an unhindered view of the sleeping quarters at the rear of the car. The train had barely come to a full stop before Louisa slid the curtain back and came sashaying out.

Not for the first time, Neil was struck by the sight of

his longtime friend. She was beautiful, absolutely beautiful. Even in black.

"Gentlemen, are we ready?"

A glance at Pritchard assured Neil that he wasn't the only one affected by Louisa. The mousy solicitor stood with his mouth opening and closing like a grounded fish.

There was no doubt that Louisa had dressed carefully for her arrival in Boston. A tiny black bonnet perched on the top of her head. An elegant veil flowed over her shoulders, contrasting beautifully with her pale skin and copper hair. At her neck a ruffle of black silk framed her chin. The jacket was severely tailored, yet still managed to offer an air of femininity with sparkling jet buttons, delicate rows of tucks and insets of velvet. From her slender waist a swath of ebony silk and velvet billowed back over a full bustle. Beneath the lower flounces of her skirt, Neil caught just a peek of black jacquard shoes with jet buckles and bits of lace.

Never in his life had Neil seen a woman look so enticing while in mourning

"Will we be waiting for the trunks?" Louisa asked as she pulled a pair of black kid gloves over her hands, then held out her wrists so that Chloe could fasten the buttons with a small silver hook.

"No." Neil cleared his throat when the word emerged with a betraying hint of gruffness. "No, we've arranged for them to be delivered. Whenever you're ready, the carriage is waiting just outside. There's no need to go through the station house."

"Really?" She bent to peer through the window, then smiled in delight. "Imagine that. I really am becoming spoiled by all of this personal attention."

She took a small collapsible parasol from Chloe and looped a crocheted black reticule over her wrist. "I'm ready whenever you are, gentlemen.'' She cast her eyes at Neil and he feared the gleam of mischief he found there. ''Mr. Smith, I hope that you've taken precautions to safeguard my person.''

Safeguard her person? The phrase sounded as if she were royalty and he a lowly servant.

''Yes, ma'am,'' he drawled slowly.

Her hand spread wide beneath her throat as if she could still feel her own leaping pulse. ''I hope so. After yesterday's fright, I don't know that I dare go anywhere without you.''

''Fright?'' Mr. Pritchard echoed worriedly. ''Has something happened?''

''Yes, Mr. Pritchard,'' she breathed, before continuing dramatically. ''Yesterday, someone tried to kill me!''

Pritchard blanched. ''No.''

''Yes!''

Louisa stepped close to Neil and hugged his arm as if she were still afraid. ''I can assure you that my heart still races whenever I think how close I came to death!''

Her fingers began to stroke Neil's arm. He steadfastly ignored the reaction the innocent gesture inspired.

Innocent?

Again he caught a hint of mischief in her gaze and wondered what had prompted it. For most of the journey, Louisa had been consumed with anxiety. Yet this morning she didn't seem to have a care in the world. Even the mention of her close call two days before didn't seem to give her pause.

So what was she up to?

He caught her eyes, searched deep into their indigo depths. But this time she kept her thoughts and emotions carefully shielded. It was as if…

As if she knew the shot that had grazed her arm had not been directed at her.

Damn. He should have known that someone would tell her. The train employees who had checked on them at each stop weren't well known for keeping secrets, and Chloe was probably no better.

Which meant that Louisa knew he had purposely misled her.

And now she was going to make him pay for it.

Under normal circumstances, Neil would have found it disconcerting to be the target of a woman's vengeful nature. But surprisingly, the only emotion he felt as Louisa clung to him was...

Anticipation.

Or would *exhilaration* be a better word?

Desire?

Sweet heaven, she was beautiful.

"Mr. Smith?"

He reluctantly banished from his mind fantasies of this woman trying her hand at seducing *him.*

"Don't you think we should be going?"

"By all means, Mrs. Winslow."

"Bitsy!"

The little dog came bounding out of the back room. She'd been recently brushed. Tiny pink bows adorned her ears and her tail. Sighing, Neil bent and picked up the animal without being asked.

Tucking Louisa's arm into his, he led her toward the door and from there outside to the waiting carriage. As Louisa climbed inside and he handed the dog to her, he could only pray that the real threat against her was not lurking nearby. She waved to railway workers and other departing passengers as if they were long-lost relatives. But she wasn't content to make a spectacle of herself alone. When Bitsy escaped, she forced Neil to chase after the animal and retrieve it.

Finally, on the second attempt, he gave up trying to take a seat on the driver's bench. To give himself some peace, he handed Bitsy to Chloe, climbed into the carriage loaded with hatboxes and parcels, yanked the shades down and slapped the wall.

The conveyance lurched forward, nearly pitching Louisa into his lap.

For the first time that morning, she seemed slightly taken aback. "Where's Chloe?"

"In the next carriage with Mr. Pritchard. Your little beastie is with her, as well."

Her brows rose. "Surely it would be more proper to have her riding with me as a…chaperon of sorts."

"Do widowed women need chaperons?"

"Not in the strictest sense of the word, but one must always do what one can to prevent gossip."

"You weren't concerned about gossip in New York."

"Ah, but I didn't plan to live in New York. Now that I'm in Boston, I must guard my every move."

"Does that include making a spectacle of yourself at the station?"

"I was merely being friendly," she said with a sniff.

"Your familiarity is dangerous."

One of her brows lifted. "Oh, really. I thought that was precisely why Charles hired you. To keep me out of danger."

"I could use some help on your part in the way of a healthy dose of common sense."

She leaned forward to touch him on the knee. "But you have already demonstrated to me how capable you are at your job." She patted her own chest as if her heart raced. "My lands, you have such quick reflexes!"

Without thinking things through, he grasped her wrist, tugging her closer. "Yes, I do," he said as her eyes grew wide. The mischief quickly disappeared.

"I am also a patient man—up to a point."

"I—I'm sure that character trait must come in handy," she said breathlessly as she tried ever so subtly to remove her hand from his grip.

"At times." He pulled her closer still. The carriage jounced over a rut, causing her to lose her balance and fall against him, her hands splayed wide over his chest. "But there are also times when patience should be abandoned in favor of other, more spontaneous delights."

Then, before she could utter a word, he covered her lips with his, kissing her with the pent-up desire that had been haunting him for days. He wasn't gentle. Instead, he hungrily sought each nuance, each sensation—and she eagerly responded, keeping nothing back.

Her instantaneous reaction was enough to turn his blood to fire. He was inundated with a need for this woman unlike any he had ever known before. The scent of her, the taste of her, the feel of her became a part of him, flowing through his veins like molten honey, and yet it wasn't enough. He wanted—needed—more.

Drawing her onto his lap, he pressed her body to his, delighting in the way her breasts flattened against his chest and her fingers clutched at his shoulders.

"We shouldn't be doing this," he gasped when finally they were forced to take a breath of air.

Her only response was a muffled sob, then her hands reached for him again, her fingers plunging into his hair and drawing him down for another kiss.

His lips began a sensual foray across her cheek, over her jaw and down the tiny sliver of her neck exposed by the high collar of her jacket.

"You've bewitched me," he murmured against her.

"I think…you are the one casting the spell," she gasped, her head arching backward, her eyes heavy with desire. "I swore that I wouldn't let you touch me again."

"Why?"

His hand spread wide over the indentation of her waist, then moved up, up, up until he touched her breast through the taut layers of fabric and the boning of her corset. She gasped, her body trembling in his arms.

"Because when you hold me, I lose all sense of reason."

His thumb stroked the sweet curve of her breast. "Perhaps this is sanity and all else is foolishness."

She shook her head. "This isn't real life. This is…"

"What?"

Bit by bit she stiffened, the fire fading from her eyes, to be replaced by an infinite sadness. "This is fantasy."

As if she'd suddenly awakened from a dream, she lifted her head and focused on the interior of the carriage, a place where they had come to the brink of making love. Gently extricating herself from his embrace, she returned to her seat. Ignoring him, she opened the blind and allowed the afternoon breeze to cool her pink cheeks.

"It mustn't happen again," she said firmly.

But Neil was certain that she knew the attraction between them would inevitably lead to…

To what?

To whisking this woman away to Oregon?

More and more, Neil was beginning to see that his original plan could never be that simple. Everything about the situation was complicated—including Louisa herself. There would be no clean escape.

Unless that clean escape came from him.

Once again, Neil considered abandoning his efforts and returning to Oregon. But even that would never be as simple as it had once seemed. When he'd come to retrieve this woman, it had been a means to an end: he'd wanted a bride to provide him with sons.

But somewhere along the way, the need for a wife had become more personal. He'd been able to see that there were advantages to marrying beyond beginning a family—such as finding a helpmate.

Companionship.

Sex.

But even as he thought the word, he shied away from it. Neil wasn't an innocent, by any means. He'd had his fair share of romantic liaisons.

But somehow this was different. More enticing. More intense.

"Yes, we'll stay away from one another," he said when Louisa continued to look at him like a deer suddenly coming face-to-face with a hunter. But even as the words came from his mouth, he knew that neither one of them believed the promise.

This would not be the last embrace they shared.

It was only a matter of time before they were intimate again.

As she stared resolutely out of the carriage window, Louisa forced herself to think about the days ahead and *only* the days ahead.

First impressions were vital. She knew that fact from years of experience. She must be on her guard as she made her way to the Winslow estates—where she would probably be introduced to a large staff and perhaps neighbors and friends who would come to pay their respects. There were funeral arrangements that would need to be made—and quickly, too, since Charles had already spent too much time "in state." Then there was Evie to think about, a household to run.

Louisa closed her eyes for a moment, feeling suddenly overwhelmed.

Was she ready for this? But even as her doubts surfaced, she knew that she couldn't afford to fail. If the truth of her identity was ever discovered, the punishment against her would be harsh. Not only would she be damned for assuming another person's life, she would also be condemned for taking an inheritance that was not technically hers.

No, the time had long ago passed for her to have second thoughts. She had to see to it that her mode of dress and air of behavior were somber and controlled...

Even though each new day seemed to hold a fresh wonder.

Trying her best to ignore the man who sat opposite her, she focused on her first glimpse of Boston. She knew that the city was "old" by American standards, but to her eyes, it looked new and quaint, with tidy brick buildings and narrow cobblestone streets. She eyed the shops and the fashions of the passersby with interest, realizing that for the first time in her life she was one of the "elegantly dressed ladies" rather than a mere servant who was expected to blend into anonymity.

"Have you been here before, Mr. Smith?"

"Yes."

"When?"

"During the war, I was stationed here for a few months."

She studied him anew. "Ah, yes. Your infamous War of the Statehoods."

His lips twitched at that remark and she wondered if she'd made a mistake in the title.

But wasn't that what Neil Ballard had called it in his letters?

"And what did you do during that war, Mr. Smith?"

Neil had been in the cavalry.

"Other than training time in Boston and Chicago, I spent most of my time dodging bullets."

She grimaced when he refused to take her seriously.

"I had a friend in your war," Louisa admitted softly. "He said it was awful."

"Yes," John agreed. "It was awful." His eyes darkened with remembered sadness. She frowned, wondering why, at times like this, she felt as if she'd met this man before.

Impossible.

For some time, there was only the sound of the horses' hooves and the squeak and rattle of the carriage. Bit by bit, the space between buildings increased. Soon verdant farmland and green, rolling hills surrounded them on either side.

"It shouldn't be much farther," John said at one point.

Leaning forward, she continued to track their progress, her pulse growing quicker.

What would she find at the end of her journey?

Excitement caused her limbs to tremble as she realized that she'd already received far more than she could have ever dreamed possible.

She could only hope that her friend Phoebe's new life had proved to be all she'd expected, as well.

For an instant, Louisa felt a twinge of guilt. She really had been beastly to Neil Ballard. She'd abandoned him to a lifetime with a stranger, all without his knowledge.

"Is something wrong?"

"No, nothing. Nothing at all. What could possibly be wrong when my life here is about to begin?"

As if on cue, the carriage slowed and turned onto a lane flanked on either side with large brick posts supporting an iron gate. The gate had been propped open in anticipation of their arrival.

"We're here," Louisa breathed.

Large trees grew on either side of the lane, plunging them into dappled shadows as the horses trotted down the winding track. Louisa inched forward in her seat, both hands resting on the windowsill. When the carriage topped the rise to disclose a castlelike manor house waiting in the valley below, her body tensed in disbelief.

Never in her wildest dreams had she imagined that her husband-to-be would prove to be this wealthy. The home before her rivaled many of the grandest she'd witnessed in England.

Immediately she was humbled by the inheritance she had received from Charles and the opportunity she had to live in a place such as this.

With that thought came the realization that she had only one way to pay her debt of gratitude, and that was to take care of Evie as if the child were her own. From this moment on, she would care for Evie's vast fortune and landholdings with infinite care. Louisa must never let it be said that she'd somehow failed in her responsibilities, no matter what personal sacrifices such a commitment might cost her.

The weight of that promise rested heavily on her shoulders. Suddenly she understood why Charles had felt it necessary to change his will so quickly after the proxy marriage. He must have been a man who prepared for every contingency in building his vast empire, and he wouldn't dream of leaving his daughter's future to chance.

The facade of the castle grew larger and larger as they descended the drive and pulled to a stop in front of the massive front staircase. Louisa didn't wait for John to help her. Instead, she opened the door to the carriage and stepped down upon a drive made of crushed pink shells.

As the other vehicles appeared on the hill behind her, she stared up, up, to the tips of the mock battlements. From this closer vantage point, she could see that the house was in need of a feminine hand. The flower beds were unruly and the windows were covered in grime.

A sense of importance caused her shoulders to straighten. The house was in need of a woman's touch.

Her touch.

The second carriage pulled to a stop behind them and Grover Pritchard climbed out. Smiling encouragingly at Louisa, he said, "You are finally home, Mrs. Winslow."

Bitsy jumped from the carriage and began to race around them in circles.

Louisa couldn't help but smile in return. "It feels good to stand on solid ground and know I won't have to leave again anytime soon."

"Perhaps your health will improve now that you aren't living the transient life."

She tipped her head. "My health?"

Mr. Pritchard's mouth worked soundlessly and his cheeks lost their color.

"Mr. Smith mentioned that you…hadn't been feeling well."

Louisa glared at John, who merely ignored her as he wrestled with her wriggling lapdog.

"I can assure you, Mr. Smith, that my...ill health has been nothing more than a bout of sadness."

Mr. Pritchard beamed at her. "I'm so pleased to hear you say that. The next few days will be challenging enough for you, I'm sure."

She nodded, at a loss for any other response. She dreaded the ceremonies to come—the laying in and the funeral. But she also comforted herself with the fact that she was done traveling for a while, and if need be, her "grief" would give her ample excuse to be alone.

The door to the manor opened and Louisa turned, eager to meet the staff who had arrived to greet her. But rather than servants, she was met with the stony glare of a tall, grim-faced man and a smaller woman with eyes the color of melted toffee.

"Mrs. Winslow, may I present your husband's family? They live here for most of the year, as well."

Family? Charles had family?

Louisa was suddenly at a loss. In all her meetings with Mr. Pritchard, he had never once said that Charles had any living relations other than Evie—nor had he mentioned that these relatives would be occupying the manor.

"This is Boyd."

Boyd appeared to be in his forties. He had angular features deeply creased and weathered from ample time in the sun. Nevertheless it was his icy gaze that caused Louisa's throat to tighten with nerves.

He didn't like her—that much was evident.

The woman, on the other hand, smiled warmly in Louisa's direction. Small and petite, she reminded Louisa of a sparrow—quite ordinary, but charming and inexplicably reassuring.

"This is Beatrice," the lawyer said.

"I'm sorry," Louisa apologized. "I didn't hear how you were related to Charles."

Pritchard's eyes widened in shock. "Boyd and Beatrice are Charles's younger siblings."

Brother? Sister? Louisa's confusion increased. There had been no mention of a brother or sister in Charles's will. She would have remembered.

So why had Charles left her a fortune and ignored his own siblings?

Moreover, why had Evie been entrusted to Louisa's care rather than that of an aunt or uncle?

Chapter Twelve

Silence settled over the little group gathered around the manor steps. An awkward, uncomfortable silence. Even Bitsy had the good grace to shrink back in John's arms and make herself as invisible as possible.

Summoning what she hoped was a gracious smile, Louisa lifted her hand and took a step forward. "I'm so please to meet you...Boyd."

The man's expression didn't soften an iota. If anything, his gaze became even harder and his lips pressed into a narrow line. He made no attempt to meet her halfway or to take her hand, and Louisa felt a betraying heat seep into her cheeks.

"So this is the latest money-grubbing ne'er-do-well that our brother has brought home," he growled.

Louisa froze, stunned by the dislike and disapproval that dripped from the man's tone.

"You must be proud of yourself. You've been the only wife to outlast the old coot—and inherit a chunk of the family wealth to boot, I'm sure."

"Boyd, please." Beatrice rushed forward to place a hand on her brother's arm. "You're being rude."

"Rude? How can a woman such as this deserve anything less? She's nothing more than a—"

"Boyd!"

Boyd stood with his hands clenched, then abruptly turned. "I've got work to do."

His boots thumped hollowly as he strode away, slamming the heavy front door behind him.

For several long moments there was no other sound, only the faint cooing of a dove—a mournful sound that merely underscored the gloomy atmosphere that had settled over the assembled group.

Beatrice wrung her hands together. "Please, I know that my brother's actions have been unforgivable, but try to excuse him. Charles's death has left so many extra burdens on his shoulders that…" Her words petered off as she realized Boyd's actions had been beyond polite explanation.

Forcing a smile to her lips, Beatrice lifted her skirts and quickly descended the steps. "I am so pleased to meet you, Louisa. It is Louisa, isn't it?"

Louisa nodded, still numb from Boyd's hostile reception.

But if Boyd's reaction to Louisa's arrival had been venomous, his sister's was delighted.

"I'm so sorry that we weren't able to make preparations for a more proper welcome. We only just received the news of Charles's death and his marriage in a telegram that arrived yesterday."

"Yesterday?" Louisa echoed, horrified.

When she turned to question Mr. Pritchard, Beatrice quickly explained, "We've been away, you see. Boyd has been in Chicago on business, and I've been tending to an elderly aunt, who has also recently passed. If we'd known that Charles was ill…"

Beatrice's voice caught, but after dabbing her eyes, she fixed a beaming smile on her lips. "You must be exhausted. Traveling always makes me so tired, even if only a short distance. Come, let's go into the house."

She looped her arms through Louisa's, drawing her forward. "With our own late arrival, the house is in turmoil, but I have managed to set up a room for you in the east turret—one of the prettiest, in my opinion. It's a bit stuffy after being closed up for so long, but I opened the windows early this morning, so it should be fairly comfortable by now."

"I'm sure it will be lovely."

With one last glance over her shoulder, Louisa allowed herself to be pulled into the house—and from there into her new life.

As he watched Louisa disappear into the dark interior of the castle, Neil felt a twinge of foreboding.

Even knowing what he did about the inheritance that Charles had left his wife, Neil hadn't anticipated that the man's wealth could be so encompassing as to include a home this large and this luxurious. By stepping within its doors, Louisa was entering a new life, a privileged future…

But damn it, she wasn't supposed to be here at all.

A slow anger built within him as Neil realized his mistake. He should have found a way to keep Louisa in New York—or to make her admit the truth about her charade. By bringing her to Winslow's home, he had allowed her to step deeper into temptation.

And what person would willingly give up such luxurious trappings for a humble home in Oregon?

Damn, damn, damn. What could he do to change her mind?

I'll do whatever it takes, he vowed to himself.

Turning to the solicitor, Neil asked, "Mr. Pritchard, does this place have a staff of any kind?" He would need to take extra precautions for safety in a house this size.

"If Boyd and Beatrice have been out of town, I doubt that more than a skeleton staff has been in residence."

"I want to interview all of them before the day is over."

"Very well." If Grover resented being ordered about by a hired man, he gave no sign. Perhaps the shooting at the station had served some purpose, after all.

Mid-Atlantic

Ritchie reluctantly approached the man who stood at the deck railing staring out at the vast, limitless horizon.

Pausing a few feet away, Ritchie waited until Horace Haversham acknowledged his presence.

"The captain says the steam sloop is making good progress. We should dock in Boston within the next ten days."

"And my brother?"

"His is a sailing vessel. He'll arrive at least a week behind us."

"Good."

Haversham gazed out at the horizon. "I swore that I would never go to sea again." He gestured to the water around them. "If anything, this should prove the depth of my anguish for the past twenty years. I had no idea how far my brother would go to reach his own ends. When I was asked to further our business interests in Hong Kong, he hired most of the crew. Little did I know that he'd arranged for pirates and renegades to make up most of the crew. We'd hardly navigated around the

Cape of Good Horn when they attacked me and a few loyal sailors. We barely managed to escape with a lifeboat and our lives before they took over the ship and set sail for regions unknown.''

His eyes closed as if the memories swamped him.

''A-at least you had the lifeboat.''

''Yes, at first glance it would seem to be a blessing, wouldn't it?'' His eyes seemed to burn. ''I soon learned there were worse fates than dying.''

Ritchie felt a cold finger trace his spine.

''There were four of us on the lifeboat. Four weeks later, when the boat ground ashore, I was the only survivor.''

Four weeks? Ritchie wondered how anyone could have survived so long.

''My brother will pay,'' Haversham growled. ''He will pay for the indignities I was forced to endure as I fought to survive.''

Indignities? Ritchie swallowed hard against the tightness gripping his throat. Surely, Haversham didn't mean…cannibalism? It wouldn't be the first time that Ritchie had heard of such a desperate plight occurring. Yet he'd never known anyone who would…who *could*…

Ritchie took a deep, calming breath, realizing anew the danger he was in. If this man had been forced to a point of eating human flesh, there was probably nothing he wouldn't do to get his retribution.

Dearest Diary,
Nearly a day has passed. Even now, as I sit in front of the turret window and peer out at the weed-infested yard beyond, I find my new surroundings hard to believe. Life at the Winslow estate is defi-

nitely not what I'd anticipated upon first seeing my new home.

When I'd gazed up at the castle from my perch in the carriage, I imagined that I'd just stepped into the realms of a fairy tale.

It took only a night in the house to help me realize the truth—and it is far from the fantasy that I had envisioned.

As Beatrice ushered me inside, the woman explained that the house truly was hundreds of years old. Charles had bought the structure for a pittance from an impoverished viscount in France. He'd then dismantled the structure and had it rebuilt in the Massachusetts countryside.

Unfortunately, the process had been done with only a few concessions to modernization. Therefore, the castle is cold, drafty and dark—

Louisa took a deep breath.

—and musty, too.

For the first time, I am inclined to believe that it might have been better for Evie to have spent so much time at boarding school. A place such as this could not be healthy for a child, and judging by what Beatrice has told me, the house is often empty, with Charles and Boyd away on business and Beatrice visiting family.

Changes will have to be made, that fact is evident. If I am determined to have Evie live at home—and I am—then the castle must be brought up to snuff. I will have to talk to Mr. Pritchard right away.

Then there is the matter of Mr. Smith.

Blast it all, can't the man leave me alone? Even now, after we are installed in the safety of the Winslow estates, he dogs my every move. He has already surveyed the castle, the estate, and interviewed the staff—a point that galls me no end, since that should have been my first duty.

My only victory came when I flatly refused to let him sleep in a room adjoining my own. Yet, after fretting most of the night over Boyd's treatment of me, I'd grown sick with nerves. When I left to visit the water closet down the hall, I found John Smith sitting in a chair outside my door.

Even now, I can feel myself blush. It's disturbing that John knows so much about me. He must think I'm a foolish, vapid woman prone to fits of swooning and vapors, with a disposition so nervous that I should be under a doctor's care.

Grimacing, Louisa forced herself to breathe deeply to ease the flip-flopping of her stomach.

In the past, I've been able to control my emotions easily enough. But the voyage to America was a continual bout of seasickness for me. The nervousness I've felt since then has not allowed my constitution to return to rights.

But now my new life has started. Today, I will make the last of the funeral arrangements and retrieve Evie from the boarding school. Then, at long last, I can begin to ease into a familiar routine. One that should serve me well as Mrs. Charles Winslow III.

* * *

When Louisa emerged from her bedroom, Neil rose from the chair where he'd spent most of the night.

"Good morning, Mrs. Winslow."

"Can't you find a room to sleep in?"

Neil resisted the urge to grin. "I don't think that would be the best idea, do you? How can I guard you if I can't even hear your cries for help?"

She offered him a pained sigh, then brushed past him without another word.

Following her, Neil studied her with narrowed eyes. Only hours earlier, she had been pale, shaky and obviously ill, yet now…

She looked the picture of health.

A niggling suspicion pushed into his head, but he forced it aside. No. It wasn't possible. This woman was so startled by his embraces, so innocent in her responses that she couldn't possibly be suffering from…

Morning sickness?

The recurring thought had the ability to blacken his mood. If it were true, it would explain a good deal about Louisa's actions—her haste to marry after so many years of writing to Neil, her willingness to trade marrying an old acquaintance for marrying a stranger.

Her quick response to his embrace.

No.

He couldn't believe it of her.

He didn't want to believe it of her.

The idea of another man touching her so intimately caused his jaw to clench. Surely the woman he'd written to for years would not have given herself away so freely. Nor would she have passed off another man's child as Neil's.

But how could he really know that? Years of sporadic correspondence could not make him an expert in judging her character. For all he knew, Louisa could be a wanton creature who routinely fell in and out of love. Her own passionate response to Neil's embraces could give credence to such behavior, as could her willingness to exchange the predictable life she would have had in Oregon for one of luxury in Boston.

No. Although he had no evidence to the contrary, Neil sensed an innocence about her.

But if she were pregnant, then that innocence had been compromised.

By choice or by force?

His scowl deepened. What desperate measures might have made Louisa lower her guard? He knew there had been some trouble with her last position. The husband or son had caused a scandal, and Louisa had been blamed.

What if there had been more to the situation than mere gossip and conjecture? What if the man had truly compromised Louisa's virtue?

What if she had been a willing participant?

A slow anger began to simmer deep in his belly. One way or another, Neil would get to the bottom of it all. If he discovered his suspicions were true, he would wash his hands of the woman and be done with the situation once and for all.

And if not…

He wasn't sure what he would do.

Breakfast was a charming affair, with Beatrice playing hostess. Beatrice and Mr. Pritchard kept a running conversation going, giving Louisa a history of the house, some information on each servant and points of interest nearby.

Again, Beatrice apologized profusely about her

brother's behavior—especially when Boyd's only appearance was to walk into the breakfast room, see the group assembled at the table, then turn on his heel and shout for the cook to take his breakfast to his study.

But the meal was delicious—hot bread, bacon, eggs, fresh fruits and thick mush drenched with cream and honey. Juices, coffee and tea were offered as accompaniments, but Louisa chose the rich steaming chocolate— a special recipe that Beatrice had brought back with her from a recent trip to New Orleans.

After Mr. Pritchard excused himself to speak with Boyd, the conversation became more personal. Beatrice soon discovered Louisa's love for romantic literature— a passion she shared. When Louisa confessed that she was trying to write a novel of her own, Beatrice invited her to join her each morning for a cup of cocoa so that they could discuss her ideas. The morning's "gentilities" proved to be a balm to Louisa's spirit, and the women vowed to make the event a daily ritual.

As she followed Beatrice on a tour through the house, Louisa's mood lightened. Until now, she hadn't realized how she had longed for a friend in her new home.

Friend.

With a rush of feeling, she remembered that she needed to get a message to Phoebe. Since Louisa had been unable to send a telegram before leaving New York, Phoebe would be worried sick if she didn't receive a message as soon as possible.

"Beatrice, is there a way for me to send a telegram— or even mail a letter—without going into town myself?"

"Yes, of course. Just let Mrs. Hillard, the housekeeper, know. She can send one of the stable boys into town for you."

"Thank you."

"Is there anyone in particular that you need to reach?"

"No. Just a friend."

But when she turned, it was to find that John had entered the room.

How much of her conversation with Beatrice had he heard?

Standing ramrod stiff, Louisa dared him to say something, but after several long seconds, the man merely stated, "Mr. Pritchard and the undertaker are waiting for you in the parlor."

Although Louisa longed to devote her immediate attention to Evie's situation, it soon became obvious that the errand would not be completed that day. Louisa had scarcely finished her tour of the castle when neighbors began to call, offering condolences.

To Louisa's utter horror, she was required to accept the visits in the parlor, with Charles's coffin mere yards away. Over and over again, she was asked to recite the circumstances of her marriage to him, the occasion of their introduction and her voyage to America—so much so that with each new guest that arrived, she embellished the story for her own entertainment.

By late afternoon, with her head pounding and her body screaming for the opportunity to stand and stretch, Louisa decided that "polite society" wouldn't dream of visiting so close to teatime without an invitation. She instructed the housekeeper to tell any tardy visitors that she had become indisposed and would not take any further calls for the time being. Then she retreated from the grimy shabbiness of the castle's central rooms to her own small apartments overlooking the garden. Unfortunately, her vantage point only seemed to remind her of the gross disrepair of the house.

Frankly, she didn't understand how a man with such an elegant personal railway car could let his own home rapidly decay. He'd spent a good deal of time and money arranging for such an elaborate structure to be rebuilt in America, but for all intents and purposes, the building was uninhabitable.

Tomorrow, Louisa would see about readying the suite of rooms next to hers for Evie. As much as she might want to send for the girl today, she felt it was important for Evie to have a comfortable place to call her own.

Tomorrow, tomorrow, tomorrow…

There were so many things that needed to be done. Louisa found it exhilarating to think that she was in charge of such decisions. It was also terrifying. If things went wrong, she had only herself to blame.

She would have given anything to have someone trustworthy to use as a sounding post. But with Phoebe thousands of miles away and Beatrice still a new acquaintance…

Louisa didn't want anyone to think she was too weak to handle the responsibilities she'd been given.

As she sank onto the swooning couch and rested her head against the padded back, she fought a wave of loneliness. Despite Beatrice's kind manner, Louisa knew she was still an interloper here—a fact Boyd made clear by throwing her frosty glares and leaving the room whenever she appeared.

How would the family feel when she began making changes to their home? She shivered, anticipating Boyd's reaction. She was sure that he would find ample reason to offer a cutting remark about her willingness to spend Evie's inheritance.

But the castle wasn't a healthy place for a young girl. If left unattended, it would be a moldering ruin by the time the child was put in charge of her own fortunes.

Louisa's temples throbbed. When she had agreed to marry Charles, she hadn't thought beyond marrying the man himself. She hadn't considered how her actions would have repercussions throughout the whole family. Indeed, she'd been so sure that Charles was without family.

A knock at her bedroom door caused her to sigh. She had asked to be left alone, yet the outside world had interrupted yet again.

"Come in."

But it wasn't Beatrice or the housekeeper who entered. It was her bodyguard. Behind him stood several servants, laden down with trunks.

Louisa nearly scrambled to her feet before she realized that she wasn't expected to rise. She was the mistress of the house.

"Where would you like your trunks to be placed?"

Gathering Bitsy against her like a shield, she motioned to a doorway that led to a small dressing room. "In there would be fine."

Since the housekeeper and the cook had been the only servants on duty the previous day, Louisa had arranged for only a few bags to be brought up to her. It had been one of Louisa's first decisions as mistress of the house to recall the rest of the staff in time for the funeral.

An army of footmen and stable hands moved in and out of her suite until the opposite wall was piled high with trunks. Looking at the sight, Louisa grimaced.

Had she really bought so many things while she was in New York? She must have been mad.

After the servants disappeared, John lingered near the door. "Tired?"

Louisa knew that she shouldn't encourage his familiarity, but she needed the sound of a voice that was not her own.

"I am beginning to see that the ceremonies of grief can be very exhausting."

"Especially for a woman who is far too young to be widowed."

Her lips twitched in a semblance of a sad smile. "I had no idea that Charles was so...well connected. Most of the visitors conducted business with Charles." Her brow creased. "I have yet to meet any of his friends."

Realizing that such a comment could be interpreted as being disloyal, Louisa quickly changed the subject. "At least you managed to be a bit more inconspicuous this afternoon."

"I wouldn't want you to think that I was completely insensitive to your sorrow."

Now why did his remark sound as if he was mocking her? She fixed him with a firm gaze. "Tomorrow I wish to retrieve Evie from her school."

"Do you really think that's wise?"

"She'll need to be here for the funeral the following day."

"Perhaps she would be safer at school."

"Safer?" Louisa shook her head. "She would never forgive me if she weren't here to offer her last goodbyes."

"But it might be better for you if you could familiarize yourself with life at Winslow Manor first."

She shrugged. "Right now I would welcome the company of the little girl." When Neil regarded her curiously, she waved her hand. "Arrange for a carriage to be ready for me first thing in the morning."

"Do you want a driver, or would you like me to do the honors?"

She opened her mouth to immediately request a driver, then thought better of it. She had no guarantees of Evie's reaction. The girl might regard her with the same disdain that Boyd had shown. If that was the case, Louisa would prefer to have only one witness to her shortcomings.

She idly petted Bitsy's silky fur before asking, "I don't suppose that you would allow me to drive myself?"

His eyes narrowed. "Do you know how to handle a buggy?"

More than anything, she wished that she could answer in the affirmative. Since she couldn't, she said instead, "I'm sure that I could get the hang of it with a few quick instructions."

John scowled. "Don't even think about it. Tomorrow I'll drive you to the school myself."

Chapter Thirteen

The air the following morning was crisp and clean as Louisa stepped from the castle and pulled the door shut behind her.

She hadn't told Beatrice that she would be retrieving Evie from school. It was Louisa's decision to collect the girl and bring her home, and she wanted to surprise the woman. Judging by the many stories Beatrice had told about nursing ailing relatives, she was a born nurturer. She would find the arrival of her niece to be a special pleasure, Louisa was sure. It would give Beatrice a family member to dote upon during such a trying time.

As if on cue, a buggy clattered over the cobbled drive, saving Louisa the trouble of walking to the stables to find John.

"Good morning, Mrs. Winslow," he said, looping the reins over the brake and touching a finger to his hat.

"Good morning, Mr. Smith."

He jumped from the wagon and held out a hand to assist her. Quickly, she tugged her gloves over her fingers, knowing that to touch the man's bare flesh this early in the morning would cause a jolt to her equilibrium.

"Will you be needing anything else for your ride, Mrs. Winslow?"

"No, thank you, John. I have the address in my reticule. The school shouldn't be too far outside Boston."

"Yes, ma'am."

The buggy dipped as he climbed onto the seat beside her and collected the reins.

"Hiyah!"

With a touch of the whip to the horse's flanks, the carriage jolted into motion.

They made their journey in silence until they were well past the estate's main gates. Then Smith asked, "Would you like a turn with the reins?"

Startled, Louisa studied him closely. She hadn't expected him to remember that she wanted to learn to drive. Moreover, she wouldn't have thought he would be willing to allow her to become proficient at anything that might give her a small modicum of freedom.

"You're sure?"

He put the reins into her own palms, and she was glad that she'd worn a pair of thick kid gloves. On more than one occasion, she'd heard the disapproving whispers of elderly women complaining that the younger generation was ruining the delicate skin of their palms by driving without proper protection.

With the buggy on the straightaway, there was no real skill required in directing the horse, but when the road bordered the winding path of the creek, she allowed John to wrap his arm around her waist so that he could help her control the skittish animal.

All too soon, she forgot the thrill of managing her own carriage. Instead, she became aware of the warmth of John's arm around her waist, his hands gripping her wrists.

A hunger like none she had ever known swelled within her. Gooseflesh raced over her skin, only to be replaced by a tide of heat.

Sweet heaven, don't let me feel. Don't let me feel!

But it was too late. She was already trembling with an awareness that was as potent as a fever. She barely noted as the carriage rattled over the wood of a covered bridge. Unconsciously, she pulled tighter on the reins, causing the horse's hooves to move slower and slower. Somewhere shy of the bright sunlight on the other side, the buggy came to a complete stop.

She would never be sure who moved first. She only knew that when she turned toward John, she found herself pulled firmly into his arms.

Her own hands slid up his chest, testing the hardness she found there. Hungrily, she plunged her fingers into the thick waves of his hair. Sighing against him, she met his lips with hers. She fell against him, allowing him to hold her weight as she became lost in the maelstrom of her desire.

Heat blossomed within her, chasing away the lingering chill of the morning and the cool air lingering beneath the bridge. Restless, she pressed herself against John, needing something more, but not knowing what she required. She only knew that her body had become a traitor, responding to a man whom she should avoid.

"No…" she whispered achingly, struggling to collect the last wisps of her control before she was completely undone. "No!"

Wrenching free, she jumped from the carriage, her heart knocking in her chest as she hurried out of the concealing shadows and leaned over the railing at the far end of the bridge.

* * *

Neil moved more slowly, knowing that he should remain in the carriage, but admitting he couldn't have stayed away from this woman for all of the gold in California.

As he closed the distance between them, she looked up quickly, her eyes shining with something akin to shame and self-loathing.

A glimpse of her guilt was enough to give Neil pause. What was it that injured her conscience? Was it the fact that she was living a charade? Or could it be something more? Something darker and far more serious?

Unbidden, he was reminded of her bouts of sickness and his earlier doubts.

No. This woman couldn't be pregnant.

Could she?

During their correspondence during the past few years, Neil had asked her several times to become his bride. Usually he had been offering the proposition in jest, trying to imagine the way such an outlandish idea would make his old friend smile. But it had only been a short time ago that she'd unexpectedly sent him a telegram, agreeing to his proposal.

A telegram, not a letter.

As if time was something she couldn't afford to waste.

Had his childhood friend found herself in trouble? Had she decided to journey to America to make a fresh start, all without telling him of her circumstances? Had she planned to have her baby and pass it off as his?

Neil's jaw clenched at the mere idea. No. He couldn't believe such a thing about her....

And yet what did he really know about this woman? He couldn't vouch for her integrity when he hadn't seen her in years. Moreover, he knew that she was living a lie in order to inherit a fortune.

Would she have lied to him about being innocent?

She stared up at him with the wild eyes of an animal suddenly aware of the proximity of its hunter, and he resolutely pushed such thoughts away.

He was jumping to conclusions, he thought, his gaze dropping to the slender span of her waist. Except for her unsettled stomach, he had no evidence of a pregnancy. Until he did, he should remain loyal to an old friend.

Even if in doing so she makes a fool of you?

Shoving that thought away, Neil leaned on the railing, his hand nearly touching hers.

Side by side, they stared down at the eddying river, the quiet of the morning settling around them like a cloak.

"I—I'm sorry," Louisa whispered. "I don't know what possessed me to…" She stopped and bit her lip. She admitted much more reluctantly, "You seem to have a very strange effect over me, Mr. Smith. When I'm with you, I forget myself."

"There's no need to apologize."

"Oh, but there is. My behavior is unforgivable and…"

"Human?"

She shook her head. "I have enough on my plate as things are."

"I'm sure yesterday was a challenge. It must be difficult comforting strangers."

She shrugged. "That has been the least of my most recent worries."

He barely resisted the urge to pull her against his chest and cuddle her there. "What has you so troubled?"

"The castle, for one thing."

He grimaced. "Was it part of Charles's plan to rebuild the house in the same disrepair he found it?"

She sighed. ''It isn't healthy. I need to bring Evie home, but the castle is so drafty and cold, I fear for her well-being.''

The mention of the girl reminded Neil that his bride-to-be would not have an easy time extricating herself from her current responsibilities.

''I don't understand why Charles left Evie's guardianship to me. Why would he do that? Wouldn't she be more at ease with her aunt or uncle?''

''Charles must have had his reasons.'' But Neil only had half a mind on his words. All the while he was studying Louisa, wondering what secrets she harbored behind her dark eyes.

Unable to stop himself, he caressed her cheek, then the soft skin of her neck. When he felt her shudder, his control weakened yet again and he pulled her to him. Despite his suspicions and the possibility of being made a fool, he could not seem to rid himself of her hold on him. Like a spider, she had pulled him tightly into her web of mystery and allure, and he was powerless to resist.

Softly, sweetly, he brushed his lips against hers. And as his body instantly reacted, he was struck with the sudden realization that no other woman had ever made him feel so alive, so...

Shying away from anything more that his heart might whisper to him, Neil lifted his head and said gruffly, ''We'd best get going.''

She nodded. ''Yes. I think you're right.''

Louisa knew that she should step out of the circle of his arms, but when John finally lifted his head, her limbs trembled so badly she could barely stand. Defeated, she dropped her forehead against the plane of his chest.

This was wrong, so wrong.

So why was she so powerless to resist?

"You must think me a loose woman."

When he didn't immediately respond, she looked up. A shadow had touched the depths of his eyes. That combined with the continued silence was enough to make her stiffen and turn away despite the weakness of her limbs.

"I can assure you that it isn't my habit to fall into a man's arms at the slightest provocation."

The silence grew thicker, fraught with a tension that she didn't understand. Even with her back to him, Louisa could feel his gaze on her like a hot hand. Yet this time the scrutiny lacked the heat of passion and felt more like the scalding blaze of recrimination.

"How did you and Charles meet?"

Her stomach lurched. "W-we were introduced by a mutual acquaintance." Louisa soothed her conscience by insisting to herself that her explanation was the truth, for the most part.

"Yet you agreed to marry a man by proxy."

She pressed a hand to her waist as her nervousness increased. "You needn't make it sound so...cold-blooded." She scrambled to think of a logical reason why any woman would marry a stranger. Heaven only knew she couldn't tell him the truth. "We corresponded for years."

"Really?"

Why did he sound so doubtful?

"Yes. We spent some time together as youngsters."

"But Charles is much older than you."

"W-well, yes...I was a child and he was...younger then." She waved her hand as if her vague reply explained everything. "We grew quite close with our letters."

"So how was it you didn't know he had a daughter?"

Blast and bother!

Her stomach lurched and she scrambled for her handkerchief.

"I think we've had quite enough questions about me, Mr. Smith. I don't think it's seemly for a hired hand to be so familiar."

"Why not?"

Her mouth worked for a moment as she sought a suitable answer. "Because you already know far too much about me, while I know hardly anything at all about you. I doubt that you would enjoy matters if the tables were turned and I was the one interrogating you."

"Feel free to ask me anything you like."

Louisa knew that she should resist the temptation he offered. She had no business asking this man about himself. Her only defense against his allure would lie in keeping him at a distance—and knowing the intimate details of his life wouldn't help.

But even as her brain churned out a list of reasons why she should call a halt to their conversation, she found herself asking, "Have you ever been in love, Mr. Smith?"

When he grinned, she flushed.

Why hadn't she begun her interview with something more bland, more mundane?

"Why, Mrs. Winslow, I'm impressed with your audacity," he drawled.

She clenched her teeth to keep from offering a pithy—and very unladylike—response.

"As a matter of fact, I am currently courting a very fine young lady."

Courting? The man was *courting* another woman and at the same time kissing Louisa?

"Her name is Betty."

"Betty?"

"She's a barmaid at a little tavern I frequently visit."

A tavern or a saloon?

"She's a fine one, Betty. Granted, she's had a tough time of it since she lost a tooth in a brawl—"

She'd lost a tooth?

"—but as long as she keeps her mouth closed, she's still a looker."

Smith suddenly stopped, then tipped his head to the side as if considering something. "I don't suppose you would help me woo the girl, would you, Mrs. Winslow?"

Her fingers curled so tightly around the strings of her reticule that she could feel her nails biting into her gloves.

"I beg your pardon?"

"She's a bit persnickity about the kind of fellow she entertains."

I'll just bet.

"She keeps telling me that my manners are too rough for her delicate sensibilities."

"I can see why."

"We'll be marrying soon."

He was nearly married to one woman, yet he was kissing her? Louisa thought, stunned. Jealousy surged through her, but was quickly doused by a slow anger.

"You're engaged?"

"No, no. Not yet. Betty hasn't agreed to my proposal. Like I said, she thinks I need some polishing."

Saints preserve them, the two of them made an appalling pair. Louisa had been widowed only a few days and John was all but betrothed—yet neither one of them could control the awareness that pulled them together time and time again.

Although Louisa might have expected as much of John, she was disturbed by her own waywardness. Had she no pride? No sense of respectability?

Without thinking, she swung out her hand and slapped John Smith hard across the cheek.

"There's lesson number one, Mr. Smith. Never, *never* toy with the affections of one woman when you are clearly involved with another."

Then, lifting her skirts, she marched back to the carriage, her chin high, her breast filled with outrage…

And her heart aching in a way she didn't completely understand.

The rest of the journey was made in an uncomfortable silence. Through it all, Louisa sat rigidly, damning the fact that she had ever met John Smith or that she'd had the lack of foresight to have melted in his arms—not once, but on numerous occasions.

Squeezing her eyes closed, she cursed herself for her foolishness, even as she tried to repair her emotional defenses.

She had a life for herself now. A full life. A meaningful life. She had responsibilities, obligations…

Pressures.

Again she laid a hand on her stomach, praying that the jouncing of the carriage wouldn't make her physically ill. She really didn't know what was wrong with her. She'd been so certain that her health would return to rights once she'd "come home."

If anything, her condition had grown worse. Rather than occasional bouts of nausea when she was most nervous or upset, she seemed to suffer continually—as if she'd eaten something that didn't agree with her. Worse yet, her condition seemed to be plaguing her with a trembling weakness and the inability to sleep. Her head pounded, her body ached with weariness....

No wonder she had been so weak as far as John Smith was concerned. She wasn't feeling well. And when a person didn't feel well, one often made mistakes in judgment.

Didn't one?

"This is it."

She jerked herself from her thoughts as John gently brought the carriage to a stop. She studied the imposing iron gates, and in the distance, the craggy, sprawling facade of Hildon Hall.

The moment her eyes began to absorb the scene, she felt a chill run through her veins. Woodenly, she lifted the veil away and tossed it backward as she read the sign that hung discreetly from a post near the front gate.

Hildon Hall
School for Unfortunates

"There must be some mistake," Louisa breathed, more to herself than to John.

"I don't think so," he said grimly.

Touching the reins to the horse's flanks, he urged the animal onward.

From the moment their carriage stopped in front of the main doors, it was obvious that their unannounced arrival was far from welcome. Hostile stares and expressions of complete disbelief followed their progress.

"Do you get the feeling that we've broken one of their

rules?'' John asked under his breath as he helped her step from the carriage.

She nodded, dropping the veil of her bonnet over her face again, needing the anonymity of the black lace to hide her instinctive reactions. Emotions crested over her, one on top of the other like an incoming tide—confusion, horror, fear.

What would cause a father to send his only child to an institution such as this?

But even as the thought arrived, she knew from her own life that such a practice wasn't completely unknown.

John took her arm and looped it around his own. Despite the fact that after their argument on the bridge she had sworn she would never let him touch her again, she clung to him for strength.

Ignoring the glare of a nearby groundskeeper, they climbed the outer steps and entered the heavy wood-and-glass doors.

Inside, the corridor held the unpleasant odors of musty books, floor wax and boiled cabbage. The tiles beneath their feet were cracked and showed distinct signs of wear. The benches that lined the walls were scarred and broken.

''Not a very cheery place, is it?''

''Charity schools rarely are,'' she said faintly. The sights and sounds caused a rush of memories to tumble through her head.

The orphanage where she'd spent most of her childhood wasn't much different than this. Even there, the air had hung thick with the pervading sense of discipline and disgust, loneliness, isolation…

She'd suffered for years.

Until she'd found a friend in Neil Ballard. They'd

become inseparable until he'd been taken back to America. It was that enduring friendship that had inspired Louisa to write to him for help when she'd found herself destitute in London.

Shame swept through her. How easily she had abandoned that friendship. And for what? Money? A life of ease?

Louisa was swiftly learning that even those with great wealth had their troubles. She was beginning to wonder if happiness was an illusion that all men sought, but no one really attained.

John stopped in front of a door with the word Office stenciled in chipped white paint. Tapping on it twice, he twisted the knob and ushered Louisa inside without waiting for a response.

A woman was bent over a desk, her brow creased as she pored over a ledger filled with numbers. At their entry, she looked up so suddenly that the pince-nez balanced on her nose trembled and the chain that secured it to her bodice shook.

"Who—"

"This is Mrs. Charles Winslow III. She has come to retrieve her stepdaughter."

Louisa was grateful for the way John took matters into his own hands. The fact that he had announced her presence in a deep, booming voice seemed to give far more credit to the spontaneity of her arrival.

The woman's eyes widened and she stood, dropping the papers on the desk.

"Mrs. *Winslow?*"

"I believe that you were sent a telegram stating that Mrs. Winslow was Evie's new guardian."

The woman snatched the spectacles from the bridge of her nose, folding them precisely.

"Yes, of course. But naturally, with all that has occurred, I was sure that Mrs. Winslow...that Evie..." Obviously rattled, she took a deep breath, then asked, "Why exactly are you here, Mrs. Winslow?"

"I've come to take her home."

The woman blinked, offered a mirthless laugh, then sobered when she realized that Louisa had spoken in earnest.

"How long will she be visiting?"

"She won't be visiting, Mrs—" Louisa read the name carved into the placard on the desk "—Mrs. Bitterman. Since the death of her father is bound to affect Evie deeply, I intend to have the rest of her education conducted at home."

The woman smiled as if Louisa had offered the punch line to a joke, but when Louisa didn't respond, she quickly cleared her throat.

"Mrs. Winslow, Evie has been with us for quite some time." When Louisa didn't respond, she said, "Years. She's been with us for years." She pressed her lips together in a thin white line. "Mrs. Winslow, I don't think that you fully appreciate the challenges that will be involved with keeping that girl at home."

Chapter Fourteen

That girl.

Louisa stiffened as Mrs. Bitterman's phrase echoed in her head. There was a hidden slur to the comment, a note of disapproval.

"Mrs. Bitterman, have you received a telegram informing you that I am Evie's legal guardian?"

"Yes, of course, but—"

"Are you also aware that my husband has died?"

"Of course. You have my deepest sympathies, Mrs. Winslow." The woman's tone was more conciliatory as she obviously remembered the money to be found behind the name. "However, I didn't see a need to let Evie know of her father's demise."

A chill swept through Louisa's body. Evie hadn't been told of her father's death? A blaze of fury followed, chasing away her last vestiges of nervousness. This…this *woman* had denied Evie the opportunity to grow accustomed to her orphaned state before she was collected to attend the funeral. Instead, Mrs. Bitterman had left it to a stranger to inform the girl that her father was dead and her new stepmother would care for her.

Such a cold handling of the affair shocked Louisa to the very core.

"Mrs. Bitterman…" she said with a sense of hauteur that conveyed she wouldn't be denied. "You will bring the girl to me. Now. Then you will have one of the teachers pack her things and have them loaded into my carriage within the next quarter hour. Is that clear?"

Two bright spots of color blazed on Mrs. Bitterman's cheeks. If possible, her lips pressed more tightly, nearly disappearing altogether. "Yes, ma'am."

She picked up a small bell from her desk and rang it sharply. Within seconds, a severe woman with a plain equine face opened the door.

"Where is Evie Winslow?"

The woman raised her eyebrows. "She's in one of the cells in the upper wing."

"*Cells?*" Louisa repeated ominously.

"She's being punished," the woman said simply.

Louisa's fury erupted. Turning back to Mrs. Bitterman, she demanded, "Take me to her." When the woman hesitated, she added icily, "At once."

Mrs. Bitterman might have protested again, but with a slight shifting of his weight, John pulled back the edge of his jacket and rested his hand on the butt of his pistol.

Clearly enraged, Mrs. Bitterman opened a drawer and removed a ring of keys. "This way," she snapped.

Louisa's horror increased with each step she took. As she traversed the halls of Hildon it became clear that this was no ordinary charity school. Despite the civility of the title inscribed on the sign at the front gate, the building didn't bear the slightest resemblance to a school. This was an asylum, a warehouse for those who were too disturbed or too ill to care for themselves.

What could possibly possess a man to allow his own

flesh and blood to live in a place such as this? Louisa could think of no infirmity, no condition that would excuse such cold-bloodedness.

"Here we are," Mrs. Bitterman said as they reached the third floor. The air here was stale and stifling. Judging by the sloped ceilings and narrow corridors, the rooms had been carved out of the attic space.

"Why is she being kept locked up?" Louisa asked in open disapproval when the woman began searching through the assortment of keys.

Mrs. Bitterman sneered at Louisa. "You women are all the same. The moment you've married, you trot over to Hildon with your sensibilities aflame. You're so sure that you'll be the one to make the difference and that a little loving care will make everything all right." She sniffed. "But you'll be back here soon enough, ready to lock her up so that you don't have to deal with the unpleasantness yourself."

Mrs. Bitterman's eyes narrowed. "Within a day or two, you'll discover that your new daughter is a demon child, one possessed by the worst characteristics to be found in human nature. Only harsh discipline curbs her willful spirit."

She gave a snort of distaste. "And don't get all high and mighty with me. I'm following doctor's orders—her own doctor! One paid for with the Winslow millions. Why, if it weren't for the tonic that she must be given every day, she would be little more than an animal."

Louisa shook with anger, a fury that blazed even more intensely as Mrs. Bitterman twisted the key in the lock and swung the door wide.

There was no light in the tiny room, no window, no lamp, no chink in the wall to provide the slightest illumination. Sensing a change in her condition, the girl started, whirling to face the open door from where she'd crouched in the corner behind a rusty iron bedstead.

As Louisa's eyes met those of her new daughter, she was stunned again.

From everything that she had heard about Evie, Louisa had expected a small child. But the figure that regarded her with suspicious, narrow eyes was well on her way to becoming a woman. True, she was small and lithe, but Louisa would say that the delicate girl was at least fifteen or sixteen years old.

"Evie?" Louisa said softly, speaking much the same way she would to a cornered, wild animal. "Evie, I've come to take you home."

The girl didn't respond. Instead, she watched Louisa with a blank, glassy stare.

"Would you like to go home?"

"She won't answer you," Mrs. Bitterman proclaimed. "She hasn't spoken in years." Her arms folded beneath her breasts. "She's more than capable of speaking, I can assure you. She remains silent in order to demand attention from everyone around her."

Louisa's hands trembled with her effort to control her temper. With a sharp gesture, she pointed at Evie. "*This* is the unruliness you warned me against?" she snapped.

Mrs. Bitterman glared down the length of her pinched nose. "Upon the advice of her physician, we felt it necessary to treat her with laudanum to soothe her nerves."

Soothe her nerves? The girl's glassy stare indicated she was only partially aware of what was going on around her.

"Rest assured that I'll be speaking to the board of trustees about this," Louisa said.

Mrs. Bitterman shrugged and offered her a sour smile. "Nothing has been done without the advice of the girl's doctor. You would be highly advised to continue with her medication as prescribed. Otherwise, she becomes violent.''

Louisa was suddenly glad that she'd come without an appointment. If she'd waited for the school's invitation, she was sure she never would have seen the horrible treatment being inflicted on the child.

''I'm taking her home.''

Without even being asked, John strode into the tiny room. Offering soft soothing sounds as if she were a skittish colt, John gently slipped his arms beneath the girl's slender frame and lifted her against him.

''You'd best hurry and get her things, Mrs. Bitterman,'' he said darkly as he brushed past the woman and began to carry the girl down the twisting staircase.

Once they reached the carriage, Louisa climbed into the rear seat first, then helped John to settle the girl beside her. Clinging to Evie with one arm, she wrapped her shawl around her shoulders, then tucked the carriage blanket around her knees.

At one point, Evie reared away, clearly disturbed by the fussing. Her eyes were sullen and suspicious, her expression rife with apprehension.

Louisa couldn't blame the girl for her reaction. Who knew how long she had been abused by the matrons of Hildon Hall?

Feeling much like a mother hen whose chick had been attacked, Louisa hugged Evie tightly as the girl's things were loaded onto the opposite seat—little more than a trunk the size of a hatbox and a worn winter coat.

The evidence of such pitiful belongings pained Louisa even more. This was the daughter of one of the wealthiest men in Boston? She had been treated with less regard than most beggars.

"See to it that she's given her tonic at each meal," Mrs. Bitterman said as she handed Louisa a bottle filled with a milky substance. "If you don't, she'll have a serious reaction."

Louisa took the bottle and stuffed it into her reticule. Then, ignoring the matron's look—one that seemed smug and confident about the fact that Louisa would soon be bringing the girl back—Louisa indicated to John that they should leave.

Louisa did her best to comfort the shivering girl on the ride home. But if Louisa had hoped that Evie would warm to her immediately, she was sadly mistaken. Evie regarded her with large suspicious eyes. Eyes that remained slightly unfocused and overly bright.

Damn that woman and damn Hildon Hall, Louisa thought time and time again. Even if Evie were ill and prone to misbehavior, Louisa couldn't imagine what the girl could have done to result in being locked in a dark, airless chamber, her frail body so drugged that she could barely hold herself upright.

Worse yet, it was obvious that the girl had not bathed in some time. Her hair was tangled and matted, her fingernails rimmed with grime. Cuts and scratches peppered her skin as if she'd run through a bramble bush.

How was Louisa supposed to tell this fragile creature that Charles had died and that Evie had been left in the care of a stranger?

"Evie?" she murmured.

At the sound of her name, the girl reared away and pressed herself into the corner of the carriage.

"Shh, shh." Louisa bit her lip.

Now wasn't the time to tell the girl anything. Although she damned herself for being a coward, Louisa decided that she would wait until Evie had been fed and bathed. Perhaps then the laudanum would have worn off enough for the girl to realize that Louisa wasn't a threat.

Tucking her shawl more securely around the girl's shoulders, Louisa gradually drew Evie into her arms again. As soon as possible, Louisa would summon the girl's doctor. Before Louisa did anything, she needed the advice of a physician. Tomorrow would be soon enough to tell Evie of her father's death. In her current state, Louisa doubted that the girl would consciously miss Charles.

The afternoon sun was hot overhead when the front gates to the Winslow estates came into view.

"We're almost home, Evie."

The girl trembled in Louisa's arms, but the time and distance had eased her tears enough that she allowed Louisa to hold her.

"Are you hungry?"

The question was asinine, given the gauntness of the girl's frame, but the constant patter seemed to calm Evie.

"We'll make you some hot soup and tea—or perhaps you'd like a cup of Beatrice's hot cocoa."

Evie stiffened in Louisa's arms as the shadow of the huge iron gate passed over them and they made their way through the darker shadows caused by the trees.

"I'm sure your aunt is eager to see you. It's probably been years...."

A whimper of distress bled from Evie's lips. Then, as they topped the rise and the castle could be seen in the valley below, she grew hysterical, crying and screaming. She pushed free of Louisa, kicking and flailing her arms, trying desperately to jump from the carriage.

"Whoa!"

John quickly calmed the gelding and turned to catch the girl around the waist before she could lunge out of the conveyance.

"What startled her?" he asked, raising his voice to be heard over the angry squeals.

"I don't know. She became restless as soon as we turned down the drive, but the moment she saw the castle, she lost control."

Still struggling with the child, John looked quickly at the castle, then down at Evie.

"Do you think she's afraid of the place? It looks a little like Hildon Hall."

Louisa peered at the castle, then down at Evie, who was frantic.

"Perhaps you're right."

"Take her for a minute."

Louisa drew Evie down upon the seat. Evie buried her face in Louisa's shoulder, sobbing piteously.

With a deft twist of the reins, John urged the horse down an alternative track to the left. The moment the trees shielded them from the view of the house, Evie's panic subsided and her sobbing took a tone of exhaustion rather than fear.

"I think you're right, John." Louisa's blood boiled. "What did they do to her at that place?"

"I sure as hell intend to find out," he muttered, more to himself than to her.

His concern tugged at Louisa's heart.

After whispering softly to the girl, Louisa said, "We can't take her home. Not like this."

John gazed around them as if the answer might suddenly show itself. "What do you want to do?"

She thought for a moment, then said, "In my inheritance, I was given the garden house. It's supposed to be nearby. From what I gathered from Mr. Pritchard's explanation, it was the overseer's home during the construction of the castle. I believe he said it was on the southeastern corner of the estate. Do you think you could find it?''

Slapping the reins on the horse's rump, John said, ''We may as well try. The way she's acting, I'd rather not go to the castle to ask for directions.''

It proved an easy task to find the garden house. The track they followed led to the stables, and from there, to another rutted road that led to the cottage.

From first glance, Louisa had fallen in love with the structure. Compared to the castle, it was a modest home. Built on a single level, it had a wraparound porch and a steeply pitched roof. Large windows let in the sunshine and lacy fretwork decorated the eaves.

John was the first to investigate. He found the rear door unlocked. After searching the house, he came out through the front.

''It's dusty and in need of a cleaning, but cloths have been thrown over most of the furniture to keep out the grime. Overall, I'd say this place is in better condition than the main house.''

He scooped Evie into his arms.

Weakly, she protested, pressing her hands against his chest, but her actions were uncoordinated.

''I'll get the two of you set up in one of the bedrooms. Then I'll take the buggy back to the stable and let the rest of the household know what has happened.''

He led them into a narrow entryway, and from there to a door at the end of the hall. Inside were two iron bedsteads and a tall shape shrouded in a dust cloth. Judging by its height, Louisa guessed it to be a highboy.

"What would you like me to fetch you from the house?" John asked Louisa as he set Evie on the bare mattress.

The girl sighed, turned her face to the wall and promptly fell asleep.

"We'll need food to carry us over until tomorrow, linens and water. Ask Chloe to bring clothes for the next few days and toiletries—especially soap." Louisa's voice gentled as she stared down at the sleeping girl. "We'll need lots and lots of soap."

In a rush, she absorbed the enormity of what had happened. Her stomach tightened, but she willed the sensation away. She'd been in the right today, and she wouldn't regret a single thing she'd done.

"She'll be happier here with you," John said softly, his hand touching her shoulder.

As much as she willed herself not to respond, Louisa melted into that caress ever so slightly.

"I pray you're right."

There was a beat of silence, one she measured by the infinitesimal stroking of his thumb.

"Are you having second thoughts?"

"About Evie?"

"About your marriage."

She quickly searched his features, wondering what would have inspired him to ask such a question.

Unless he'd guessed somehow that she'd had a choice in the matter.

No. Not possible. Her identity was still a secret.

"Why would I regret anything about my life to date?"

His eyes seemed to plumb her very soul and she forced herself to hold his gaze without flinching.

"Why, indeed?"

To her infinite relief, he dropped his hand. His boots

thumped against the wooden floor, marking his depar-
ture, so that in time she heard the bang of the front
screen and the hollow sound of a horse's hooves retreating up the drive.

Feeling suddenly faint, Louisa stripped off her bonnet
and gloves, tossing them onto the other bed. Then she
unbuttoned her jacket and slid it from her shoulders.
More than anything, she longed to strip to her under-
things and stretch out on the mattress to take her own
nap, but such an indulgence was out of the question.

As soon as Chloe arrived with a change of clothing,
she would dress in something more suitable for cleaning.
Since the funeral was scheduled for tomorrow afternoon,
time was of the essence. She needed to ensure that the
cottage was habitable.

Leaving the door ajar should Evie need her, Louisa
began to explore. Besides the bedroom, she soon discovered two more sleeping areas, a kitchen, parlor, din-
ing area and pantry as well as a screened porch to the
rear. A search of the cupboards revealed a few canned
goods, linens and cleaning supplies.

Rolling her sleeves up, Louisa began stripping dust
sheets from the furniture. Bit by bit, she revealed strong,
high quality pieces—perhaps not the newest or the prettiest to be found, but serviceable nonetheless.

With each discovery, a deeper pleasure grew in her
breast. All of this was hers—*hers!* To a woman who for
most of her life had owned little more than what would
fit into a trunk or a carpetbag, she felt like a queen.

If the truth were known, she found the cottage to be
much more to her liking than the castle. As grand as the
other structure might be, there was something…ominous
about it. Perhaps the walls held secrets from its past

inhabitants and the house did not appreciate being taken so far away from where it had originally stood.

Louisa shook her head brusquely. "Preposterous," she murmured to herself, turning her attention back to her labors.

What secrets could possibly be contained within the Winslow mansion?

Chapter Fifteen

Within an hour, a bevy of servants had arrived at the garden house, and Louisa put them to work dusting, cleaning and scrubbing floors, while she and Chloe changed linens. In the kitchen, Beatrice filled the larder, then made a pot of thick soup that she put on the back burner to simmer.

By nightfall, the tired women had set up housekeeping. After a meal of bread and cheese, they retired to their rooms, with John relegated to the screened porch to sleep.

It was the last real moment of peace that Louisa would have for several days. The following morning, Charles's coffin was again displayed for early visitors. Then there was the procession to the church, a lengthy funeral and the graveside service.

Through it all, Louisa tried her best to play the grieving widow. The charade wasn't entirely impossible. With all of the heartfelt words being offered and the flowery condolences, she grew teary thinking that she would never have the opportunity to meet such a paragon of virtue.

It was only when the mourners followed her back to

the rectory for a late meal—then stayed and stayed until darkness had begun to fall—that her emotions wavered. As the hours wore on and the clock wound past the appropriate hour for Evie to be in bed, impatience bubbled within Louisa and she felt she might scream soon if everyone didn't go home. It wouldn't seem polite if she were to leave early.

Glancing up, she caught John looking at her, a hidden smile teasing his lips. That fact only seemed to increase her irritation.

Why did this man always seem to find humor in her situation? It was as if he knew she didn't belong here. She was a crow among peacocks. Although she might have donned the plumage necessary to hide herself among society's elite, she still felt like an interloper.

Did he somehow sense that?

Her temples throbbed as she finally saw the last guest out the front doors and leaned against the heavy panels.

"I have the carriage waiting for you."

She started at the deep voice that came from a spot just behind her shoulder.

"Evie?"

"Beatrice has already collected her."

Louisa didn't flinch as he settled her wrap over her shoulders.

"It's all over, Louisa. Let's take you home."

She shuddered ever so softly, some of the tension easing from her body. For the past hour, she'd held herself so tightly that she feared she would shatter.

His hand was warm against her waist as he reached around her to open the door. Louisa took the pastor's hand as he offered his last encouraging words, but she caught only a small portion of what was being said. She was conscious only of the man who stood behind her and the strength that he represented.

John quickly ushered her to the carriage and helped her to climb inside. Beatrice sat on the opposite bench, her arm around her niece.

"Is she asleep?"

Beatrice nodded. "The day has worn her out, poor thing."

Louisa doubted that Evie had been aware of much of anything that day. She'd awakened late and docilely taken the tonic that Beatrice had given her. The rest of the afternoon she'd watched the proceedings with glassy eyes. Only at the graveside had she cried, huge, silent tears that were more heartbreaking than the piteous sobbing Beatrice had displayed.

Sighing, Louisa rubbed her temples. "Perhaps I shouldn't have brought her."

Beatrice shook her head. "It wouldn't have looked right."

Louisa didn't really care if Evie's absence would have caused tongues to wag or not. Her primary concern had been for the girl. When Louisa's mother had died, she had been told she was too young to attend the services and she'd been left at home. Without the finality of a funeral, the entire affair had seemed incomplete to her. For years Louisa had believed that if she was good enough, clever enough, faithful enough, her mother might return. After all, she had no proof that her mother had truly been placed in the ground. In her childish brain she had envisioned all sorts of possibilities—that she'd merely been asleep, or that a prince would kiss her and bring her back to life....

Louisa wouldn't do such a thing to another child. Despite her…diminished faculties, Evie deserved the chance to mourn her father properly.

"Boyd stated that he would be sleeping at his club tonight," Beatrice murmured.

At that moment, Louisa didn't care what Boyd did. By moving to the garden house, she'd avoided his icy glares—something she hadn't been able to do at the church.

"You really needn't stay with Evie and me, Beatrice. I know that you're probably accustomed to living in the castle."

Beatrice bit her lip in indecision, then shook her head. "I wouldn't dream of remaining there while you are with Evie. You're my family."

Louisa hesitated before finally asking, "Beatrice, why didn't your brother leave Evie to your care?"

She tried to read the woman's expression, but even with the outside lanterns, the shadows in the carriage were too deep.

"My brother and I…didn't get along well," Beatrice said stiffly.

"But why not?"

There was a long silence, and a small sliver of moonlight limned Beatrice's profile as she stared out the window.

"Did you know that I am older than Charles?"

"No."

"Yes. By a year." Her voice hardened ever so slightly. "But being a girl as I am, my father didn't think it…appropriate for me to be involved in the family business."

"Did you want to be?"

"Yes. Oh, yes." Her head tilted in a proud angle.

"I've always been very good with numbers. In fact, I'd dare say that I was much more clever than Charles."

Louisa heard the rustle of silk as her sister-in-law shrugged.

"I had the bad fortune to be a woman." Her voice took on an edge. "I thought that once Father died Charles might allow me to participate, but he didn't. If anything, he was even more backward thinking than Papa. We had quite a row about the subject, I can tell you." She sniffed in disgust. "The next morning, I discovered just how precarious my position could be. My father had left me nothing, you see. His estate was left to Charles's discretion, and since I'd become a source of irritation to my brother, he decided that I should go to the country to live with a pair of maiden aunts." Beatrice's voice throbbed with remembered anger and regret. "Thus began my long career as the family nurse."

Louisa was so shocked by her late husband's callousness that she didn't know how to respond. "I'm sure that your efforts weren't wasted," she said at last.

Beatrice took a deep breath, and when she spoke again, it was with an affected lightness. Nevertheless, Louisa could feel a measure of the woman's hurt.

"Yes, I know fully well that I brought them a sense of peace. Many of my elderly relations mentioned me in their wills, allowing me a small amount of independence. There was just never enough to remove myself from my brother's control once and for all."

Bitterness filled the air around them, causing Louisa's mood to blacken even more. "What about Boyd? Was your father as restrictive with him?"

A short laugh cut through the chilly evening. "Boyd has been little more than my brother's lackey for years. He's added as much to the family fortune as Charles, yet he's been given little more than a yearly salary. To be honest, I wouldn't have been surprised if there'd been foul play involved in Charles's death. Boyd has often wished that he had the nerve to do something.''

"Beatrice!" Louisa was truly shocked. As badly as Boyd had treated Louisa herself, she wouldn't have thought Beatrice could think such a thing about her own brother.

"You needn't sound so surprised. I'm fully aware that Boyd was here in Boston when Charles's death occurred. I'm merely trying to convey to you the depth of animosity my brothers had for one another. They worked together, but only grudgingly. It's simply too bad that Charles didn't have enough heart to recognize all that Boyd has done for the company, and reward him accordingly.''

Louisa bit her lip, realizing that she had benefited from Charles's largesse, while his own family had been ignored. When she caught sight of the familiar iron gates that led to the Winslow property, relief surged through her.

As much as she might wish to set things to rights with Charles's family, tonight she didn't have the strength or the energy to even think clearly. Tomorrow she would speak to Mr. Pritchard. Surely there was a way to sort out the injustices that had occurred.

Beatrice sighed. "Louisa, if it isn't a bother, I do believe that I'll change my mind about sleeping at the garden house. I've grown a bit set in my ways, and with Boyd gone, the silence of the castle might do me good.''

Louisa heard the gruffness of Beatrice's voice and sensed she was trying to hold back tears.

"Yes, of course."

After knocking on the side of the carriage and offering

instructions to John, Louisa peered out of the window, watching as the huge, looming shape of the manor rose out of the darkness.

A shiver coursed down her spine. In the black shadows, the house seemed ominous and overwhelming. Even with several windows alight, the facade's Gothic architecture gave it an abandoned appearance.

"I've left a tin of my special cocoa at the garden house," Beatrice said as she stepped from the carriage. "Be sure to make yourself a cup tonight. It will help you sleep."

"Thank you, Beatrice."

As her sister-in-law climbed the front steps, Louisa took her place, resting Evie's head against her shoulder and wrapping her arm around the girl's fragile waist.

"Good night, Louisa," Beatrice said as she slipped through the front door. "Don't worry. I'll make a point of joining you for breakfast each day as well as helping with Evie. I wouldn't want to shirk my duties in that respect."

"Good night."

Louisa was inestimably weary as she, Evie and John made their way to the garden house.

Home.

Home?

Louisa loved the little house. The simplicity of its design offered a sense of security that she never would have thought possible of any building. And yet…

Perhaps her sense of restlessness was merely a cause of the tumult of the past few days, but she didn't feel completely at ease in her new house. She still felt like a visitor rather than the rightful owner.

The carriage rolled to a stop. Within moments, the

door opened and John reached for Evie. "I'll carry her in."

Lifting her skirts, Louisa climbed from the carriage herself, then quickly moved ahead so that she could hold the door for him.

She bit her lip at the tenderness that he displayed as he carried the exhausted girl into her room and laid her on the bed. As he reached for the lamp, Louisa removed Evie's shoes, then pulled a quilt over her shoulders.

Within seconds, Bitsy ran into the room and jumped onto Evie's bed. Burrowing into the pillow, she cuddled next to the girl. Since meeting Evie, the small dog had clearly shifted her allegiance, and the delight was mutual. Although Louisa missed the companionship of the animal, she was pleased that Evie had something to dote upon.

"I would like to have Evie examined by another doctor," Louisa said as she lingered near the bedside.

John nodded. "I think that would be wise."

He held the lamp aloft, offering them a mellow glow of welcome as they returned to the sitting room. When the silence pressed around them, Louisa felt a shiver of disquiet…as if things were not quite right.

Sighing, she removed the hatpin from her bonnet and dropped the concoction of satin and lace onto a small table. Crossing to the window, she peered into the darkness beyond, then swiftly drew the blind. "I must confess that I am glad of your company tonight."

The fact that she'd uttered the words aloud surprised her as much as it did him.

"I'm pleased that I can be of help."

Overcome with the events of the day, Louisa stood immobile. In her mind, she played out the hours spent at the church and then again at the graveside. A montage of faces swam in front of her eyes—mostly business associates who had come to pay their respects before worriedly conferring with Boyd about whether or not shipments would continue as usual. Through it all, Louisa was left with the impression that Charles had been too busy with augmenting his fortune to develop many personal relationships. Even the minister had admitted that he knew Charles by reputation alone.

"You should go to bed," John said after long silent moments had passed.

"Yes." The word was a bare whisper of sound.

Before she could anticipate what he meant to do, he crossed the room, scooping her into his arms much as he had done with Evie.

Louisa knew that she should resist, but the strength of his arms was more comforting than she would have thought possible, and she was tired, so tired.

Her arms looped around his neck and she settled against him, her head resting against his shoulder as he moved down the hall to her room. Once there, he laid her on the bed, then tenderly removed her wrap, jacket and shoes. Then he tucked her beneath the covers, clothes and all.

The man's infinite gentleness brought tears to her eyes. She couldn't remember a time when she had felt so...cherished.

Had she made a mistake in assuming Louisa Haversham's life? Had she forfeited all hope of happiness with a man...like John?

Before she could fully formulate an answer to her inner query, he leaned toward her, his hands braced on either side of her pillow. Softly, sweetly, he placed a kiss on her lips. The gesture was so rife with tenderness and his own tightly reined desires that when he drew away, it took all of the will she possessed not to pull him back. Instead, she clutched the bedclothes, knowing that she could not give in to her own hunger.

To lose control now would be her undoing.

To reach out to him now would mean that she did not wish to sleep alone, yet she could not, would not, *must* not deepen her confusion even more.

"Good night," John whispered, backing from the room.

For long moments she couldn't speak. She was afraid that if she uttered a word it would throb with the unmitigated desire that raged within her. Therefore, he was already gone when she finally offered a husky, "Good night…my friend."

Newfoundland Waters

"Do you have an update for me, Mr. Ritchie?"

Ritchie snapped the door to the private cabin shut and leaned against the panels to keep his balance against the pitching sea.

"The weather has caused a delay. The captain has been forced to ride out the storm. Nevertheless, he believes we'll arrive within a day or two of our original schedule. At the very least, the weather has to be giving your brother fits. There's no telling how long he'll be delayed."

For the first time, Ritchie saw the man smile—a slow feral smile that made the hairs at the back of Ritchie's neck stand on end.

"Excellent. I'll expect you to make contact with Badger the moment we arrive. Hopefully, he will have taken care of our western problem by then."

The man was so cool and calm when he spoke of the planned murder that Ritchie shivered.

Horace's eyes narrowed. "Is something wrong, Mr. Ritchie?"

"No, sir," Ritchie said quickly—perhaps too quickly.

"You aren't getting soft on me, are you, Mr. Ritchie?"

"Not at all."

"Good. It wouldn't do for you to become a…problem as well."

"My only wish is to please you, milord," Ritchie said.

Because if I don't, you'll see me dead like the two Haversham women.

Chapter Sixteen

Dearest Diary,

With the funeral over and my husband's body safely interred, I prayed that my life would return to normal. But within a few days, I have been forced to admit that I no longer know what the term "normal" means.

Since my primary concern is for Evie, I have turned my attentions to the girl. Already horrified by the treatment she received at the asylum, I didn't think that I could be surprised with any new discoveries. But I soon realized I was sadly mistaken.

Evie continues to be fractious—so much so that I can sometimes understand why Mrs. Bitterman was so forceful in her warnings. The girl's emotions are volatile—sobbing one minute, then overly calm and glassy-eyed the next. A visit by Evie's physician has done little to resolve the matter. Other than informing me that Evie inherited a "nervous disposition" from her mother, and supplying a bottle of his usual tonic, he had no alternative treatments that he could offer.

My only small victory came from the fact that Evie appears to trust me. Unfortunately, such emotions don't extend to anyone else in the household. Evie is rude and suspicious of Beatrice and openly hostile toward John. But what pains me most is that the girl clearly expects to be returned to the asylum at any minute.

Hoping to reassure Evie of the permanence of our relationship, I began interviewing craftsmen to refurbish the castle. Under Mr. Pritchard's guidance and wholehearted approval, I have arranged for the building to be cleaned, repaired and modernized. Whenever possible, I include Evie in the planning so that the girl will realize that the changes have been made on her behalf.

To my disappointment, Evie remains unmoved by such efforts. Her only real moments of calm seem to come after she has taken the tonic prescribed by the doctor. Then her emotions cease their wild seesawing and she contents herself with sitting on the porch swing hugging Bitsy, or taking walks in the nearby woods.

Dear, sweet girl. My heart aches for her. It is tragic that one so young and beautiful could be so afflicted.

Hearing John Smith walking down the hall, Louisa slid her diary into her highboy and stood. Peering into the looking glass, she made the last few adjustments to her toilette. As she was doing so, she became aware of Evie at the far side of the room.

Thinking she was unobserved, Evie was delving into the contents of Louisa's steamer trunks. Due to a lack of wardrobes in the garden house, Louisa had positioned the full-size trunks in the corner of her room as make-shift closets. Evie was apparently mesmerized by what she found in the compartments. She tried on several bonnets, lovingly stroked the velvet of a cape, then knelt down to finger a pair of shoes. Through it all, there was a simple reverence to her actions.

Sensing that she may have stumbled upon a way to strengthen her bond with the girl, Louisa called out, "Mr. Smith?"

Within seconds, John stood in the doorway, his fingers hooked over the upper jamb in such a way that she couldn't ignore the breadth of his shoulders tapering down to narrow masculine hips and muscled thighs.

For a moment, all coherent thought scattered. She could do little but stare at the man, her heart pounding in her chest, her blood pooling deep in her belly in the first coilings of desire.

Silence spooled between them, fraught with awareness and remembered passions. It had been days since she'd felt his arms around her—and although she'd sworn she would behave with all of the decorum and severity of spirit of a new widow, she couldn't deny that she hungered for his touch.

"Did you want something?"

Yes. Yes, she wanted something. She wanted to wallow in the warmth of his embrace. She wanted to feel his lips against hers. She wanted…

More than she could ever have.

Turning resolutely away, she donned what she hoped was a bright, cheerful facade.

"Mr. Smith, arrange for a carriage. I think the time has come for me to take Evie shopping."

At that, Evie looked up, and for the first time, Louisa

caught something in the girl's eyes that looked very much like a glint of hope.

"Do you think that's wise?" John drawled. But even he had caught the change in Evie's manner, because when she glared at him, he grinned and straightened.

"Very well, Miss Evie. I'll get the team myself and bring it around front."

If Neil had thought shopping with Louisa on her own was a chore, shopping with Louisa and Evie together was a nightmare.

Although Evie had come to accept the fact that John would accompany them everywhere they went, her feelings about him were mixed. At one moment she regarded him with overt suspicion and dislike, yet in the next she clung to him for reassurance.

It was the latter reaction that worried John the most. He'd never encountered anyone so…fragile. Evie's emotions were often chaotic, her grasp on reality tenuous. He feared that if she began to form any sort of attachment to him, she would suffer once he was gone—because he would leave. With Louisa or not. He didn't belong here. This wasn't his life.

That fact was brought home to him time and time again as he accompanied the women through the shops of Boston. As Louisa and a shopkeeper dithered over the merits of a single yard of ribbon, and Evie looked on as if the entire process fascinated her, Neil was filled with a raging impatience.

He should be home, tending to his stock and his property. The narrow streets of Boston made him itch at the confinement, and the need to dog Louisa's every move was…

Well, it was disturbing. In more ways than one.

So what did he intend to do? So far, there had been no overt attempt made on Louisa's life. Indeed, except for Boyd's obvious enmity, there hadn't been a hint of trouble.

Why? If Horace Haversham was intent on removing the threat of his brother's heirs, why was he focusing his attention on Phoebe Gray rather than Louisa? According to the telegram Neil had received, there had been an attempt made in Oregon.

Yet everything here had been peaceful.

No, not peaceful. Since joining Louisa, Neil had found his existence to be confusing, chaotic, arousing and confining.

And yet…

As much as he might tell himself that there was nothing to fear and that a mistake must have been made about Louisa's predicament, he still felt uneasy. Years as a scout in the war had taught him that instincts should never be ignored—and Neil's instincts refused to grow quiet. He knew the danger was there, waiting, crouching in the darkness, like an animal ready to spring.

So he continued to bide his time and keep a wary eye. Even if it meant hours of shopping and inane feminine prattle. In the meantime, he had a pair of men patroling the grounds while the others investigated Haversham's business practices in the U.S. in the hopes of discovering his whereabouts.

"Let me see you in this bonnet, Evie!"

Neil had lost count of the number of hats that Evie had modeled. But then, as he saw the women stand in front of the mirror, Louisa's hands resting lightly on Evie's shoulders, Neil suddenly realized that Louisa wasn't really intent on gathering clothing for the girl as much as she was on forming an emotional bond between them.

In a rush of clarity, Neil felt his impatience drain away. Evie's eyes were alight and clearer than he'd ever seen them. Her cheeks were pink and her eyes sparkled with hope and delight.

"Do you like it?"

The girl nodded.

"We'll take this one, Mrs. Beem."

"And the ribbon?"

"Yes, the ribbon, too. But let's make it two yards rather than one."

"Very good."

As the shopkeeper went to cut the ribbon, Louisa slipped her arm around the girl's waist.

Neil noted that Evie actually stepped into the embrace rather than shying away like a skittish colt. So much progress had been made in a single afternoon.

"Would you like to wear the bonnet or carry it home in a hatbox?"

Evie's hands settled on the hat and Louisa grinned.

"I don't blame you. It's a wonderful bonnet. It brings out the green in your eyes. We'll have to find the perfect fabric and have a dress made to match. Silk, I think. Every girl your age should have a beautiful silk dress in her wardrobe."

Evie raised herself on tiptoe and threw her arms around Louisa's neck. But what began as a quick hug became a desperate clench.

"There, there, Evie. You're safe with me. You won't be returning to Hildon House. I promise," Louisa whispered.

Neil looked away, a curious pang striking his heart. Louisa was so earnest, so openly affectionate with the girl—and Neil couldn't fault Louisa for her methods. It was clear that she was willing to do everything in her power to make Evie feel loved and accepted.

But inwardly, he cringed at the rapport the women were developing. The longer he and Louisa stayed here, the more she became embroiled in a life he would have her leave behind.

If he thought such a tactic would work, Neil would take Louisa in his arms, tell her his real name and whisk her back to Oregon to be his wife, as she'd once promised to become. But more and more, he was beginning to realize that he wanted something more from her than mere obligation. He wanted Louisa to truly care for him—just as he was beginning to care for her.

The thought was so sudden, so piercing, that Neil had to look away from the women. In a heartbeat, he realized that he was jealous of Louisa's open affection with Evie—and the whole idea rankled. How could he possibly deny her one moment of happiness?

Yet he also couldn't deny that he would give anything to have Louisa touch him, spontaneously, innocently, then look up at him with a quick smile and her eyes alight with laughter. He wanted her to feel free around him, to enjoy his company.

If he thought that revealing his true identity might cause such a thing to happen, he would shout the truth out right now. But he feared that he would only complicate things even more. Louisa would probably be angry with him for playing her for a fool. Worse yet, she might refuse his offer of marriage and send him packing.

So he had no choice but to stay a little longer, to become more embroiled in his role as Louisa Haversham Winslow's bodyguard. His only hope was to make her feel something for him that she could neither deny nor refuse.

"Is something wrong, Mr. Smith?"

Neil shook himself from his ruminations to discover that Evie and Louisa were staring at him.

"You look awfully grim," Louisa remarked. "Are you growing tired?"

The question was an open challenge.

"Not at all." He gestured to Evie. "I like the bonnet. It's very fetching."

Evie looked down, but the pink that touched her cheeks told him she was pleased by the compliment.

"If I'm looking grim, it's because I'm hungry. And I think Evie is hungry, too," he said.

Evie couldn't prevent a quick smile.

"There's a hotel down the block that is famous for its desserts."

Louisa's brows rose. "Dessert? Don't you think we should concern ourselves with a proper meal first?"

"The food is good, even if the waiters tend to fuss. But the real treat is the assortment of ice cream and cakes that follow."

Evie's eyes grew wide.

Louisa reverently echoed, "Ice cream?"

For an instant she looked so much like his childhood friend that he could have laughed. How many times in the orphanage had they dreamed of rich foods and smooth, sweet ice cream? Although neither of them had ever tried the stuff, they'd heard about it and longed to taste the sweet treat.

"Do you think I could tempt either one of you to break off your shopping for an hour or so?"

"By all means, Mr. Smith." Louisa gestured for Evie to collect the packages they'd left on a nearby bench.

When the shopkeeper returned and began to help the girl, Neil took the opportunity to bend close to Louisa.

"Is that all I can tempt you to do, Mrs. Winslow?"

He saw a tide of pink rise in her cheeks. "Behave, Mr. Smith."

"I have been the model of decorum all day, Mrs. Winslow." Out of sight of Mrs. Beem and Evie, he traced a finger down the length of her spine. "I would like you to know that such measures of restraint have been very…taxing."

He felt her breath quicken.

"Oh?"

"Yes. It is difficult to spend so much time with you."

She stiffened. "I didn't think my company was so onerous."

"Quite the contrary. It's keeping my hands away from you that has become the chore."

Her lashes flickered shut for only a moment, and he thought he heard her say, "As it has become for me."

Then she stepped away, calling, "Come along, Evie. Let's discover for ourselves how wonderful this ice cream can be."

"…as Mr. Rochester…"

Louisa allowed her voice to trail away into silence. Evie lay fast asleep in her bed, her arms tightly clutching a beautiful china doll.

Even now, Louisa felt a tug of tenderness at the sight of Evie's affection for the doll. Soon after finishing a tantalizing meal of roast chicken, new potatoes, hothouse asparagus—and all of the sweet, delicious ice cream they could eat—the three of them had been on their way back to the seamstress, when Evie had seen the doll.

Louisa had often seen finer creations in the arms of

her young charges. But this doll's bustled skirts, gold curls and paperweight eyes had immediately entranced Evie. She'd stared longingly at the toy for several seconds before resolutely turning away and following Louisa into the next shop. There she'd patiently put up with being measured and having countless fabrics and trims held up to see how they complimented her coloring. With the promise that the seamstress would come to the Winslow estates for final fittings at the end of the week, Louisa had finally ushered Evie into the waiting carriage.

And there, wrapped in paper and tied with a satin ribbon, lay a package.

Seeing Evie's name on the tag, Louisa handed the object to the girl. Evie had torn the outer coverings free with the eagerness of a child at Christmas. When she'd seen the doll, her eyes had filled with tears—as had Louisa's.

She'd known the instant she'd seen the golden curls who had purchased the toy. Glancing down at John, she'd offered a gruff, "Thank you," unable to say anything more past the tears that knotted her throat.

Those tears flowed more strongly when Evie launched herself at John, offering him an exuberant hug before self-consciously returning to the carriage.

Standing now, Louisa crossed to the window, pushing aside the curtain and staring out at the darkness beyond.

She still had no idea why Charles had arranged for a bodyguard. John had insisted that there were those who wished to harm her, but other than Boyd, she'd sensed no discontent from anyone. She had been treated with respect and gentility.

So why was John here?

More importantly, how long would he stay?

She wrapped her arms around her waist, suddenly chilled.

When had she begun to depend on him, even…care for him?

Shaking her head in impatience, she crossed the room and began to hang Evie's new things in the wardrobe with savage efficiency. But she had barely begun the job before she was inundated by a wave of restlessness and discontent. A loneliness she couldn't deny.

Hanging the last of Evie's petticoats on a peg, Louisa closed the doors, resting her forehead on the cool panels.

Had she no shame? No pride?

But even her inner castigations were unable to derail her thoughts. Squeezing her eyes shut, she knew she was on a one-way track toward disaster. She was a widow, a guardian. She should be a bastion of respectability.

But she was also a woman.

Behind her, the door opened, and she knew immediately who stood there. She could feel him with every part of her being. She knew the instant that he found her in the darkness. She felt his gaze as if it were a hand stroking down her spine.

A yearning swelled within her, filling her with a sweetness that she had come to know well. As she turned to face him, she felt the tension of her body ease into a deep, delicious languor. She became infinitely conscious of her own femininity.

"She's asleep?"

"Yes."

"Any problems?"

Louisa shook her head.

"She missed two doses of her tonic," John said softly.

Louisa flushed when she realized that she'd forgotten such an important detail.

"She seemed a little more clear without it," he noted.

Louisa realized he was right. The more the day had worn on, the sharper Evie's awareness had seemed to be.

"Perhaps her dosage needs to be changed. I've always thought she's seemed…drugged."

"Yes."

Silence pooled between them, reminding them that Evie was safely sleeping and any precautions they might need to take would have to wait until morning. Until then…

When John took a step forward, Louisa met him halfway. The moment he touched her, she felt as if she were home, melting into his arms with a familiarity that frightened her.

Her arms swept around his neck at the same instant that he took her weight, lifting her against him, his lips covering hers.

A storm of sensation rushed through her, sapping the strength from her body and leaving her trembling but oh, so alive. Clutching at his broad shoulders, she met each of his caresses with one of her own, absorbing the taste of him, the feel of him.

When he finally drew back for breath, she rested her face in the hollow of his shoulder

"We shouldn't be doing this," she whispered.

"Why not?"

For a moment, she couldn't think of a single objection. "My situation is…complicated," she finally managed to say.

"The only thing that complicates matters is you."

She nodded, wondering what he would say if he knew

just how complicated her life had become. "So why am I so willing to make things even more difficult?" she murmured.

She felt him take a deep breath, felt the beating of his heart beneath her cheek. "I've asked myself the same question, but I don't have any answers. I only know that...around you—" he tipped her chin up "—I can't seem to resist the temptation."

Then he was kissing her again, his mouth firm, insistent. She willingly opened her lips, allowing him to search her intimately. She was so tired of being "good." She didn't want to push him away any longer. When he held her in his arms, she felt beautiful and desirable.

"What have you done to me?" she whispered against his cheek, gasping for air. "I have always been a sensible person."

"Always?" There was a smile in his voice.

"Most of the time."

"And have you never been tempted to do something outrageous?"

Her laughter was rueful. "Yes, but I have rarely allowed myself to give in."

He drew back suddenly, taking her hand. "Then come with me. Now."

Before she knew what he meant to do, he was tugging her out of the room, down the hallway and out the rear door.

The night was thick and black around them as they left Beatrice and Evie sleeping in the house behind them and made their way to the nearby trees.

"Where are you taking me?"

"Shh. Don't talk. Just surrender to the experience."

She didn't need a second invitation. Laughing softly, she allowed him to pull her along a convoluted path, her skirts whispering in the grass, stray branches teasing her hair from its pins.

Soon she became aware of the gurgle of water and she wondered at its source.

"Is there a brook up ahead?"

"Wait and see."

She didn't know how she was supposed to see anything at all. The thick leaves overhead obscured what little light the moon might have to offer. But before she could wonder any more, the trees suddenly gave way to a small clearing.

"Oh, John," she breathed.

In front of her lay a deep pool surrounded on all sides by verdant grass and patches of wildflowers. Overhead, the moon shone high, seeming to hover in the center of a frame of leaves and tree branches.

"Let's go in."

She gasped. "I couldn't possibly. I—I don't have…I couldn't…"

Before she could protest any further, he silenced her with a soft kiss.

"For once, don't analyze what you should or shouldn't do. Follow the dictates of your heart."

The dictates of her heart…

What would he say if she were to tell him that her heart begged her to do anything that would allow her to be closer to him?

John gave a low, throaty chuckle. Drawing her to him, he stroked her back with his hands. Strong hands. Broad hands. They were big and powerful, yet still had the ability to soothe her or bring her to a fever pitch of desire.

"Don't think so much, Louisa. Follow your instincts.

It's only by listening to one's heart that anyone can be truly happy.''

Happy.

Was she happy? She'd been given everything she'd ever wanted—a home, wealth, a family. So why did she feel so hollow inside? Why did she sense that in accepting the sudden windfall, she was missing or forgetting something?

''Are you happy, John?'' she asked, grasping his wrist when he would have touched her face. She wasn't sure why, but she wanted to absorb his answer without the clouding affects caused by his touch.

''I have known happiness.''

''When.''

''As a child. I had an…unconventional upbringing, but there were moments of superb happiness.''

''What made them so wonderful?''

''A good friend.''

Louisa smiled, realizing that in that respect they were alike.

''Was childhood your only source of happiness?''

''No. I was lucky enough to be raised on a sprawling bit of land that offered me a chance to work hard and see things grow.''

''But you still feel…unsatisfied.''

''That's an interesting choice of words.'' His tone was wry.

She felt the heat of embarrassment seep into her cheeks, but refused to be derailed.

''You know what I mean.''

''Yes. Unfortunately, I do.''

He thought for a moment, holding her in the circle of his arms, his fingers laced together.

''No. There are things I still long for.''

"Such as?"

"Children. Sons."

"Would they have to be sons?"

He stared into the darkness, but she sensed that he was seeing something with his mind's eye.

"No. I don't suppose they would." There was a hint of wonder in his response, as if he'd never considered the alternative before.

"What else?"

"A wife."

"That goes without saying."

"Not necessarily."

Again, she felt the heat seep into her cheeks.

"Does Betty know of your plans?"

"Betty?"

He stared at her blankly and she prompted, "The barmaid you spoke of."

"Ahh, yes. Betty. She's a real corker."

"And is she to be the mother of your children?"

He didn't speak for the longest time. Instead, he regarded Louisa with such intensity, such thoughtfulness that she would have squirmed away if he hadn't held her fast.

"I don't know if Betty is the gal for me, after all."

Louisa's stomach flip-flopped, but this time, it wasn't from nerves. Instead, it felt very much like pleasure. Joy.

"Why would you say that? I thought the two of you seemed very much alike."

"Mmm. Perhaps. But in the last few weeks, I've broadened my outlook. I've begun to see that there are other types of women."

"Oh?"

"Yes. I've discovered that women can smell sweet and smile prettily and act with all of the gentility and propriety that a person could ever imagine. Yet simmering beneath that facade of respectability is something else.''

Louisa felt as if the breath were being squeezed from her body. ''And what would that be?''

''The sensuality of a siren.''

''Didn't sirens lead sailors to their doom?''

''Yes.''

She felt his body tense. Moonlight revealed the gravity of his expression.

''What about you, Louisa? Will your sweet passion lead me to my doom?''

Chapter Seventeen

Louisa opened her mouth to offer an immediate denial, but the words wouldn't come.

Would she lead him to his doom?

Or would she cause both of them to suffer for her weaknesses?

In that instant, Louisa realized that she was trapped in the life she had chosen. As much as her heart might urge her to surrender and indulge in this man's heated embraces, she knew she mustn't. She was a newly widowed woman in a society where appearances were everything. If she was to ensure the proper place for Evie and indeed, for herself—in Boston's upper elite, she must behave in a way that was above reproach. Indulging in a romance with one's bodyguard did not fit into the scheme of things.

Neither did losing one's heart to one's employee.

The thought was so shocking, so wrenching, that Louisa shied back, covering her mouth with her hand.

Had she allowed herself to fall in love with John Smith?

No, not love. This surely wasn't love.

But it could be.

Horrified at how she'd stupidly allowed her emotions to hover on the precipice of commitment, she took another step backward, then another, and another. Then, knowing she must flee from her thoughts as much as from the man, she picked up her skirts and raced back to the garden house. She didn't stop her headlong flight until she had closed herself in her room, shut the door behind her and turned the key in the lock.

Sobbing, she rested her forehead against the wood. How could she have done such a thing? How could she have allowed herself to become emotionally involved with that man? He was everything she had fought to escape, the very life she had sought to avoid. He was living from job to job, pay to pay. He had no real home to call his own and his only real family was…was…

A barmaid named Betty.

Sinking to the floor, Louisa cried even harder, her heart feeling as if it were actually cracking in her chest.

Why hadn't she been smarter? Why hadn't she found a way to make him leave? And barring that, why hadn't she guarded herself against him more carefully? She'd been such a fool, such a brazen, wanton, lonely fool….

Swiping at the tears that coursed down her cheeks, she crossed to her bed and threw herself upon the mattress.

Too late, she had learned that money truly didn't buy happiness. She'd thought that she would lead a life free from responsibilities—or at least none greater than running a household and arranging flowers. All too soon, she had found that even wealth had a host of taxing duties that could not be denied.

So what was she going to do? She had already tried everything in her power to make John Smith leave—and it was evident that she would not be able to resist him if he were near.

Squeezing her eyes shut, she realized the time had come to "make a scene"—something she had hoped to avoid. On Mr. Pritchard's next visit, she would consult with the man and see if he could have John removed through legal avenues.

Even if it meant hiring another man to take his place.

The tears came again, stronger, faster.

No. No man could ever take his place.

After their stolen embrace by the pool, Neil became more troubled with the mysteries surrounding his old childhood friend.

When he'd asked if she would lead him to his doom like the sirens of old, he had expected her to laugh at the comment—or better yet, to respond to the challenge. But to his infinite regret, he had seen her expression settle into something akin to horror. Then she had turned and fled.

What had caused such a reaction? Until that moment, Neil had known that she shared his passion and his overwhelming need. When he'd drawn her into the forest, he'd envisioned that they would laugh and swim, kiss, perhaps even...

Make love?

Staring up at the ceiling of the screened porch, where he'd been assigned to sleep, Neil rested his arm on his forehead, his fingers absently tightening into a fist, then releasing again.

What had gone wrong? Something had scared her.

But Neil could think of nothing. She'd gone with him quite willingly. The way she'd reacted to his kisses had been heartfelt and immediate. And then...

What? What had he done?

He grew still when he realized that it might not have been anything that he'd said or done, but rather what they had been about to do.

Had the thought of making love to him scared her? If so, was it because she was innocent of such intricacies of physical love?

Or was she familiar with lovemaking and didn't want him to know that fact?

His eyes squeezed shut as he remembered the look that had settled over her features. Not hesitancy, not even fear. But horror.

Dear sweet heaven above, *was* she pregnant? Had she known that by undressing in front of him—even if it were only for a midnight swim—she would reveal her condition?

Should he ask her bluntly?

As he pondered such a course of action, Neil realized that knowing the truth was only half the problem. The larger dilemma lay in his response once he had the knowledge he sought.

Rather than acting, Neil did nothing. Despite their correspondence, he really knew nothing about her other than that he'd claimed her as his own—and therein lay his greatest weakness.

In his mind, their engagement had been as binding as marriage. When he'd discovered that she'd donned a new identity, he'd refused to believe that any woman would scorn him in favor of a stranger. But after spending time with Louisa, after experiencing her beauty and passion, he was learning just what a prize he had lost. For the first time, he was forced to acknowledge that his emotions involved love, not just passion. He wanted to spend his life with her.

But he was also honest enough to know that he wanted her on his terms. He didn't want "Charles's widow." He wanted Phoebe Gray, the innocent Scottish lass who had befriended him as a child and written to him for years.

He couldn't seem to reconcile his earlier dreams with the reality that confronted him now. If Phoebe's innocence had already been compromised, would he be willing to play father to a child who was not his own? Would he be able to live with a woman who had originally agreed to marry him only to provide her baby with an unwitting father? A woman who had been willing to trade a life with him for a fortune from a stranger?

Despite his reservations, Neil found himself growing even more protective of Louisa…and yet, protective of what? There still had been no threats made against her, no signs of attempted violence.

As the days continued to unwind without incident, Neil grew puzzled. He knew that his time as her bodyguard was limited unless he could prove that his concerns were justified—especially if she enlisted the aid of Mr. Pritchard. Neil sensed that she had already considered such a move since she'd grown particularly agitated when a note to the lawyer's offices had been returned with an explanation that Pritchard was away on business for a week.

One week. Neil had so little time to resolve his situation, one way or another.

With each day that passed, he grew increasingly restless. He supposed that he should be pleased that his concern for Louisa's safety was unnecessary. And yet his instincts continued to warn him that disaster was about to strike.

Needing something to keep his mind occupied, Neil decided to investigate the sudden death of Louisa's husband. Yet even in that respect he found nothing suspicious, despite the whisperings of his spirit. Instead, what he uncovered was more information about the character of the man Louisa would have married.

Neil often wondered if Louisa knew how close she'd come to disaster. From more than one source, Neil had learned that Charles was a brilliant businessman. But Charles Winslow was also an ornery, cantankerous despot. He'd been a stingy, mean old man who had thoughtlessly shipped his daughter to an asylum soon after her mother's death so that she would be ''out of sight.'' No wonder Evie was distraught at the mere sight of the castle.

Dearest Diary,
The days have melted into one another as I've become accustomed to my new life and responsibilities.

If I'd thought that being Charles Winslow's bride would lead to a life of leisure, I would have been sadly mistaken. From dawn to dusk, I am responsible for a myriad of tasks. I have taken charge of the household budget for the castle as well as a fleet of servants who have returned to service to bring things to rights.

From the first, I insisted that the castle be given a thorough scrubbing. As each room is cleaned, the furnishings are inventoried and slated for repair, refurbishment or refuse. Any elements of disrepair or need for improvement are then noted in the housekeeper's ledger so that I can review the list each evening.

As the servants tackle the castle, Beatrice and I have seen to the garden house, turning it into a home for Evie. There are lessons for the girl— which, as of yet, focus more on rest and rejuvenation than academics.

Yet with all of the demands on my attention, I continue to be drawn more and more to the mysterious man who serves as my bodyguard. Although I have tried my best to remain unaffected, I cannot deny that I am growing fond of him. Too fond.

In an effort to slow the tender emotions burgeoning within me, I have compiled the lists gathered by the housekeeper and dedicated my energies toward refurbishing the castle. I have conferred with Mr. Pritchard, who has approved the expenditure and helped me interview a host of artisans and craftsmen to complete the restoration as well as a thorough modernization....

"How is she today?"

Louisa started. Glancing over her shoulder, she saw that Beatrice had come up behind her. Slipping her diary into her pocket, Louisa rose from where she'd been resting in the porch swing.

Folding her arms, she regarded Evie as she sat beneath the trees in the distance. Knowing that the girl would eventually need to return to the castle and leave the cramped confines of the garden house, Louisa had begun to spend a small portion of time each day near the larger house.

At first, Evie had reacted with open hysteria at being

so near the castle. But as the bond of friendship between Louisa and her had strengthened, she'd gradually accepted the fact that she would spend part of her day here.

"She's had a...difficult day."

Louisa's comment was an understatement. The afternoon spent shopping had proved to be the exception to Evie's usual behavior. More and more, she tended to vacillate between being fractious—or even violent—and passive and completely unaware of her surroundings.

Beatrice touched Louisa's shoulder. "You mustn't blame yourself. She's been to the finest physicians possible. She simply...isn't well."

"There must be something we can do. No one should have to live like this."

"Her tonic is a godsend."

But Louisa wasn't completely sure of that. From what she'd seen, the tonic did little to help matters. It merely drugged her enough to make her more manageable.

"I'd like to take her to someone else."

Beatrice shook her head. "There *is* no one else. She's been from Boston to New York. Charles tried everything." Her eyes shimmered with tears as she watched the girl aimlessly pace back and forth among the trees, mumbling to herself and casting fearful glances at the castle. "Her mother was the same way, poor thing."

"What was she like?"

Beatrice wrapped her arms around her waist as if suddenly chilled. "Frightening."

Louisa was shocked by the way her features hardened. "In what way?"

Flushing, Beatrice hastened to explain. "Virginia was a beautiful woman, truly. She was so young when Charles brought her home—all wide-eyed innocence and golden curls." Beatrice stopped, choosing her words carefully. ''I was gone a good deal of the time, but when I returned after Evie had been born, there was a change. She was overly protective of the child, to the point of locking them both in the nursery and refusing to let anyone in. Day by day, things grew worse until...''

Evie's aunt shuddered, biting her lip. ''She used to scream and scream. Charles had to take the baby away from her, but that merely made her more frantic. Then one day...'' A sob burst from her lips and she shook her head, clearly too upset to continue. ''I see the same thing happening to Evie.''

Louisa shook her head, refusing to believe that anything so horrible could ever happen to the girl.

''Are you sure that you don't want to return her to Hildon Hall?''

''No!'' Louisa was horrified that Beatrice could even suggest such a thing. ''I'll arrange for an army of doctors and nurses to come here before I'll ever take her back.''

Intent on escaping Beatrice and her abhorrent suggestion, Louisa turned, planning to rush down the stone stairs that led to the garden, but she found her way blocked by Boyd.

Sure that the man had overheard the conversation, Louisa waited for him to make a cutting remark. But he simply stared at her with dark, hooded eyes before stepping aside to let her pass.

Rushing through the weedy garden to the orchard beyond, Louisa took Evie's hand, urging her to return to the garden house with her.

Louisa would never allow Evie to be taken back to the asylum.

Never.

From that moment on, the rest of the day seemed to go from bad to worse. Evie grew more unsettled by the minute. Her emotions began to seesaw wildly. One moment she was weeping hysterically, the next she laughed and talked to herself in a feverish manner that frightened Louisa. Even Bitsy ran beneath one of the beds and refused to come out.

Alarmed, Louisa finally sent for Evie's doctor, but as the man emerged from the bedroom, he shook his head. "I've given her a sedative to help her sleep through the night."

More drugs. In Louisa's opinion, the last thing Evie needed was something to cloud her mind even more, but she held her tongue.

Her gaze bounced helplessly to John. He stood at the far end of the hallway, his large frame nearly filling the doorway to the kitchen.

"Is there nothing else that we can do?" she asked.

The doctor shook his head. "Evie has always been a delicate, nervous child." He made a tsking noise with his tongue. "I'm afraid that she has required special care since birth—and the demands she makes will only grow, I'm sure." He settled his hat on his head and donned his cloak. "I've left a stronger tonic on the bedside table. Administer it every three hours without fail. Other than that…" He regarded Louisa gravely. "May I be frank with you, Mrs. Winslow?"

"By all means."

"The child will never recover. Never. In my opinion, the best recourse would be to return her to the asylum, where professionals can manage her."

"Manage her?" Louisa stiffened. "Do you call locking a growing child in the attic 'managing' her?"

The doctor sighed. "I would not expect a woman of your delicate breeding to react to the situation with anything other than a soft heart, Mrs. Winslow. But the fact of the matter is that caring for the insane is neither pleasant nor easy.''

''Evie is not insane.''

The doctor eyed her pityingly. ''It is only a matter of time, Mrs. Winslow.''

Louisa drew herself up to her full height. ''I refuse to believe your doomsday predictions.''

''One day you will be forced to believe them. Even you must admit that her condition has deteriorated visibly since her return from Hildon Hall. I must agree with your sister-in-law in begging you to consider Evie's stay here a short holiday.''

Incensed, Louisa gestured to John. ''Thank you for your time, Doctor, as well as your…personal opinion. Mr. Smith will see you to the door.''

The doctor was not so obtuse as to misunderstand that he'd been given his marching orders. Bowing slightly, he gathered his things and strode down the corridor.

It wasn't until she'd heard the click of the door closing that Louisa lost her temper. ''How dare that man say such vile things!'' she hissed aloud as she stormed into the sitting room.

''He is a physician,'' John stated.

''Is he? Is he really? So far, I don't like the kind of medicine that he's peddling, thank you very much. I have always believed that doctors were humanitarians. But what kind of humanitarian would condemn a child to the kind of life she would have in Hildon Hall? He's offered her nothing, nothing at all.''

''There is the tonic.''

Louisa hissed in disapproval. ''Frankly, I'm beginning to wonder about the harm such a powerful medicine could have over time. I don't even know what is contained in the brew! The doctor insisted the ingredients were a secret concoction that had not yet been patented, so he refused to give me any details at all.''

John was watching her carefully. "So what do you want to do?''

Biting her lip, Louisa came to a stop in front of the window. Rather than seeing the blackness outside, she saw her reflection, and behind her, that of John.

"I want to take her to another doctor.''

"According to Beatrice, Evie has seen every specialist.''

Louisa's throat grew thick with tears as logic wrestled with instinct within her.

"I don't care,'' she finally said, her voice gruff with emotion. "I refuse to accept the fact that nothing can be done. I—I won't have Evie sent back to…to that place.…''

In an instant, John was turning her toward him, his arms folding her against his chest as she wept openly. "Shh, shh, we'll find someone.''

She gazed up at him through her tears. "We?''

"Yes, we.'' John's thumb gently wiped the moisture from her cheeks. "You aren't the only one who is upset by the thought of sending her back to that place.''

For long moments, Louisa could only stare at him, basking in the warmth she saw in his eyes. She found it amazing that, of all the people who should care about Evie's future, the person to give her the most support was someone outside of Evie's family.

"Why would you help me?''

His expression grew so still, so intent, that she trembled. "Don't you know?''

She shook her head.

His eyes narrowed, his gaze focusing on her lips. Softly, gently, he traced his thumb over the fullness.

"I've grown quite fond of you, Louisa Haversham Winslow."

It took every ounce of strength for her to keep from melting into his arms then and there. He cared for her—moreover, he'd been willing to voice his feelings, something she never would have expected of the great John Smith.

In that moment, the last of her defenses tumbled and she was left open and vulnerable. When had John ceased to be her adversary? When had he become her closest ally, her...

Her what? Their relationship had grown much too personal for employer and employee. How should she describe it?

Louisa instantly shied away from calling him a beau; the term was far too childish. And yet to refer to him as a lover was not quite true.

Even if she wanted to become his lover.

The thought shocked Louisa to her very core. Her hands clutched fistfuls of his shirt and she stood in indecision, wondering if she should push him away or bring him closer.

How could she have allowed this to happen? How could she have let her feelings for John grow so... personal? For they were personal. In fact, if she dared to probe her emotions, she knew she would have to admit that she was more than slightly in love with her bodyguard. She had grown so attuned to his vitality and power that she had begun to rely on him with much the same intensity that a flower needed rain.

Resting her head on his chest, she closed her eyes, listening to the beating of his heart.

What was she going to do? It would be the height of impropriety for her to suddenly marry her bodyguard.

Louisa's eyes squeezed shut in horror at the reaction her highbrow neighbors might have at the news. Even after a suitable period of mourning had passed, she would cause plenty of scandal by marrying an employee....

But wasn't she presuming far too much? Louisa stiffened, pushing away from John. There had been no mention of marriage, no mention of love, merely a growing fondness. True, they had exchanged fervent kisses and stolen embraces, but she had no guarantees that John was in love with her.

When she looked up, she discovered that he was watching her closely. Embarrassed, she prayed that he had not been able to read her thoughts. If he had...

"I do care for you, Louisa. More than you will ever know."

Before she could respond, he bent down, his lips softly caressing hers. But when she would have lifted on tiptoe to deepen the embrace, he stepped back, his hands circling her wrists and drawing them away from his neck.

"No," he murmured softly.

"But—"

"If I kiss you, Louisa, I won't stop." He waited for his pronouncement to sink in before continuing. "When we make love, it will be for all of the right reasons, not because you are worried or sad or lonely. It will be because you want it as much as I do."

She opened her mouth, then closed it again, knowing that he was right. There was still enough of the Puritan in her to make her balk at lovemaking without commitment.

Silence filled the room around them, a sticky, uncomfortable silence fraught with might-have-beens. Then, when Louisa was sure she could not bear it any longer, John nodded in her direction and said, "I'll be on the porch if you need me."

Within seconds, she was left alone with her whirling thoughts. Yet, through it all—her worry over Evie, her distrust of the doctor, her weariness and her inner angst—one thought stood out.

He loves me.

John Smith loves me.

Chapter Eighteen

The next day Neil stood in the shadow of a tree, watching as Louisa directed an army of gardeners in how best to plot out the formal rose garden at the rear of the house.

"What have you discovered?"

"Nothin' you'll be wantin' t'hear." Tucker shook his head. "Matter of fact, it wasn't difficult fer Parker t'get the information. Seems folks are more than willin' to gossip about Charles Winslow and his poor unfortunate brides."

Neil felt a prickling of warning slither up his spine. When Albert Parker had joined them, Neil had sent him nosing around the community to gather information.

"Go on."

"Seems the first Mrs. Winslow died in childbirth."

"Sad, but hardly unusual."

"Ahh, but it gets better." Tucker nodded his head in Evie's direction. "The girl's mother managed to live nearly three years after marrying Winslow. Then she went mad and committed suicide."

Neil winced. "So the…condition Evie suffers afflicted her mother as well?"

"So it 'ppears. Accordin' to reports, the woman was fragile from the start, but as time went on, she became overly emotional. She would scream about how her joints ached. She would tear her hair out in fistfuls and scratch at her skin until it bled. One day she couldn't take the torment any longer and she leaped from the roof of the castle. Some say that Evie witnessed the suicide and she's never been right since."

Neil stared up, up to the battlements, suddenly understanding Evie's reluctance to live in the place.

"What about the other wives?"

Tucker shook his head. "Bad luck plagued them all. The third one died in a riding accident, and the fourth after an extended illness. She all but wasted away in bed."

Neil's unease deepened. At that moment, he would have liked nothing better than to carry Louisa away from this house, but she was already too deeply embroiled in her role as lady of the manor for such a thing to occur.

"So what are you goin' t'do, Cap'n?"

Neil inhaled, holding the air in his lungs before releasing it slowly. "I don't know. But I think it's time we hired some men to help us."

"Y'think something's going t'happen?"

"I don't have any doubts."

Neil had spoken the truth to Tucker. With each day that passed, his worry increased—and not just because of the aura of imminent danger that he could sense in the air around him. No, what worried him even more was that he was starting to believe Louisa might never consent to leave Boston and become his wife.

As he watched her overseeing the flower beds and the placement of rose bushes, it was clear that she was enjoying her life as a woman of society. She had every luxury that a woman could ask for—money, servants, fine clothing, good food. She had the pleasures of Boston a short drive away and the privacy of the walled Winslow estates when she wished to remain apart from the bustle of the world.

What could possibly entreat her to exchange everything for life on the frontier? And as comfortable as Neil's house might be, it wasn't a castle by any stretch of the imagination.

As for her possible pregnancy…

Was he three times a fool? With each day that passed, the thought of a baby worried him less, because he could no longer ignore the fact that he loved Louisa.

His lips twitched in the barest semblance of a smile as he watched her bend over a delicate peach-colored bloom. The silky texture of the rose paled compared to the beauty of Louisa's skin. Indeed, he was sure that the blossom's petals could never be as soft as Louisa's cheek.

Resting his hand against the pillar of the porch, he admitted to himself that he was totally besotted. The emotion was completely new to him and even more disturbing because of its intensity. True, he'd enjoyed the company of women on more than one occasion. He'd even fancied himself in love once or twice. But now that he had experienced the true depth of caring, he realized that he'd never really known what it meant to be in love.

He had only to look at Louisa for his pulse to quicken. But more than that, he felt each of her emotions as his own. When she ached, he ached. When she laughed, he experienced her joy. He *knew* this woman and her character, in a way that went beyond outer trappings. He knew what gave her joy and what regrets lingered in her heart. She was a good woman, a caring individual. She had an infinite capacity to inspire the best in others…including himself.

If Louisa had encountered trouble in England and her virtue was compromised, Neil didn't care. He would help her to see that the incident meant nothing to him. He would raise her child as his own.

A few evenings later, Louisa settled heavily onto the porch swing. Her body was weary and her head throbbed.

She'd had another trying day with Evie. The girl had alternated between being dazed and glassy-eyed, and violent.

Louisa rubbed her temples, wondering what had happened to make Evie so angry. Even the sight of her beloved doll hadn't been able to calm her. Louisa had barely managed to save the toy from destruction.

She sighed. Unfortunately, a good many of the ironstone dishes hadn't fared so well. Evie had nearly emptied the cupboards, smashing the stoneware onto the floor and throwing it against the walls before John had been able to restrain her.

Unfortunately, it was Evie's latest outburst that had forced Louisa to concede to at least one of Beatrice's suggestions. Tomorrow they would all move back into the castle. Once there, Louisa would have a full staff to help her with the girl—as well as a nursery suite, which had been updated and carefully furnished with Evie's "special needs" in mind.

So why did Louisa feel as if she'd failed the girl? Why did she feel as if she were abandoning Evie?

Her only comfort lay in the fact that John had located a physician who specialized in "nervous ailments."

Louisa had arranged for him to examine Evie at the end of the week.

Pushing at the floorboards with her toe, Louisa set the swing in motion, hoping that the gentle swaying would ease the tension gripping her muscles.

As she pondered the upcoming doctor's visit and her stepdaughter's decline, Louisa decided that, come morning, she wouldn't force Evie to take her tonic anymore. The new dosage only seemed to aggravate the girl—indeed, her newfound aggression could be directly linked to the hour preceding her next dose.

Several times, Louisa had noted that delaying the tonic caused Evie to grow more and more volatile and agitated. But on the other hand, her eyes lost their glassy sheen and she seemed to grow more coherent.

Perhaps the tonic no longer agreed with her. In any event, Louisa hoped the new doctor could offer some alternate methods of treatment.

As for herself, Louisa feared she was working too hard and worrying too much. Her nights had become sleepless and her body ached with weariness, despite her efforts to rest. But what concerned her most was her inability to concentrate. She felt as if she were moving in a fog, sleepwalking through her days and pacing the floor all night. Worse yet, her nervous stomach was a constant affliction. She was unable to eat anything more than the tiniest portions of bread or soup. If not for the calming effects of Beatrice's hot chocolate, she didn't know what she would have done. She was swiftly losing weight—so much so that she knew her physical state was attracting far too much attention from John Smith. She knew it was only a matter of time before he forced her to see a doctor herself.

Sighing deeply, she supposed that maybe she should

see someone. Heaven only knew she hadn't been feeling well since her arrival in America. If only…

Not for the first time, she wished there was someone to talk to. She had written at least a dozen letters to Phoebe, sending them to be mailed via one of the groomsmen, but she had yet to receive an answer. She would have given anything to have a friend to converse with. Even writing in her diary failed to clear her thoughts. More and more she discovered that she didn't have the energy to put pen to paper—and her dreams of becoming a novelist had been put on the back burner.

Sadly, she realized that in severing her ties to her old life, she had not taken into account how much she would miss her correspondence with Neil Ballard. She had grown so used to pouring out her sorrows and triumphs on paper. She truly missed the comfort and advice that her friend had offered on countless occasions.

But he was lost to her now. She had chosen this life rather than the one he would have offered her.

"Problems?"

Her eyes flew open. John stood with his shoulder resting against one of the porch supports.

How long had he been there? How long had he been watching her?

She couldn't bring herself to answer him.

"You look tired," he said when the silence grew fraught with awareness.

"Yes. Yes, I'm tired. But that's to be expected, I suppose. I spent most of the day getting the north wing of the castle ready so that we could move in tomorrow morning. It's a good sign, I think. When I showed Evie where she would be staying, she actually grew excited about having a larger room and her own water closet."

So why did Louisa feel as if she wanted to burst into tears?

"You're doing too much, Louisa."

She shook her head. "I'm not doing enough."

"You can't right years of injustices in a few weeks."

Was that what he thought she was doing? Making things "right" for Evie?

With a sigh, Louisa realized that he was correct. She felt a moral obligation to the girl. She wanted to erase Charles's indifference and the years of abuse in the asylum. But would she ever really be able to do that?

"She's my responsibility."

"But she's not your child."

Louisa shrugged. "She may not be blood of my blood, but I already care deeply for her."

"Why? Because you were commanded to oversee her future?"

"It's more than that. This may have started because of the stipulations made in Charles's will, but soon after meeting Evie I began to care for her."

"But she isn't your child," John insisted again.

"Does that matter?" She bit her lip before whispering, "There was a time when I was sure that I would never marry and have children of my own. Now that I am experiencing the joys and tribulations of parenthood, I am discovering that there is nothing so wonderful—or so terrifying—as to have someone look to you for their every need."

"So you like being a mother?"

Her smile was rueful. "Yes, I suppose I do."

"And Evie is to be only the first of many?"

Louisa shrugged, wondering at the intent of his question. Was he suggesting that he…that they…that the two of them might one day have a child? Together? Or was he merely speaking rhetorically?

Suddenly too weary to deal with the complexities of the conversation, Louisa stood. "I'd best be retiring myself," she murmured softly.

As she brushed past him, he offered silkily, "Yes, you'd better...or there's no accounting for what might happen."

Dearest Diary,
We have moved back into the castle and I do not know how I am going to bear living here. The moment I stepped inside the door, I felt as if a heavy weight pressed into my chest.

The workmen have done remarkably well in the short amount of time they've had, but there is still so much for them to do. At least some of the mustiness has been banished by the cleaning. I...

I'm still not feeling well. What is happening to me? More than anything, I want to curl up in bed and sleep, but I can't. Too many people are depending on me.

I still have not heard from Phoebe. I'm so worried. What is she doing now?

How, oh, how I sometimes wish that I could see Neil just once. How is he? If he were to know how I treated him, could he ever forgive me?

As Louisa settled her diary in her bureau and stood, she was suddenly overcome with a wave of dizziness.

Dear sweet heaven above, what was wrong with her? Sweat beaded her skin even as she was racked with chills.

Had she caught a bug? Or was it something more

serious? Except for her nervous stomach, she'd rarely been ill.

As she struggled to catch her breath, she knew that she should seek medical attention as soon as possible, but she hesitated to do such a thing. Not because she feared doctors, but because she hated to show such a blatant sign of weakness.

Especially with Boyd nearby.

Boyd was clearly displeased at having the women move back into the castle, but he had yet to say anything. As Louisa and Beatrice lingered over hot cups of cocoa in the parlor, he'd entered the room, unaware of their presence until he'd come too far to gracefully retreat. Once he'd realized his mistake, he had glowered briefly at them both, then retrieved his newspaper, a cup of coffee and a handful of cookies, before retreating again, all without comment.

Louisa prayed that his actions meant a truce was imminent.

The waves of dizziness returned again. Closing her eyes, Louisa released the buttons of her bodice and stumbled in the direction of the balcony.

Air. She needed some air.

Her legs trembled as she stepped onto the balcony and reached for the wrought-iron balustrade. But as she rested her full weight against the railing, the moorings suddenly pulled free.

A scream ripped from her throat even as she clutched the iron with all her might. Sure that she was caught in the grips of a horrible nightmare, she watched as the world spun sickeningly. Then her arms felt as if they would be ripped from the sockets as the balcony grillwork slammed into the wall, being held in place by a single set of screws.

More screams ripped from her throat, and just when she thought she couldn't hold on for another second, John appeared above her.

"Hold on, Louisa! Hold on!"

Sobbing, she clenched her teeth, using every last ounce of strength she could summon, until John's strong hand grabbed her wrist.

She saw the muscles of his arm tremble and strain as he lifted her, inch by inch. Finally he hauled her back to safety with a rush that took her breath away.

For long moments, they clung to one another in panic and relief. Louisa wrapped her arms tightly around his neck, absorbing the frantic rhythm of his heart and the strident measure of his breathing.

What would she have done without him? He'd saved her life!

As their terror subsided, their awareness bloomed. Louisa didn't know who made the first move or who surrendered. She only knew that in the space of a heart beat, they were kissing, their embrace fierce, their emotions unfettered. When he reached for the rest of the buttons to her gown, she did not resist. Her own hands were trembling as she stripped his shirt from his shoulders.

When John drew her own bodice away, she felt the chill against the bare skin of her shoulders. She shuddered as his hands, large and callused, grazed her back, then slid down the length of her corset.

"You are so beautiful," he murmured into the hollow of her throat.

"No."

"Yes, yes. I've never seen a woman so vibrant. So passionate, so loving, so seductive."

Her laughter was rueful. "Then you've clearly been blinded by love."

"No. I'm seeing clearly." He drew back, framing her face in his hands. "You've changed me, Louisa."

When she tried to shake her head, he kissed her again, then trailed his lips over her cheek, down the curve of her throat to the sensitive hollow between her collarbones.

"I've never felt like this with any other person before. It doesn't even matter to me that you're pregnant. I only know that I—"

Louisa's blood turned to ice and the sensual spell that had filled her body with an enervating energy swiftly drained away.

Pregnant?

"Pregnant!" She uttered the word aloud.

When he straightened, she could only gape at him in horror.

John thought that she was pregnant?

Ice seemed to flow through her veins and she woodenly took a step back, then another and another until she'd put several yards between them.

"You think that I'm pregnant?"

His expression became guarded. "Aren't you?"

"What would make you think such a thing?"

He waved a hand helplessly. "It's the only explanation for the way you're always huddled over the chamber pot."

She stiffened in fury. "I can assure you there are many other reasons for my apparent malady, none of which will result in the birth of a child."

Suddenly, the ramifications of his belief hit her like a slap in the face. Not only did John think she was a woman of loose character, he also believed that she had wed a man without informing her husband of her condition.

"Get out," she said softly.

"Louisa, you have to understand—"

"I already understand more than I care to." She shuddered as the full impact continued to seep into her consciousness. John was no better than any of the others. He'd judged her by her appearance and had decided that she was a wanton woman. Worse yet, she had fallen into his arms like a ripe apple.

"Leave my house. Now."

"Louisa—"

When he tried to take her in his arms, she ran to her bedside table, removing the derringer that he had given her so long ago.

"I want you out of this house and off my property within ten minutes or I'll summon a constable. Whatever obligations you feel you had toward my husband are finished. If I catch sight of you ever again, I'll have you charged, do you understand?"

"Damn it, you were nearly killed!"

She gave a scoffing laugh. "Don't you dare turn an accident caused by the disrepair of this building into something for your own gain. I'm through with listening to you, do you hear? I don't believe there ever was a threat against me—and frankly, if there is, I don't care. I simply want you gone!"

He opened his mouth, clearly intent on arguing. But at the last moment, he apparently changed his mind. Turning on his heel, he strode from the room.

As soon as he was gone, Louisa sank to her knees, her body shaking convulsively. Dear sweet heaven above, was she forever doomed to being treated badly by men? Was there something in her character that made them think she could be so ill-used? Or that she could be so lacking in moral fiber? Was it merely the color of her hair? The fullness of her figure? Or was there something more, something buried deep in her character, something lacking in her spirit?

Heartache gripped her chest like a crushing vise. Sobs shook her body, making her sick and feverish and weak.

For the first time since coming to America, she actually regretted the fact that she hadn't chosen a simpler life and married her childhood friend.

Chapter Nineteen

When Louisa awakened the following morning, she still didn't feel well. The aches and pains she'd experienced for days had intensified. Added to that were the strained muscles in her shoulders and arms from having John pull her back through the window.

Shuddering, she tried not to remember her near-fatal accident. Today she would meet with the workmen and insist that each of the railings be tested thoroughly.

Sighing, Louisa forced herself to swing her legs over the side of the bed. Her head swam with dizziness and she was forced to sit hunched over until the sensation passed.

More than anything, she wished she could spend the day in bed. But since this would be her first full morning at Winslow Manor, she wanted to ensure that everyone present knew she was in charge. She mustn't show a hint of weakness—not when she was about to live so closely with Boyd and his disapproval.

Standing, she steadied herself against the bedpost, then crossed to her dressing table. Sinking onto the cushioned seat, she wished that she found her reflection more encouraging. In her opinion, there was nothing worse than a redhead who wasn't feeling well. Her skin was deathly pale. Dark circles were carved beneath her eyes and her cheeks were gaunt.

Ringing the bell that would summon Chloe from the neighboring rooms, Louisa took the brush and began to stroke her hair. But when she looked down to see tufts tangled in the bristles, she gasped. Dropping the brush, she ran her fingers through the tresses, thcn offered a horrified cry when many of the strands came free in her grasp.

Louisa's eyes filled with tears. Horror swept through her body. What was happening to her? For days now she'd tried to convince herself that it was merely the strain of arriving in America or in assuming the duties of her new family that had affected her health. But she knew now that there was far more to her condition. Something was wrong, terribly wrong.

A knock sounded at the door and she struggled to assume a blank face. "Come in."

But it wasn't Chloe who stood on the other side. John Smith stood in the doorway, his trunk slung over his shoulder, his rifle in his hand.

"I came to offer my goodbyes."

She steeled herself against the instantaneous joy that had rushed through her at the sight of him.

Remember what he's done to you. Remember what he's been thinking of you all along.

"I believe I made my views quite clear when I told you to leave last night, Mr. Smith."

"Since I don't have a horse of my own, I had to wait for someone from the staff to take me into Boston."

It was a weak excuse at best, but Louisa didn't bother to point out that fact. It would require more energy than she had.

"Goodbye, then."

Her spine remained ramrod straight, despite the effort it cost her, but John didn't immediately leave.

"I thought I'd ask you to reconsider and let me stay."

The idea was tempting, so tempting, but Louisa managed to answer firmly, "I don't think such an arrangement would ever work out, Mr. Smith."

"Then come with me."

His audacity caused her mouth to fall open. He wanted *her* to go with *him?* To drop her life and her responsibilities and run away with a man who had…who had…

Who had treated her no better than any of the other men she'd encountered in England.

No. She wouldn't deign to consider the idea. Her only real mistake had been in falling in love with this man.

So why was she so tempted to accept his offer? Why did every instinct in her body urge her to run into his arms and leave this place now?

"I don't think I would care to do that, Mr. Smith."

Liar.

"Then at least promise me that you'll see a doctor. You look like hell."

"Perhaps the strain of an imagined pregnancy is catching up with me."

He had the grace to flush. "I'm sorry about that. I jumped to conclusions when I should have come to you personally."

She tipped her chin, giving him her best haughty stare. "Perhaps your first mistake was in presuming *anything* of a personal nature about me, Mr. Smith."

Rather than responding to her comment, he said again, "Promise me that you'll see a doctor."

"I hardly see how my health is any of your affair."

"Promise me."

She pressed her lips together. As much as she might wish for the opinion of a physician, she knew now wasn't the time. She mustn't appear weak. Not yet. Not until Boyd had learned to accept her and Beatrice didn't rely so heavily on Louisa to oversee the refurbishment of the castle. And then there was Evie...

Evie needed Louisa, and Louisa had made it her goal to bring the girl's properties back to fruition.

"Goodbye, Mr. Smith."

He turned as if to leave, then stopped. Dropping his trunk to the floor, he crossed the room in a half dozen quick strides. Before she could react, he'd cupped her head in his hand and bent to place a searing kiss on her lips. Then, without another word, he released her and closed the door behind him.

"Mr. Smith! This just arrived for you."

The last thing that John wanted was to be delayed as he left the Winslow estates. After his row with Louisa the night before, he'd made his peace with himself. He would be leaving this place—and Louisa—without a backward glance. She was the one who had chosen this life and it was now up to her to see it through. The time had long since come for him to return to Oregon and wash his hands of the whole affair.

"Mr. Smith?"

Sighing, he stopped at the bottom of the stairs and turned.

"Yes?"

The maid curtsied and handed him a familiar envelope. "Telegram, sir."

As he took the message in his hand, Neil felt a familiar surge of foreboding—and with it came the realization that his association with Louisa Haversham Winslow was not over yet.

Neil's knock on the door of the honeymoon suite of the Plymouth Hotel had barely faded away before the door swung wide and he found himself staring into a pair of eyes that were oh, so familiar.

Dear heaven above, Louisa and her sister were incredibly similar in build and coloring. But in looking at Phoebe, Neil was forced to acknowledge just how sick Louisa had become. Compared to her sister, she now looked gaunt and pale—a mere shadow of her twin.

"Mr. Ballard! How good of you to come so quickly."

"Miss…" He paused, wondering just what to call her. This was the true Louisa Haversham, but he knew her as Phoebe Gray.

"Mrs. Cutter," she said with a small smile. "For now, I think that's the most logical solution, don't you?"

"Yes, ma'am."

He swept the hat from his head and stepped into the hotel suite.

As if on cue, the far door swung wide and Gabe Cutter stepped into the room. He'd been swiping shaving cream from his chin, but at the sight of Neil he threw the towel onto a settee and strode forward.

"Ballard. It's good to see you."

Neil nodded in his direction. "Your telegram stated that you had information concerning Horace Haversham."

Gabe crossed to a table where a holster and revolver had been folded next to a pair of saddlebags. "That's right. Horace Haversham is on his way to Boston—as is Oscar."

"The two of them?"

"That's right."

Neil shook his head, his mind whirling. Throughout his stint as Louisa's bodyguard he'd continually wondered why there had been no attempts on her life.

A rustle of skirts caught his attention. "How is my sister, Mr. Ballard?" Cutter's wife asked.

"She's fine…that is—" He broke off, his mind still focused on the information Gabe had given him. "You're sure that both of the Haversham men are on their way to Boston?"

"They should arrive within days of each other. From what I was able to determine, Horace booked passage on a steam sloop, but Oscar is only a few days behind."

"So Horace is planning something. And he wants his brother to be here when it happens."

Phoebe clasped her hands together. "That's the same conclusion we came to a few days ago. That's why we altered our plans and came here immediately."

"Have there been any attempts on my sister-in-law's life?" Cutter asked.

Neil shook his head. "None whatsoever."

Gabe strapped the holster to his hips. "Then I think it's safe to say that Horace must be planning to make his move as soon as Oscar arrives."

Neil looked at the man in amazement. "How did you get all of this information? I thought you'd left Oregon and were planning a leisurely trip east."

"We were." Phoebe and her husband exchanged glances. "Until another attempt was made on my life."

Gabe's expression grew fierce. "With the help of some friends of mine, we were able to track down the man responsible. Before his…unfortunate demise, he had the forethought to confess everything he knew."

Neil had no doubt that Gabe had managed to wrestle the admission from the man himself.

"Apparently Oscar Haversham hired a man named Phillip Badger to oversee his plots. It was Badger who hired the first assassin sent to kill my wife. When he didn't receive a report from his henchman, he arranged for a second man to complete the job."

"The same gunman who offered his confession to you."

"That's right."

"What about Louisa? Did he have any information on the plans made against her?"

"No, but he did offer me Badger's address. It's right here in Boston."

Neil felt a hot wave of anger rush through him, followed by an icy chill of determination. "Where is he?"

Gabe gestured toward Neil's pistols. "Are they loaded?"

"Yes."

"Then why don't you and I find ourselves some mounts and have a chat with Mr. Badger."

"On three," Gabe said with a grin.

Neil wasn't even willing to wait that long. "Three!" he called out, lifting his foot and bringing it smashing down on the doorknob.

The force splintered the lock, causing the door to fly open and bounce against the opposite wall. Within seconds, the two men were inside the hotel room, guns drawn.

A pair of figures sprang up from the bed, one a woman who clutched a blanket in front of her and screamed. The male reached for the nightstand, but before he could retrieve the pistol that lay there, Neil had grabbed him by the hair and placed the muzzle of his own revolver at his temple.

"Don't give me an excuse to shoot."

The man held his arms out, his hands wide.

"Where is he?"

"Wh-who?"

"Horace Haversham."

Badger closed his mouth, pressing his lips together mutinously, but when Neil pulled back the hammer, he sagged against him.

"H-he's arriving in Boston later this afternoon."

"Did he hire you to kill Phoebe Gray?" Gabe snarled.

Badger dared a slight nod. "I was to arrange it."

"So you hired a henchman to follow her west?"

"Yes. Some old fellow who was making the voyage on the same ship said he'd do it for me."

"He wasn't successful, was he?"

"No. When he didn't report, I contacted an old friend to look into things."

"Then you hired him to kill Phoebe Gray, didn't you?"

Badger didn't reply, but it was obvious that Gabe had guessed correctly.

This time it was Gabe who grabbed a fistful of the man's hair and yanked his head up.

"Anyone else?"

"N-no! He's an ace tracker. I figured he could take care of the job!"

"Well, you thought wrong," Gabe growled. "He's facedown in the Snake River right now—that is, if the wolves haven't already picked his bones clean."

Badger paled.

"What about the other sister?"

"I don't know what you—"

Neil dug his revolver into the man's skin, making him cry out. "We haven't got time for your lies. Tell us what we need to know and tell us now!"

Badger licked his lips. "Originally she was supposed to be taken care of quickly, but Haversham changed his mind. He didn't want her dead until he could get to Boston."

"Who?" Neil growled. "Who did you get to do the job?"

Badger began to laugh. "You'd never expect a woman to do the job, would you?"

"Who?" Neil shouted.

Badger's face contorted into a grimace of rage. "Go to hell. Do you think you scare me? I'm a dead man anyway. I knew that the minute Haversham said he was coming to Boston. Do you think he's going to leave any witnesses to his plots?" He laughed bitterly. "The man is feeding on rage, don't you see? He won't last until his brother and his nieces are dead. Then he'll turn on the rest of us!"

Without warning, Badger lunged toward the table, grasping his revolver. Before either Gabe or Neil could react, he turned the pistol on himself and fired.

Louisa clasped her hands together as Dr. Browne opened the door of Evie's bedroom. Bitsy— who'd been banished from the room for the examination—went racing back to the bedside of her beloved Evie.

"How is she?"

Gesturing to Louisa, Browne ushered her into the adjoining sitting room and motioned for her to take a seat.

"I'm very concerned about your stepdaughter, Mrs. Winslow."

Louisa's grip tightened so fiercely that her knuckles turned white.

"Can you help her?"

He nodded. "Yes, I think so. But…" He took a place on the settee beside Louisa and reached out to cover her hands with his in a comforting paternal gesture. "Mrs. Winslow, what exactly do you know about your stepdaughter's condition?"

Louisa's shoulders rose in a helpless shrug. "Very little, I'm afraid. I've been told that her mother went mad. Some say that Evie witnessed her mother's suicide," she began.

When she'd finished relating what she knew, Dr. Browne patted her hand, then leaned back in the settee. Stroking his goatee, he seemed to digest the information, then stood.

"I'd like your permission to take Evie's tonic with me. Before I offer a diagnosis, I need to make a few tests to see what the tonic contains."

Louisa's heart pounded in her chest. "Yes, of course. Do you think she's been improperly treated?"

Browne took a deep breath and held up a cautioning hand. "As I said, I would like to study the liquid before I make a definite statement on the matter, but from my preliminary exam, I would say that your daughter displays all of the symptoms of being drugged, and quite heavily."

"Drugged?" Louisa echoed weakly. "But the medicine was prescribed by her physician."

Browne shook his head woefully. "Many of the medicines being prescribed as miracle cures are mere quackery concocted in back-room laboratories." When Louisa would have spoken, he held up a silencing hand. "I'll say no more on the matter until I can investigate things more conclusively. In the meantime, I want you to watch Evie carefully. If she has been drugged over an extended period, she may show a serious reaction in the next few days—fever, delirium, agitation. If she gives any of these symptoms, contact me immediately.''

''Yes, Doctor.''

''I'd also like to see her gain a few pounds. She's far too weak and slight for her age. Broths are the ticket until she asks for something more specific.''

Louisa stood. ''I'll collect her tonic for you.''

Slipping into Evie's room, she paused only momentarily to tuck the blankets more securely around her chest and brush a strand of hair from her forehead. Then she took the bottle and returned to the sitting room.

''I'm afraid I don't have any of the original medication. This is the dosage that Evie's physician prescribed a few days ago.''

Dr. Browne took the bottle from her hand, removed the stopper and sniffed. Other than grunting softly to himself, he made no comment, but slipped the bottle into his jacket pocket and grasped his bag and his hat.

''I'll see myself out, Mrs. Winslow. No need to trouble yourself.'' He winked. ''It appears to me that you could use a dose of beef broth yourself. Don't be worrying yourself sick about the little lady. We'll get to the bottom of her malady, I promise.''

The clock in the hall was striking noon when Louisa heard a soft clanking noise. Looking up, she saw that Beatrice had come into the nursery to relieve her. The noise was from the chatelaine suspended from her waist.

''You look in need of a breath of fresh air,'' she commented, taking Louisa's needlework from her hands and tugging her to her feet. ''I absolutely forbid you to return

to this room until you've had something to eat and some
fresh air.''

''Y-yes, I...''

Fresh air.

A sudden thought popped into Louisa's brain. She had
no one watching over her shoulder, no one to tell her
what she could or could not do. Why wasn't she taking
advantage of the fact?

''If you don't mind, Beatrice, I think I'll take a short
drive into town. I'm in need of more embroidery floss
as well as some other notions.''

''Go. Have a good time.''

Needing no other bidding, Louisa hurried from the
room with a rustle of skirts. John Smith might have been
the bane of her existence for the past few weeks, but
he'd also done her a favor. He'd taught her to drive a
carriage. Today she intended to use that fact to her own
advantage. As soon as she arrived in Boston, she'd stop
at the telegraph office. Since her letters had probably not
arrived yet, she desperately wanted to get a message to
Phoebe Gray.

''Chloe!'' she called out as she entered her own apartments. ''Chloe, I need your help in changing into my
visiting attire.''

Louisa was just descending the front steps to the waiting carriage when the noise of a team and the faint scent
of dust caused her to look up.

''Blast and bother,'' she muttered under her breath
when Grover Pritchard came into view.

''Good morning, Mrs. Winslow!''

''Mr. Pritchard.'' Not wishing to be forced into returning to the house to pay court to the officious solic-

itor, she continued to tug on her gloves. "I pray you haven't come looking for me to conduct business."

"No, no." He held up a basket filled with a nosegay of flowers and art supplies. "I heard Miss Evie was feeling under the weather, so I brought her a little something to cheer her up."

"How thoughtful of you. I was just about to go into Boston for an appointment, but Beatrice is sitting with Evie. I'm sure she can help you."

Pritchard's face fell. During the past few visits, he'd made it clear that he would be willing to make their relationship far more personal. Louisa had purposely ignored the overtures, knowing that to give the man any encouragement, no matter how slight, would merely lead to awkwardness.

"If you'd care to wait a moment, Mrs. Winslow, I'd be happy to take you into Boston myself. I could bring you back later this afternoon—perhaps after a spot of lunch."

Louisa took her handkerchief from her reticule, gazed at Pritchard mournfully, then whispered in a voice that she hoped sounded choked with emotion, "What a dear, dear man. Truly, Mr. Pritchard, your friendship touches my heart." She sighed heavily. "But I'm afraid that I'm feeling rather melancholy today. I thought I would pick a few wildflowers and visit Charles's grave on my way." She held the handkerchief to her lips and paused as if struggling for control, "You'll forgive me if I wish to make the pilgrimage alone."

Grover Pritchard paled, clearly worried that he'd overstepped his bounds. "Oh! But of course...I wouldn't dream...!"

He hurried to help Louisa step into the wagon. As he handed her the whip, he suddenly beamed. "Bless my soul! I have a piece of news that will brighten your day, and I nearly forgot to pass it on.''

Louisa prayed the man wouldn't take too much longer. She really was anxious to get to the telegraph office.

''Your father has changed his mind about traveling to Italy for his health.''

Louisa waited, wondering why such news was supposed to prove so meaningful to her.

Pritchard paused dramatically before saying, ''He's decided to come here instead! To visit you!''

Louisa's blood immediately turned to ice.

Oscar Haversham was coming here? *Here?*

Dear sweet heaven above, what was she going to do now?

Chapter Twenty

Every muscle in Louisa's body urged her to flee—now! She had to leave this place before the marquis arrived and her masquerade was revealed.

Granted, she and her friend Phoebe were quite similar in appearance, but a father would know the difference immediately. He would recognize her as the woman he'd hired to accompany his daughter to America.

Her stomach heaved and she felt suddenly unsteady.

"Mrs. Winslow?"

She waved aside Pritchard's concern and the hand he'd put out to help her.

"I'm fine. I'm just...overjoyed with the news. I'll have to pick up a few of ...Papa's favorites while I'm in Boston, to help him feel at home."

Pritchard was eyeing her strangely, but she ignored the man. Climbing into the carriage, she prayed that she could make her way to the edge of the Winslow estates before she became deathly ill. Only after she was out of sight would she dare to stop the buggy.

Settling the woolen rug over her skirts absentmindedly, she urged the horse into a walk, and then, once she'd rounded the drive and was nearly out of sight of the house, a trot.

What was she going to do? What was she going to do?

As much as she might want to ride into Boston and never come back, she knew she couldn't leave Evie. Not now, when the girl was at her most defenseless. Nor could she take the girl away when Dr. Browne felt that he might be on the verge of a diagnosis. If Louisa left, she was afraid that either Boyd or Beatrice would be tempted to return the girl to the asylum, since both of them doubted that anything more could be done for the child.

What could she do?

Now more than ever, Louisa knew that she needed to contact her friend in Oregon. Hopefully, Phoebe would have a solution to the dilemma.

The journey to Boston was made in a daze. Once at the station, Louisa found a gaggle of boys waiting near the boardwalk for the opportunity to carry baggage into the station for pennies. Offering one of them a dollar, she asked him to watch her horse while she went into the telegraph office.

Once inside, it took only a moment to send the message, pleading for Phoebe's help and advice. Louisa was turning to leave the establishment, her mind still focused on the thought of Oscar Haversham suddenly appearing on her doorstep, when she accidentally ran headlong into another patron.

"Excuse me, I…"

Whatever she'd been about to say slipped away as she stared up, up, up into the piercing gaze of John Smith.

"Oh."

He didn't speak, merely took her by the elbow and

led her outside. Tossing a handful of coins to the boys who huddled near her buggy, he lifted her bodily onto the bench, then climbed up beside her. Within seconds, they were barreling down the lane.

"You shouldn't be here," John stated gruffly.

Louisa knew that she should stiffen in indignation, berate the man for his high-handedness and demand that he leave her alone, but she was so tired. So, so tired.

"Have you been following me?"

"No. One of my men followed you."

"Your men?"

"I've had two men watching the property since we arrived in Boston."

"I see." Again Louisa supposed that she should rail against John for failing to inform her of such precautions, but she couldn't. Nor could she control the jolt of joy she experienced when she realized that John had not left her completely alone even after she'd forced him off the property.

"How are you, Louisa?"

Ill. I am truly ill and there is no one I can turn to for help.

A faintness was stealing over her. Her head ached abominably and she couldn't seem to think. She didn't even resist when John pulled her tightly against him, resting her cheek on his chest.

"As soon as we arrive, I'm summoning a doctor," he said firmly.

No. Tell him no.

But Louisa was unable to tell him a thing. Instead, she wound her arms around his waist and focused on the beating of his heart as if it were the last tangible grasp she had on reality.

* * *

As they made the journey home, Neil was beset with worry. Louisa looked pale and weak, and he was sure that she had lost weight. What could possibly be the matter? How could she have deteriorated so much in only a day?

The moment they arrived at the castle, Neil sent Beatrice to find a groomsman to summon the doctor, then carried Louisa up to her room. But when he set her on the bed, an icy finger of warning slid down his spine. On her pillow he saw several strands of brilliant red hair.

Damn it, why hadn't he realized? Why hadn't he guessed? Louisa had never been pregnant, she'd been ill. Gravely ill. Instead of succumbing to his pride and his suspicions, he should have taken her symptoms seriously.

As her breathing grew labored and her skin clammy, Neil realized the depth of his love for this woman. He could only pray that he'd sent for the doctor in time.

Don't let her die. Please don't let her die.

If she recovered, he would do anything she asked. He would be John Smith, forsake his life in Oregon and live out the rest of his days as her bodyguard if that was what she wanted.

Please, God, don't let her die.

It was much later when Neil looked up to see Evie standing in the doorway. With her bare feet peeking from beneath the hem of her ruffled nightdress, she looked younger than her sixteen years. Her eyes, still retaining a portion of their sleepiness, bounced from Louisa to Neil then back again.

As the severity of Louisa's condition sank into her consciousness, the blood drained from Evie's face. She came into the room slowly at first, then started running toward the bed. Darting past him, she reached for Louisa's hand, grunting, tugging on her arm, clearly wanting her to rise.

When she didn't respond, Evie became frantic. Rushing to Neil, she beat her hands against his chest, her mouth working, primitive noises ripping from her throat. Slowly, as if priming a rusty pump, she began to produce words, becoming more and more coherent.

"'Ouisa… 'ick."

Even with his concern over Louisa, Neil felt a burst of pride. Evie was speaking. According to what he'd learned, she hadn't spoken since her mother's death.

"Yes, Louisa is sick." He tried to take Evie's hands to calm her, but she shook her head, her breathing coming in strident gasps.

"Ma…ma…sick…"

Was she remembering the last time she'd spoken? Was she remembering the night her mother had committed suicide?

Evie grasped his hands, pulling him toward the bed. "Sick…mur…mur…er."

Neil offered soft shushing noises, hoping to calm her before she woke Louisa. "She'll be fine, Evie. I've already sent for the doctor."

"No! The word was more a scream than an order. "Mur…mur…er…poi…son. Mama. Murder. Poison."

Murder. Poison.

Evie's warning became stunningly, startlingly clear.

"Poison? Your mother was poisoned?"

Evie nodded, still frenzied.

In a flash, all the pieces to the puzzle fell into place and Neil realized what a fool he had been. He had been guarding against an overt outside threat, when all the time Louisa was being systematically poisoned from within her own home.

By a woman.

Badger had said that a woman had been hired to kill Louisa. He'd said that Horace had insisted that the attempts on her life be suspended until Horace and Oscar Haversham arrived. Neil had assumed that he had time to fortify his defenses and investigate the staff at the castle. He hadn't realized that the murder weapon had already been used.

The knowledge sank into his brain like a bitter brew, chilling his body and coating his tongue.

A woman. The assassin is a woman.

Who had access to Louisa? Who could have offered her the lethal dosages without causing suspicion?

Evie tugged on his hands. "Be…trice."

Just as the word reverberated in his brain, Beatrice appeared in the doorway and leveled a pistol in his direction.

"Don't move," she ordered, her tone hard as flint.

Easing into the room, she closed the door behind her. Her features were cast in bitterness, adding years to her appearance.

"So," she drawled, her eyes momentarily cutting in Evie's direction. "You've finally remembered." Her mouth pressed into a thin line. "I should have killed you long ago. Heaven only knows you haven't been worth the effort of keeping you drugged and exiled all this time."

She grimaced. "But then, you were so honestly traumatized by your mother's death. The physician I bribed to admit you to Hildon Hall assured me that your memory loss was most likely permanent. I should have taken him for the fool he was."

Sighing, she eased closer, supporting the pistol with both hands. "Honestly, I would have taken care of things in my own way if I hadn't been so sure that Charles would catch on to my shenanigans if something happened to you."

"Shenanigans?" Neil repeated. "Don't you mean murder?"

Beatrice shrugged. "Call it what you will. The truth remains that Charles could barely be bothered by the death of his wives. He considered each of their premature demises unhappy accidents—or sheer carelessness on their part. But if something had happened to his sole heir…" She shuddered at the mere thought.

"Why, Beatrice?"

Her grip on the revolver trembled as anger swept through her body.

"I should have inherited the business. But, no…my father was old-fashioned and wouldn't hear of it. But Charles—he was a man of the world. I was so sure he would do the right thing once Father died."

Her voice became shrill as her fury increased. "But Charles was a stingy, greedy bastard. He kept everything for himself—the business, the money, the estate. Boyd and I received nothing. Nothing!"

A sob burst from her throat. "He denied me everything—my future, an education, even the man I loved. My brother wouldn't part with a penny on my behalf."

As her rage increased, the mask of refinement dropped completely away. "So I swore that I would get even with him. Moreover, before I was finished, the Winslow fortune would be mine."

Her laughter sounded more like a cackle. "It was easy, so easy. Charles's first wife taught me a good deal about poison. I'm afraid that I allowed her to die too quickly. I worried for months that Charles would choose to investigate the matter. But he didn't. When he decided to marry again, I took my time, poisoning her bit by bit over several years until she finally snapped and went mad.''

The woman's eyes narrowed as she stared at Evie, registering the dawning realization that began to fill the girl's eyes.

''Yes, my dear. She caught on in the end. I was fortunate that no one believed her ramblings, but I was forced to take matters into my own hands. Everyone believed that Mary threw herself from the rampart. In reality, I offered her some…help.''

When Evie would have launched herself at Beatrice, Neil caught her around the waist, holding her fast.

Beatrice made a tsking noise. ''Poor pet. All of this time you thought the images were merely the remnants of your nightmares. You had no idea that the dreams came from reality. It was so easy to convince Charles that you were as ill as your mother and a danger to yourself as much as those around you. And since he was a busy man, he told himself there would be other children, other heirs. If not, there would be time enough to deal with your illness. Little did he know that I made sure that none of his other wives lived long enough to ever conceive.''

Neil held Evie tight as she fought against him.

Beatrice sneered. ''I should have known that you would cause problems the moment you left the asylum. You were developing a tolerance to the tonic your physician prescribed. Mrs. Bitterman reported to me that you were more aware of your surroundings. But I was so sure that Louisa would prove to be no different than Charles's other wives. I didn't think you would last the week before she sent you back.'' Beatrice frowned, then took a deep, calming breath.

"It's too bad, really. If Louisa hadn't interfered, you would have been wallowing at Hildon Hall in a laudanum-induced haze. As it is, I'm afraid I won't be able to let you leave this room. I haven't quite decided how to explain your death to Boyd—or those of Louisa and her bodyguard. But I suppose I can blame it on a reoccurrence of the same madness that afflicted your mother.''

Screaming, Evie wrenched free, running for the door. With Beatrice's attention diverted, Neil dived toward the older woman, knocking the gun from her hands.

But Beatrice was filled with hatred. Grasping a pair of scissors from the chatelaine she wore, she whirled, plunging them into Neil's arm.

Blackness swam in front of his eyes as he fell to his knees. He was unable to grasp the woman as she ran past him, heading toward Louisa's supine shape, her arm upraised.

"No!''

Neil lunged forward, trying to grasp Beatrice's skirts, but fell to the ground, blood pouring from the wound on his arm.

A gun shot sounded through the din. For a moment, Beatrice seemed frozen in place, then she crumpled to the floor, a pool of blood forming beneath her. Gripping his own injured arm, Neil looked up. Above him, Evie stood with her arms still outstretched, Beatrice's pistol held in a death grip.

It was later that evening when Louisa awakened to find John leaning over her bedside.

"John?''

"Shh. The doctor has been here. I'm afraid rest and plenty of beef broth are all he could prescribe. That and time."

"Am I dying?" she asked, appearing confused.

John's smile held a tinge of sadness. "No, no thanks to me. You'll be right as rain soon enough."

She shook her head, still confused by the odd dreams she'd experienced. Troubling dreams that involved screams, angry shouts and the report of a pistol.

Then her eyes fell upon a bandage wrapped around John's arm. The bright stain of blood was unmistakable.

"What happened?"

Taking her hand, John began to explain a fantastical tale of murder and madness—with Beatrice as the author of the tragedy. As each twist and turn of the events unfolded, Louisa discovered to her horror that her dreams had been a reflection of what had really occurred.

Before she could completely digest the events, the door opened to admit Boyd and Evie.

Louisa stiffened at the sight of her brother-in-law, but when Evie ran toward her, throwing herself into Louisa's arms, she held her close.

"You were so brave, Evie. So brave."

Evie sobbed and Louisa held her tightly, rocking her to and fro until the girl quieted in her arms.

It was only then that Boyd stepped forward.

"I'd like to apologize to you, Louisa."

She blinked in surprise. Of all the words she'd expected to leave his mouth, these weren't the ones.

She stroked Evie's hair, wondering how she should respond.

"I have been rude and boorish, but it has taken my sister's death for me to realize just how much." He looked down at the floor, clearly uncomfortable, but determined to continue. "Beatrice wasn't the only one affected by our father's callousness and Charles's greed. I'm afraid I allowed myself to become just as bitter, just as cynical." His brown eyes grew dark with regret. "I only hope that you can forgive me. I should have seen that you only meant to help my family."

He held out his arms and Evie ran into his embrace. "I am also eternally indebted to you for liberating Evie from a life that was hell on earth. I swear to you that I will spend the rest of my life ensuring that she is never harmed again. It's the least I can do after ignoring her plight for so long."

Louisa's eyes filled with tears. Looking beyond Boyd, she caught John's gaze—and in an instant, she knew that she didn't belong here. This was not her life or her identity. She was tired...tired of living a lie and tired of pretending. As much as she had grown to love Evie, Louisa knew that she could never be happy immersed in a fantasy. She wanted her life back—*her* life, not that of a stranger. And if she didn't claim it now, she would be haunted by might-have-beens.

Especially where John was concerned.

Please, please forgive me, she prayed silently, her gaze locked with John's.

"I'm afraid I have my own confession to make. One that I hope you will someday understand...." She bit her lip, then said, "I am not Louisa Haversham. My name is Phoebe Gray—and you were right from the beginning, Boyd." Her gaze skipped to him, then back to John. "You were right to call me a gold digger. On the journey to America, I was paid to serve as a hired companion to the real Louisa Haversham. We look very much alike, you see. So when each of us voiced our fears about the life we were about to lead in America, we stumbled upon an unorthodox solution, that of switching places.''

The room shuddered in silence.

''I'm sorry,'' she whispered hoarsely. ''I honestly did not know that Charles had any family. We were told that he was alone in the world. I only agreed to switch identities with Louisa because I was sure that Charles could provide me with a comfortable life. One without fear and want.''

Phoebe braced herself for Boyd's response, knowing that he would be furious—and rightly so. But even as she cringed in anticipation of his tirade, he stared at her in stunned disbelief, then offered a rusty sound. A laugh.

A laugh!

Soon the room was filled with chatter and mirth. Phoebe was quickly told of all that had transpired since she'd lost consciousness. As Evie wearily curled on the bed beside her, Boyd spoke of the way the doctor had arrived at breakneck speed after being summoned by John. He'd come with the news that the tonic Evie had been given was primarily laudanum and that she should be carefully weaned from it over the space of many months to prevent serious withdrawal symptoms. Upon his arrival, however, he'd found John bleeding from a gaping wound, Evie sobbing piteously and Phoebe unconscious.

''He was able to determine soon enough that you were suffering from arsenic poisoning,'' John said, squeezing her hand.

''Arsenic!''

Boyd nodded. ''A search of Beatrice's things revealed that the hot cocoa she made each morning was liberally laced with the substance. In time, you would have died in the same slow, painful manner as Evie's mother—

perhaps even going mad in the process.'' He shook his head. ''How could I have been so blind? Besides Charles's wives, there were other relatives who died prematurely—all of them under Beatrice's care.''

Phoebe shivered and John squeezed her hand. ''I think we're tiring you,'' he said.

Boyd immediately rose to his feet.

''Once again, I've proved to be insensitive. John is right. You need your rest. There will be time enough to sort all this out later. In the meantime, I think I'll tuck my niece into bed.''

Gently Boyd scooped the girl into his arms and carried her into the hall.

John followed them with the lamp, and for several long minutes a heavy silence filled the air.

Closing her eyes, Phoebe wondered what the next few minutes would bring. How would John react to her confession?

As he stepped back into the room, she braced herself for his recriminations. But the eyes that met hers were gentle.

Closing the door behind him, he settled on the side of the bed. Tenderly he skimmed the curve of her cheek with his fingertips. ''You do look tired.''

''I'm fine.''

''Perhaps.'' He studied her for long moments, then said, ''I am so pleased to make your acquaintance, Phoebe Gray.''

For a moment she couldn't comprehend what she was hearing. And then she understood. He wasn't angry with her. If anything, he appeared...relieved.

Sobbing, she wrapped her arms around his neck and hugged him close, whispering, ''I'm so sorry that I deceived you.''

"Shh, shh." For long moments he held her close, his hands rubbing her back through the thin layer of her nightdress. A rash of gooseflesh followed in their wake. "I should be asking for your forgiveness."

Sure that he meant to apologize for his boorish behavior as her bodyguard, she was astounded by the words he spoke next.

"For you see, I've been living a lie myself. I'm not John Smith. My real name is Neil Ballard. And I've been waiting for years to meet you once again, Phoebe Gray."

Chapter Twenty-One

Phoebe could scarcely believe the words she heard. "Neil?"

Her fingers curled into the fabric of his shirt as she sought something, anything within his features that would remind her of that scared little boy she'd known in the orphanage. But try as she might, she couldn't reconcile the frail image she'd carried in her mind's eye with this giant of a man. His hair was darker, his skin tanned and healthy.

But the eyes...I should have recognized him by the eyes alone.

Sobbing, she buried her face in her hands. "You must hate me for what I've done, for the cavalier way I've treated you."

He drew her into his embrace, his body warm and comforting. "I'm as much to blame as you. I should have insisted that we have some time to get reacquainted before marrying. Barring that, I should have told you immediately who I was."

She tipped her head back to see if he truly wasn't angry with her. "Why didn't you?"

His grimace was rueful. "At first out of pride. I was

hurt that you could have chosen another man over me. Frankly, I wanted to make sure you were worth the bother.''

She laughed when a hint of color touched his cheeks.

''But after I saw you for the first time, I knew I would be staying—and I didn't plan on leaving again until I'd convinced you to come with me.''

''What if Charles hadn't died?''

''I can assure you that it was one of the best days of my life when I discovered he would never have the power to claim you.''

Her brow creased. ''So that day at the station…you pushed me to the ground simply to thwart my first meeting with Charles?''

''No. I honestly thought that you were in danger.''

''But why?''

He took her hands, his long callused fingers stroking her own. ''There are a few details to this story that you still don't know.'' He paused for a moment, as if waiting. ''You haven't asked me yet how I knew you were in New York.''

The truth dawned on her slowly. ''Phoebe.''

''Don't you mean Louisa?''

She touched her forehead with her fingertips. She had lived so long as Louisa Haversham, she was having difficulty remembering her true identity.

''You met…my friend then.'' She stiffened slightly. ''You refused to marry her?''

Neil laughed. ''I did not refuse to marry her. She refused to marry me.''

''What?'' Phoebe breathed.

''Your…friend, as you call her, had the audacity to fall in love with an undercover Pinkerton along the way.''

Louisa shook her head in confusion. "I don't understand."

He patted her hand. "I'll let her explain everything to you. She's here. In Boston."

"Louisa is here? But why?"

Neil tucked a strand of hair behind her ear. "I'm afraid that so many explanations are awaiting you, and I'm not sure that you have enough strength to deal with them yet. You need to rest first."

"But…" Instinctively, Phoebe knew he was right, but she had to know one thing first. "Why did you think I was in danger?"

"Because several attempts had been made on Louisa's life while she'd been pretending to be you."

Again, the words made little sense. "Why would anyone ever want to hurt me?"

"Because you are the daughter of a great man."

"Nonsense."

"Did you ever know who your father was?"

She shook her head. "My mother refused to speak of him. She said the memories were far too painful. I was still so young when she passed away that I didn't have an opportunity to press her for details."

"Then you never knew that your father came from the titled aristocracy."

She laughed. "That's absurd. I couldn't possibly…" Her words trailed away as she remembered her mother's harsh attitude toward London's elite. Susanna Gray had been an unhappy woman. Although she'd loved her daughter with every fiber of her being, Phoebe had sensed a tide of anger and hurt just boiling beneath her mother's outward facade.

"Did she never tell you that you had a sister?"

"No, I…"

Vaguely, Phoebe remembered that when her mother had been ill and delirious, she had often talked of her "girls."

Girls.

No. It wasn't possible.

Even before Neil could continue, she whispered, "Louisa?"

She'd always thought the similarities in their build and appearance had been eerie. Was it possible?

Neil nodded. "She's your twin."

Phoebe shook her head, still unable to fathom how such a thing could be true. "It isn't possible. We look similar, yes, but not…"

Neil's smile was gentle. "Not all twins are identical."

Like rain seeping into parched ground, Phoebe absorbed the truth. She wasn't alone in the world. She had a sister. A twin.

Suddenly everything made perfect sense. There had been a bond between the women from the first. Phoebe had felt as if she'd known Louisa forever. From the onset, they'd shared things about themselves that Phoebe, at least, had never told another soul.

Except Neil.

Suddenly it was all too much to take in. Sobbing, she gripped his shirt while the room seemed to dip crazily.

Seeing her distress, Neil laid her down against the pillows. "Shh. We'll talk about all of this later. Louisa will be arriving for a visit around teatime. I couldn't put her off any longer than that. Until then, you need to sleep."

She still gripped him tightly, afraid that if she let him go she would discover that all of this was merely a dream and she was alone again.

Neil smiled, stretching out on the bed beside her and pulling her into the warmth of his arms.

"Sleep, little one. I won't leave you." Smiling at her gently, he reached into his pocket and withdrew a gold circlet studded with rubies.

"Will you forgive me, Phoebe? Will you overlook the fact that I was so thoughtless and shallow in my treatment of you that I allowed myself to look upon you as a possession rather than the woman I loved? Will you reconsider becoming my wife and spending your life with me? Not as a servant, but as my soul mate?"

Tears filled her eyes and she held out her hand. "There is nothing on earth that I would rather be than your wife."

"Say it."

She regarded him in confusion.

"Say my name."

Her smile was brilliant.

"Neil."

As he slipped the ring on her finger, she drew his head down. Their kiss was slow, sweet and filled with the heat and reverence that only mutual love could bring. And with it came a melting of the last lonely corners of her heart.

As Neil folded her in his arms, she realized that life had a funny way of coming full circle. She had been searching her whole life for a family and a place where she felt she belonged. Little had she known that by surrendering everything she had once held so dear—her life, her identity and her future—she would discover that she'd had everything she'd ever wanted all along.

In the days that followed, both Phoebe and Evie began to recover. Of the two of them, Evie had fared the worst—which was understandable, considering the length of time that she had been drugged. Even with the gradual weaning away of the tonic, she suffered from chills and trembling one minute, bouts of anxiousness and rage the next. But through it all, her mind grew clearer, and more of her memories returned—not all of them happy recollections. Nevertheless, she was determined to make a full recovery. Never again did she want to feel the helplessness she'd experienced when stringing a complete thought together was more than she could manage.

Phoebe stayed by her through it all. Despite the truth of her identity being exposed, she had still formed a bond with Evie, and she would not abandon the girl at such a needy time.

The greatest surprise came from Boyd. When Mr. Pritchard was informed of Phoebe's true identity, he determined that Boyd should become Evie's guardian and the recipient of the inheritance that would have gone to Charles's wife.

Phoebe wasn't sure if it was self-sufficiency due to his sudden fortune or the fact that the empire he'd helped to create now fell under his sole discretion, but Boyd's mood transformed overnight. His eyes, which had once been filled with bitterness and suspicion, were alight with joy. Even more touching, he seemed to honestly endeavor to build a relationship with his niece. Again and again he expressed his sorrow at not helping Evie sooner, and vowed to spend the rest of his life in search of recompense.

As if sensing that Phoebe would not be able to stay with her for much longer, Evie eagerly accepted her uncle's attentions, confessing to him that after years in the asylum, she wanted to see more than the countryside surrounding Boston. When Boyd proposed a year's tour of Europe—with proper tutors and companions to see to Evie's education—she eagerly accepted the idea.

Phoebe supposed that she would have felt a trifle lonely if not for the arrival of Louisa. Their reunion was filled with laughter and tears—the emotions even more poignant at the realization that they were sisters. Twins.

As Phoebe gained her strength, Louisa related all that had occurred on her journey west. Phoebe was astounded to discover that she and Louisa Haversham had become the prey of an uncle she hadn't even known existed.

When Neil urged Phoebe to be careful and remain under the protection of the men who had been stationed around the Winslow estate, she remained skeptical that anything more could happen. Gabe and his Pinkertons had already been posted at the harbor, waiting for Horace Haversham to appear. She had no doubts that her uncle would be arrested as soon as he docked. So why did she have to endure more confinement? But even as she silently protested, she kept her thoughts to herself. After all that Neil had been through in ensuring her safety, she knew she would have to humor him.

Especially since the confinement would not interrupt their plans to be married.

As they entered the stone chapel on the outskirts of town, she squeezed his hand. "I'll be ready in just a minute," she promised.

Neil kissed her hand before allowing Phoebe to hurry with Louisa and Chloe into a side room where Phoebe would dress for the wedding.

Since Louisa's marriage in Oregon had been a rushed affair with little time for such niceties as a gown and flowers, she had insisted on Phoebe's nuptials being a bit more grand. A half-dozen seamstresses had been working day and night to finish her dress—an elaborate creation of ivory silk and Chantilly lace. Tailored to Phoebe's slight frame, the bodice was low and sleeveless, and the skirt cascaded at mid hip over a modest bustle into rows of ruched satin, silk and velvet.

As she stared at her image in the vicar's warped mirror, Phoebe could scarcely believe the woman dressed so elegantly was herself. Never in her life had she dreamed that she would marry for love rather than convenience.

"You look beautiful," Louisa said, offering Phoebe a small hug and a kiss on the cheek. "This really is so romantic. You're about to marry a childhood friend, yet you fell in love with him without even knowing that he had ties to your past."

Her sister handed her a bouquet of delicate pink blossoms. "May your life with him be as happy as my own marriage to Gabe." Then, backing out of the door, she said, "I'll tell them you're ready."

As the latch snapped shut again, Phoebe took a deep breath, taking a moment to gather her thoughts. Behind her, Chloe turned away, offering her a modicum of privacy.

Was Phoebe really about to marry Neil Ballard? The man she had so carelessly offered to another woman only a few short weeks before? The fact still seemed so hard to grasp.

And yet the love she now felt for him had grown out of changes made within themselves.

"Miss Phoebe?"

"Yes, Chlo—"

In a rush, Phoebe took in a hundred details at once. Chloe's voice had lost its French accent.

Her face was contorted with contrition, her skin flushed and beaded with sweat.

Then, before Phoebe could comprehend what the woman meant to do, Chloe looped a thick length of ribbon around Phoebe's neck and began to choke her.

"I'm sorry, I'm sorry," Chloe sobbed as she pulled tighter and tighter. "I don't want to do this, but don't you see? I have no choice. If I let you escape, Horace Haversham will hunt me down, as well. He paid me money to kill you, a great deal of money. I didn't know that you would be so kind, that you would offer me clothes and gifts."

Chloe's laughter held a tinge of hysteria. "I'd already started to poison you, bit by bit, you understand. But then I caught Beatrice lacing your cocoa with the same stuff—imagine my relief. I wouldn't have to finish what I'd begun, but Horace would never know the difference.... I truly have grown to love you, but...I'm sorry!"

Phoebe scarcely heard the words. She clawed at Chloe's hands and her own throat in an effort to breathe. A red haze swam in front of her eyes and her head pounded.

As the strength ebbed from her body, Phoebe realized that she was about to lose everything—the man who loved her, her future happiness, her very life.

The thought offered her a spurt of strength. She flung her hand back, striking Chloe in the eye and catching her off guard. With the stricture imperceptibly loosened, she reached for the lamp on a nearby table and swung it at Chloe with all her might.

Blessed air filled her lungs as she took a deep breath through a throat that seemed to be on fire. Knowing that Chloe would have the power to overtake her if she were caught again, Phoebe stumbled toward the door, threw it open and ran into the chapel.

Time seemed to grind to a halt. In slow motion she saw Neil turn toward her, then Gabe, then Louisa. To her horror, she remembered that the vicar had forced the men to leave their weapons at the door.

Glancing over her shoulder, she saw Chloe in quick pursuit, this time with a knife in her hand.

Screaming, Phoebe turned to Neil for help, but to her horror, her toe caught in the hem of her gown and she fell to the ground. Within seconds, Chloe was looming over her, while Neil and Gabe were still yards away.

Without warning, a shot rang out, shattering the reverence of the church. Chloe stopped in her tracks, a bloom of red appearing on her chest.

Screaming again, Phoebe scrambled to her feet, whirling to find the source of the shot.

It was Louisa who stood mere feet away, still sighting down the length of a tiny derringer. As Gabe rushed to her side, she lowered the weapon, then lifted her skirts and returned it to a delicate kidskin holster strapped to the top of her boot. Then, collapsing into her husband's arms, she declared in a trembling voice, "No one hurts my sister. No one."

Epilogue

August 12, 1870

Dearest Diary,
Our journey west to Oregon was made in the Winslow private car. With no schedules to meet or appointments to keep, we took what Nell called the "scenic route," indulging in the beauty to be found along the way.

It has been a leisurely honeymoon—just as I'd requested. Neil had suggested that we journey with Evie and Boyd and "take a season" in Europe, much like newlyweds of "quality," but I quickly refused. For one thing, the expense would be frightful and I do not wish to tax my husband's income so severely. But more important, I no longer feel a need to chase the whims of fashion. My only wish is to spend time with the man I love. Moreover, I've lost any desire to roam from pillar to post. I simply want to go home.

Besides my marriage to Neil, my greatest joy is

having my name back. I no longer have a desire to look or act a certain way in order to please others. Through my experiences I've learned to appreciate those things that make me who I am. Indeed, rather than writing a romance—since I have had my fill of gothic adventures—I am seriously considering a volume expounding on the "home arts," with young ladies of Evie's age in mind.

Closing her eyes, Phoebe paused in her writing as she was flooded with memories.

So much has happened since the attack in the church. Chloe revealed on her deathbed that she once tried to kill me at the railway station in New York. She began poisoning me soon after that— accounting for the way my stomach seemed continually unsettled. The poison was administered in the tea that I had requested while we were in New York. It was only when she caught Beatrice spooning rat poison into the "cocoa mix" that she stopped.

When I marveled at the way both women had used the same methods to harm me, Neil merely shrugged and said that poison was a woman's weapon.

Before she died, Chloe also revealed where Horace would dock upon arriving in Boston. With only a few hours to spare, Gabe and Neil organized a contingent of men to meet him there.

In my mind's eye I can still see Horace's astonishment when he realized his plots were spoiled before he'd even set foot on American soil. He was immediately taken into custody. I had to feel some pity for the man. He had exchanged the prison of a deserted island for that of a prison cell.

It was days later—and only after Neil was assured of my safety—that we were we able to return to the church to be married.

Phoebe smiled at that particular memory. She and Neil had been so intent on solemnizing their vows that they had awakened the rattled pastor at an indecent hour so that the ceremony could be performed and they could return home to Phoebe's bedroom as man and wife.

After our marriage, Neil and I did not reappear from our suite until well into the second day of our honeymoon.

A blush stained her cheeks at writing even that much in her diary.

We emerged just in time to see a carriage rattling through the gate, the distinctive crest of Lord Haversham on the door.

Knowing instinctively how to handle the situation, I waited at the top of the stairs as my father appeared.

I don't know what I had expected. How was a great titled man supposed to look—especially one who had hurt so many people in so many ways? I thought I would react to him in anger or remembered girlish hurt. But when I saw him, I felt nothing but pity. This man had been so intent on having a son that he had denied himself the love he could have received.

As I walked down the stairs, I offered him my

haughtiest stare. Then, pulling Neil close, I introduced Lord Haversham to my husband.

My pleasure grew tenfold when my father realized that it wasn't Charles Winslow who stood before him, but a total stranger. When Louisa and Gabe Cutter appeared next, Oscar Haversham's defeat was complete. He grew pale, stumbling and clinging to his valet for support. It gave me great pleasure to inform him that neither of his daughters had married into wealth.

I suppose that I should have felt sorry for the man, but I didn't. It was his fault that my mother was forced to steal one of her own children and run away. It was his fault that my sister and I were raised apart. Moreover, it was Oscar Haversham who put us in danger by sabotaging his own brother and forcing Horace to seek his own revenge.

With Louisa at my side, I told Oscar Haversham of his brother's machinations and our own marriages to men completely "unsuitable to his needs." Bit by bit, it became apparent that our father finally understood the extent of his daughters' "betrayal." Without the Winslow fortune in the family, he was ruined. Worse yet, I knew that the scandal of his treatment of his own daughters and his brother would destroy him socially. It was only a matter of time.

And now…now I am savoring my last taste of luxury. This morning Neil and I will arrive at our destination, and my real life will begin in earnest. Boyd and Evie generously allowed us to use the private Winslow railcar, but from this point on, I will be the wife of a humble homesteader….

"What are you doing, sweetheart?"

Phoebe smiled as a pair of strong hands curled around her shoulders. "Merely adding to my…memoirs."

"Am I featured in your writing?"

"Of course."

Putting her diary away, she allowed herself to be pulled into her husband's arms. Despite the proximity of their destination, they were soon wrapped in an embraced, enjoying the passion that inevitably ignited between them.

When Neil pulled her onto the bed, she did not resist. Instead, she reveled in the familiar joy of being together. He brought her to the very pinnacle of passion, then joined her in ecstasy.

It was much later, after the train had been at the station for some time, when she and Neil reluctantly dressed. Outside, they loaded her trunks—filled with all of the clothing and accessories she'd purchased as Mrs. Charles Winslow III—into a rough wagon.

Climbing onto the bench beside Neil, she took his hand.

"Ready?" he asked her.

"Yes."

Neil eyed her with concern. "Are you sure you're well enough to make the journey today? We could spend the night in town if you'd like."

Phoebe shook her head. "I feel fine."

Recovering from being poisoned was taking much longer than she had ever supposed. She still had frequent bouts of weariness and her strength was limited. But in time, Dr. Browne had assured her, she would make a full recovery. He'd prescribed lots of broth, as well as a special diet rich in fruits and vegetables and grains.

As she melted against Neil's side and his arm slid

around her waist, she absorbed the intense green of the Oregon countryside. Although she was accustomed to the rolling green hills of Scotland, she had never seen such tall, towering pine trees jutting up against rugged mountains.

"It's beautiful," she murmured.

Neil's embrace tightened. "I hope you'll be happy here."

"I know I will be."

She marveled at how much she had changed since leaving England. During her voyage she'd dreaded all thought of Oregon, considering it a heathen land. Now she welcomed the peace and beauty that surrounded her. Although she knew that a rough cabin and a wilderness in need of taming awaited her at the end of her journey, she wasn't the slightest bit disappointed. In fact, she relished the challenge that lay ahead.

Nearly an hour passed before she felt Neil tense. Looking up, she saw that his features had sharpened in anticipation.

"Are we here?"

"Just over that rise."

Although she was already beginning to tire, she felt a fresh wave of energy. Straightening, she eagerly watched as the horses reached the top of the hill and she could finally glimpse the sprawling valley below.

A gasp lodged in her throat. "Neil? This is yours?"

"Yes."

"All of it?"

He laughed. "Yes, all of it."

Her eyes swept down the winding track of road to the compound below. Hundreds of cattle grazed on the verdant pastures as far as the eye could see. Fenced paddocks housed several dozen horses—and even from a distance, Phoebe could discern the quality of the animals' bloodlines. There were stables, two barns and a half-dozen outbuildings. A large pond glistened in the sunlight, and at the far end, nestled amid a shady stand of pine trees, was a sprawling ranch house made of rough-hewn logs and river rock.

"*That* is our home?"

Neil nodded in evident pride. "Do you like it?"

"Like it? I…" She waved a hand, unable to summon words to describe her astonishment. "I was expecting a cabin."

"It began as a cabin."

"But—"

He laughed, hugging her close. "I suppose I didn't tell you the whole truth because I wanted to see your face when you saw what I'd done with my life."

"B-but you told me I would be helping you to run your household."

"I need someone to oversee the staff."

"Staff?" When Phoebe had originally agreed to marry Neil, she'd feared she would become nothing more than a servant. She'd had no idea that he would be so…so…

"But you're rich!"

Neil laughed again. "I can assure you that my bank balance pales in comparison to Charles Winslow's."

Stunned, Phoebe realized that she had married a man of great wealth. Yet now that a life of ease was within her grasp, she discovered that such things didn't really matter anymore. With all that had happened, she'd learned that happiness was not dependent on a healthy bank ledger. Instead, what mattered most was giving and receiving love.

Turning to Neil, she threw her arms around his neck.

"I didn't marry you for money. I didn't know that you…that we…"

Neil smiled, holding her close, his hand caressing her back. "I know. You married me because you adore me."

Her laughter joined his.

When he bent to place a soft kiss on her lips, then another and another, her worry disappeared. In that instant she realized that Neil already knew the depth of her love. He had encountered his own brand of suspicion and self-growth during their misadventures in Boston. Together, they had emerged stronger and more appreciative of the miraculous gifts of life and love that they'd been given.

"I love you more than life itself," Phoebe whispered against his lips.

"As do I." He offered her a smile filled with happiness and devotion. "I think it's time I showed you your new home. I have the strongest desire to carry you over the threshold—" his voice deepened "—especially the one to the master suite."

Neil spurred the team into a brisk walk. Phoebe rested her head on his shoulder and sighed in utter bliss as the wagon wound its way downhill, taking them closer and closer to their future.

And when the looming shape of the house came into focus, she snuggled deeper into Neil's embrace, realizing that she had finally found a home. It wasn't a rambling ranch house or a castle.

It was here…wrapped tightly in her husband's love.

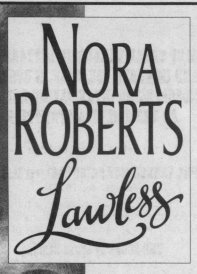
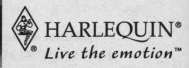

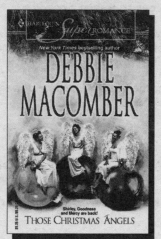

✂ **Your opinion is important to us!** Please take a few moments to share your thoughts with us about your experiences with Harlequin and Silhouette books. Your comments will be very useful in ensuring that we deliver books you love to read.
Please take a few minutes to complete the questionnaire, then send it to us at the address below.

Send your completed questionnaires to:
Harlequin/Silhouette Reader Survey, P.O. Box 9046, Buffalo, NY 14269-9046

---

1. As you may know, there are many different lines under the Harlequin and Silhouette brands. Each of the lines is listed below. Please check the box that most represents your reading habit for each line.

Line	Currently read this line	Do not read this line	Not sure if I read this line
Harlequin American Romance	❑	❑	❑
Harlequin Duets	❑	❑	❑
Harlequin Romance	❑	❑	❑
Harlequin Historicals	❑	❑	❑
Harlequin Superromance	❑	❑	❑
Harlequin Intrigue	❑	❑	❑
Harlequin Presents	❑	❑	❑
Harlequin Temptation	❑	❑	❑
Harlequin Blaze	❑	❑	❑
Silhouette Special Edition	❑	❑	❑
Silhouette Romance	❑	❑	❑
Silhouette Intimate Moments	❑	❑	❑
Silhouette Desire	❑	❑	❑

2. Which of the following best describes why you bought *this book*? One answer only, please.

the picture on the cover	❑	the title	❑
the author	❑	the line is one I read often	❑
part of a miniseries	❑	saw an ad in another book	❑
saw an ad in a magazine/newsletter	❑	a friend told me about it	❑
I borrowed/was given this book	❑	other: _____	❑

3. Where did you buy *this book*? One answer only, please.

at Barnes & Noble	❑	at a grocery store	❑
at Waldenbooks	❑	at a drugstore	❑
at Borders	❑	on eHarlequin.com Web site	❑
at another bookstore	❑	from another Web site	❑
at Wal-Mart	❑	Harlequin/Silhouette Reader	❑
at Target	❑	Service/through the mail	
at Kmart	❑	used books from anywhere	❑
at another department store or mass merchandiser	❑	I borrowed/was given this book	❑

4. On average, how many Harlequin and Silhouette books do you buy at one time?

I buy _____ books at one time	❑
I rarely buy a book	❑

MRQ403HH-1A

5. How many times per month do you shop for any *Harlequin and/or Silhouette* books?
   One answer only, please.

1 or more times a week	❑	a few times per year	❑
1 to 3 times per month	❑	less often than once a year	❑
1 to 2 times every 3 months	❑	never	❑

6. When you think of your ideal heroine, which *one* statement describes her the best?
   One answer only, please.

She's a woman who is strong-willed	❑	She's a desirable woman	❑
She's a woman who is needed by others	❑	She's a powerful woman	❑
She's a woman who is taken care of	❑	She's a passionate woman	❑
She's an adventurous woman	❑	She's a sensitive woman	❑

7. The following statements describe types or genres of books that you may be
   interested in reading. Pick *up to 2 types* of books that you are most interested in.

I like to read about truly romantic relationships	❑
I like to read stories that are sexy romances	❑
I like to read romantic comedies	❑
I like to read a romantic mystery/suspense	❑
I like to read about romantic adventures	❑
I like to read romance stories that involve family	❑
I like to read about a romance in times or places that I have never seen	❑
Other: _____	❑

*The following questions help us to group your answers with those readers who are
similar to you. Your answers will remain confidential.*

8. Please record your year of birth below.

   19 _____

9. What is your marital status?

   single ❑   married ❑   common-law ❑   widowed ❑
   divorced/separated ❑

10. Do you have children 18 years of age or younger currently living at home?

   yes ❑   no ❑

11. Which of the following best describes your employment status?

   employed full-time or part-time ❑   homemaker ❑   student ❑
   retired ❑   unemployed ❑

12. Do you have access to the Internet from either home or work?

   yes ❑   no ❑

13. Have you ever visited eHarlequin.com?

   yes ❑   no ❑

14. What state do you live in?

   _____

15. Are you a member of Harlequin/Silhouette Reader Service?

   yes ❑   Account # _____   no ❑   MRQ403HH-1B